Dear Reader,

The Midnight Palace *is the second in a series of novels I wrote for young adults in the 1990s, back when even I was probably more young than adult myself! Writing for the young, or the young at heart, is a risky business and I learned that teenagers are a notoriously demanding and honest audience. My intention when crafting these books was to create stories that would appeal to them; also that they would hopefully be enjoyed by more mature and experienced fellow travellers for whom they might rekindle memories of the first books they had read, those magical tales of mystery and adventure that every reader hoards in the treasure chest of their brain. So whether you are young or young at heart, I hope you will enjoy this ride into the twilight world of Calcutta in the 1930s, where the shadows of the night are thicker than blood. Never mind the number of candles on your birthday cake – for those in the know, it's what lies beneath them that matters! Enjoy.*

Carlos Ruiz Zafón

February 2011

Praise for Carlos Ruiz Zafón

The Midnight Palace

'Zafón's young adult fiction was published in Spain long before he became an international sensation, and it's fascinating to see, in his second book, premonitory glimpses of *The Shadow of the Wind* . . . Zafón makes it look so easy but he's in a class of his own'
Financial Times

'Murders most foul, chilling crimes and dark deeds . . . Carlos Ruiz Zafón, author of *The Shadow of the Wind,* locates his ghost story in *The Midnight Palace*' *Vogue*

'It's fast-moving and never hesitates, and it quickly sketches the eight young people who inhabit its pages as quirky and likeable individuals, from the taciturn artist, Michael, to the fiery and intelligent Isobel. It's also a story about stories: tales from the past are woven into the narrative in an elegant way, with the whole book framed by the narrative of the last surviving member of the group'
Guardian

'A cracking mystery . . . A thoroughly ripping yarn' *The Times*

'This novel's plot is as dark and threatening as the Calcutta night that envelops the opening scenes . . . *The Midnight Palace* should not be overlooked by adults in search of literary excellence'
USA Today

The Prince of Mist

'The first book from *The Shadow of the Wind* author – published in English at last – is an atmospheric thriller following a young hero as he explores his new house in the country. Described as a cross between Stephen King and Neil Gaiman, it proves young adult fiction can be as gripping as the adult version'
Times Educational Supplement

'Everybody's talking about Carlos Ruiz Zafón, the bestselling author of *The Shadow of the Wind*, and *The Angel's Game*, who returns with *The Prince of Mist*. This very scary ghost story stayed at the top of the Spanish book charts for two years and is now translated into English for the first time. The haunting tale is aimed at readers of all ages, so is one to share with the whole family'

Good Housekeeping

'In this page-turner, a young hero finds himself in a house haunted by secrets he is fated to uncover – but at what cost? Magical and, even though I'm a grown-up, SCARY!'   Lauren Laverne, *Grazia*

'Addictive page-turner with things that go bump in the night'

Essentials

'Zafón mixes youthful romance, devilish pacts, salty seadogs, scary clowns and haunted shipwrecks with a generous hand, and you might not want to go diving again after reading this'

Financial Times

The Angel's Game

'The prose is intelligent but unpretentious, and the author is clear in his intentions to provide a rollicking, fun read . . . the novel's themes address the power of narrative, and many sharp lines pertain to storytelling . . . hugely enjoyable'   *Daily Telegraph*

'In this book about books, Zafón writes about Spain's harrowing history with literary aplomb'   *The Times*

'Revisits some of Zafón's much-loved urban landscapes in old Barcelona. Yet this novel stands alone, a complement or even an antagonist to its forerunner. If the previous book celebrated the ecstasies of reading, then this one – no less in love with literature, and no less crammed with archetypal plots – explores the agonies of writing'   *Independent*

'Readers familiar with *The Shadow of the Wind* will find themselves back in the Cemetery of Forgotten Books, the echo of Eco where, from a labyrinthine library, volumes seem to select their readers . . . rattling good Gothic fun' *Spectator*

'Summer and reading go together like buckets and spades, and sultry days are made for chunky page-turners such as *The Angel's Game* . . . It unfolds in twenties Barcelona where a young man undertakes to write a book that will change people's lives. The task is daunting and the stakes perilously high' *Daily Mail*

'The Cemetery of Forgotten Books – "a colossal labyrinth of bridges, passages and shelves" – is a wonderful creation, and there are many thrilling set pieces' *Sunday Telegraph*

'Starts off as an intelligent literary thriller, but morphs into action-packed adventure with a hefty body count' *Daily Express*

'The tale is rich, evocative and literate, with *Great Expectations* and Faust among its more nakedly displayed influences. Zafón is a great describer, with a cinematic flair for murders and sexual encounters' *Evening Standard*

The Shadow of the Wind

'If you thought the Gothic novel died with the nineteenth century, this will change your mind . . . in Zafón's hands, every scene seems to come from an early Orson Welles movie . . . one gorgeous read'
Stephen King

'*The Shadow of the Wind* is a triumph of the storyteller's art. I couldn't put it down. Enchanting, hilarious and heartbreaking, this book will change your life' *Daily Telegraph*

'What makes this novel so irresistibly readable is the emotional energy generated by the ups and downs of a big and varied cast of memorable characters . . . His conviction of the importance of literature in real life comes shining through . . . Walk down any street in Zafón's Barcelona and you'll glimpse the shades of the past and the secrets of the present, inscribed alike in the city's material fabric and the lives of its citizens' *Guardian*

'Everything about *The Shadow of the Wind* is smooth. The language purrs along, while the plot twists and unravels with a languid grace . . . Zafón's novel is atmospheric, beguiling and thoroughly readable' *Observer*

'One of those rare novels that combine brilliant plotting with sublime writing . . . word of mouth alone is sure to make it a bestseller'
Sunday Times

'Carlos Ruiz Zafón's wonderfully chock-a-block novel *The Shadow of the Wind* starts with the search for a mysterious author in Barcelona in the aftermath of the Civil War and then packs in as many plots and characters as it does genres - Gothic melodrama, coming-of-age story, historical thriller and more. It is a deeply satisfying, rich, full read' *Sunday Telegraph*

'Set in the author's native Barcelona in the years after the Spanish Civil War, this gripping novel has the feel of a Gothic ghost story, complete with crumbling, ivy-covered mansions, gargoyles and dank prison cells . . . this is just the sort of literary mystery that would have found favour with Wilkie Collins' *Daily Mail*

The
MIDNIGHT
PALACE

CARLOS RUIZ ZAFÓN

Translated from the Spanish by Lucia Graves

WEIDENFELD & NICOLSON

A W&N PAPERBACK

First published in Great Britain in 2011
by Weidenfeld & Nicolson
This paperback edition published in 2012
by Weidenfeld & Nicolson,
an imprint of Orion Books Ltd,
Carmelite House, 50 Victoria Embankment,
London EC4Y 0DZ

An Hachette UK company

9 10 8

A CIP catalogue record for this book
is available from the British Library.

ISBN 978-0-753-82924-0

Printed and bound in Great Britain by Clays Ltd, St Ives plc

The Orion Publishing Group's policy is to use papers
that are natural, renewable and recyclable products and
made from wood grown in sustainable forests. The logging
and manufacturing processes are expected to conform to
the environmental regulations of the country of origin.

www.orionbooks.co.uk

For MariCarmen

© Jackie Freshfield

I'LL NEVER FORGET THE NIGHT IT SNOWED OVER *Calcutta. The calendar at St Patrick's Orphanage was inching towards the final days of May 1932, leaving behind one of the hottest months ever recorded in the city of palaces.*

With each passing day we felt sadder and more fearful of the approaching summer, when we would all turn sixteen, for this would mean our separation and the end of the Chowbar Society, the secret club of seven members that had been our refuge during our years at the orphanage. We had grown up there with no other family than ourselves, with no other memories than the stories we told in the small hours round an open fire in the courtyard of an abandoned mansion – a large rambling ruin which stood on the corner of Cotton Street and Brabourne Road and which we'd christened the Midnight Palace. At the time, I didn't know I would never again see the streets of my childhood, the city whose spell has haunted me to this day.

I have never returned to Calcutta, but I have always been true to the promise we all made to ourselves on the banks of the Hooghly River: the promise never to forget what we had witnessed. Time has taught me to treasure the memory of those days and to preserve the letters I

received from the accursed city, for they keep the flame of my memories alive. It was through those letters that I found out our palace had been demolished and an office building erected over its ashes, and that Mr Thomas Carter, the head of St Patrick's, had passed away after spending the last years of his life in darkness, following the fire that closed his eyes for ever.

As the years went by, I heard about the gradual disappearance of all the sites that had formed the backdrop to our lives. The fury of a city that seemed to be devouring itself and the deceptive passage of time eventually erased all trace of the Chowbar Society and its members; at which point, I began to fear that this story might be lost for ever for want of a narrator. The vagaries of fate have chosen me, the person least suited to the task, to tell the tale and unveil the secret that both bonded and separated us so many years ago in the old railway station of Jheeter's Gate. I would have preferred someone else to have been in charge of rescuing this story, but once again life has taught me that my role is to be a witness, not the leading actor.

All these years I've kept the few letters sent to me by Roshan, guarding them closely because they shed light on the fate of each member of our unique society; I've read them over and over again, aloud, in the solitude of my study. Perhaps because somehow I felt that I had unwittingly become the repository of everything that had happened to us. Perhaps because I understood that, among that group of seven youngsters, I was always the

2

most reluctant to take risks, the least daring, and therefore the most likely to survive.

In that spirit, and trusting that my memory won't betray me, I will try to relive the mysterious and terrible events that took place during those four blazing days in May 1932.

It will not be easy and I beg my readers to forgive my inadequate words as I attempt to salvage that dark Calcutta summer from the past. I have done my best to reconstruct the truth, to return to those troubled days that would inevitably shape our future. All that is left for me now is to take my leave and allow the facts to speak for themselves.

I'll never forget the fear on the faces of my friends the night it snowed in Calcutta. But, as Ben used to tell me, the best place to start a story is at the beginning ...

© Mark Rusher

The Return of Darkness

Calcutta, May 1916

SHORTLY AFTER MIDNIGHT A BOAT EMERGED OUT of the mist that rose like a fetid curse from the surface of the Hooghly River. The faint glow of a flickering lantern attached to the mast revealed the figure of a man wrapped in a cape, rowing with difficulty towards the distant shore. Further to the east, under a blanket of leaden clouds, the outline of Fort William in the Maidan – a sort of Hyde Park carved out of tropical jungle – stood out against an endless expanse of street lamps and bonfires that spread as far as the eye could see. Calcutta.

The man stopped for a few moments to recover his breath and look back at the silhouette of Jheeter's Gate Station rising from the shadows on the opposite bank. The further he went, the more the station made of glass and steel seemed to melt into the city – a jungle of marble mausoleums blackened by decades of neglect; naked walls once coated in ochre, blue and gold, their colours peeled away by the fury of the monsoon, leaving them blurred and faded, like watercolours dissolving in a pond.

Only the certainty that he had just a few hours to live – perhaps only a few minutes – kept him going, leaving behind in that ill-fated place the woman he had sworn to protect. As Lieutenant Peake made his last journey to Calcutta, aboard an old river boat, the rain that had arrived in the early hours of darkness was washing away every last second of his life.

While he struggled to row the boat towards the shore, the lieutenant could hear the crying of the two babies hidden inside the bilge. Peake turned his head and noticed the lights of the other boat twinkling only a hundred metres behind him. He pictured the smile of his pursuer, savouring the hunt for his prey. Relentless.

Ignoring the children's tears of hunger and cold he applied his remaining strength to steering the boat towards the threshold that led into the ghostly labyrinth of streets. Two hundred years had been enough to transform the thick jungle growing around Kalighat into a city even God did not dare enter.

In a matter of minutes the storm looming over the city had unleashed all its fury. By mid-April and well into the month of June, the city withered in the clutches of the so-called Indian summer, with temperatures reaching up to forty degrees and a level of humidity close to saturation. But with the arrival of violent electric storms, which turned the sky into a battle scene, thermometers could plunge thirty degrees in a few moments.

The curtain of rain hid the unsteady jetties of rotten wood that dangled over the water's edge, but Peake didn't stop until he felt the hull hit the planks of the fishermen's dock. Only then did he thrust the anchoring pole into the muddy riverbed and rush to extract the children, who lay wrapped in a blanket. As he took them in his arms, the crying of the babies permeated the night like a trail of blood calling out to a predator. Pressing the bundle against his chest, Peake jumped ashore.

As the rain pelted down, he saw the other boat approaching the river bank, slowly, like a funeral barge. Gripped by fear, Peake ran towards the streets bordering the southern edge of the Maidan, a district known by its privileged residents – mostly British and other Europeans – as the White Town.

He clung to one remaining hope of being able to save the children, but he was still far from the heart of North Calcutta and Aryami Bose's house. The old lady was the only person who could help him now. Peake stopped for a moment and scanned the gloomy expanse of the Maidan, searching for the distant glow of the street lamps that flickered in the northern part of the city. The dark streets, cloaked by the storm, would be his safest hiding place. Holding the children tight, Lieutenant Peake set off again, heading east, hoping to find cover in the shadows cast by the palatial buildings of the city centre.

Moments later, the black barge that had been pursuing him came to a halt by the dock. Three men jumped ashore and moored the vessel. The small cabin door slowly opened and a dark figure wrapped in a black cloak crossed the gangplank the men had laid from the jetty, ignoring the rain. Once ashore, the figure stretched out a black-gloved hand and, pointing to the place where Peake had disappeared, gave a sinister smile.

THE WINDING ROAD that cut across the Maidan, rounding the fortress, had turned into a swamp under the pounding rain. Peake vaguely remembered having crossed that part of the city in the days when he was serving under Colonel Llewelyn. But that had been in broad daylight, on horseback and surrounded by an armed cavalry regiment. Ironically, fate now took him along the same stretch of open fields that had been levelled by Lord

Clive in 1758 so that the cannons of Fort William could enjoy a clear line of fire in all directions. Only this time he was the target.

Lieutenant Peake ran towards an area of trees, sensing the furtive gaze of those hidden in the dark, the nocturnal inhabitants of the Maidan. He knew that nobody here would try to waylay him and snatch his cape or take the children who were crying in his arms. The invisible presences could smell death clinging to his heels, and not a soul would dare come between him and his pursuer.

Peake jumped over the railings separating the Maidan from Chowringhee Road and entered the main artery of Calcutta. The majestic avenue had been built on top of the old path which, only three hundred years earlier, had crossed the Bengali jungle southwards, leading to the temple of Kali, the Kalighat, which gave the city its name.

Because of the rain, the swarms of people who usually prowled the area at night had retreated and the city looked like a large, empty bazaar. Peake knew that the veil of rain that blurred his vision, but also shrouded him, could vanish as instantly as it had appeared. The storms that entered the Ganges Delta from the ocean quickly travelled north or west after discharging their deluge on the Bengali Peninsula, leaving behind a trail of mist and flooded streets, where children played in filthy puddles and carts ran aground in the mud like drifting ships.

The lieutenant ran along Chowringhee Road until he felt the muscles of his legs give way and he was barely able to support the weight of the babies. He could see the lights of the northern district, but he knew he would not be able to keep up this pace much longer, and Aryami Bose's house was still a good distance away. He had to make a stop.

He paused to get his breath back under the staircase of an old textile warehouse, the walls of which were covered in official notices announcing its imminent demolition. He vaguely recalled having inspected the place years ago after some rich merchant had reported that it concealed a notorious opium den.

Now, dirty water poured down the crumbling stairs like dark blood gushing from a wound. The place seemed deserted. Lieutenant Peake lifted the children close to his face and looked into their bewildered eyes; the two babies were no longer crying, but they were trembling from the cold and the blanket that covered them was soaking. Peake held their tiny hands in his, hoping to give them some warmth as he peeped through the cracks in the staircase, keeping an eye on the streets leading off the Maidan. He couldn't remember how many assassins his pursuer had recruited, but he knew that there were only two bullets left in his revolver, two bullets he would have to use with all the cunning he could muster – he had fired the rest of his ammunition in the tunnels of the railway station.

Peake wrapped the children in the drier part of the blanket and left them lying on a bit of dry floor he spied in a hollow in the warehouse wall.

He pulled out his revolver, slowly peering round the side of the stairs. He strained his eyes and recognised the line of distant lights on the other side of the Hooghly River. The sound of hurried footsteps startled him and he moved back into the shadows.

Three men emerged from the darkness of the Maidan, the blades of their knives shining in the gloom. Peake rushed to gather the children in his arms once again and took a deep breath, aware that if he were to flee at that moment, the men would fall on him like a pack of wolves.

The lieutenant stood motionless against the wall, watching his pursuers as they stopped to search for his trail. The assassins exchanged a few mumbled words and then one signalled to the other two that they should separate. Peake shuddered as he realised that the one who had given the order was now approaching the staircase; for a split second he thought that the smell of his fear alone would lead the killer to his hiding place.

Desperately, he scanned the wall below the staircase in search of some gap through which he could escape. He knelt down by the hollow where he had left the babies a few seconds earlier and tried to dislodge some planks which were loose and softened by damp. The rotten wood yielded easily and Peake felt a breath of noxious air

11

escape from the dilapidated building. He turned his head and saw the murderer standing only twenty metres away, at the foot of the staircase, brandishing his knife.

Peake wrapped the babies in his cape for protection and crawled through into the warehouse. A sharp pain, just above his knee, suddenly paralysed his right leg. He patted his leg with trembling hands and found a rusty nail sunk into his flesh. Stifling a scream, Peake grabbed the tip of the cold metal and pulled hard. He felt the skin tear and warm blood trickled through his fingers. A wave of nausea and pain clouded his vision. Gasping, he gathered the babies and struggled to his feet. An eerie passageway with hundreds of empty shelves spread before him. Without a moment's hesitation, Peake ran towards the other end of the warehouse, the wounded structure creaking beneath the storm.

When Peake re-emerged into the night after running hundreds of metres through the bowels of the ruined building, he discovered he was only a stone's throw from the Tiretta Bazar, one of the commercial centres of North Calcutta. He thanked his lucky stars and set off towards the jumble of narrow streets, heading straight for the house of Aryami Bose.

It took him ten minutes to reach the home of the last woman in the Bose family line. Aryami lived alone in a sprawling house built in the Bengali style that rose amid the dense wild vegetation that had invaded the courtyard over the years, making the place look abandoned. Yet no inhabitant of North Calcutta – an area also known as the Black Town – would have dared go beyond that courtyard and enter the domain of Aryami Bose. Those who knew her loved and respected her as much as they feared her. And there wasn't a soul in the streets of North Calcutta who hadn't heard of Aryami Bose and her ancestry. For the people of the area she was like a spirit: an invisible and powerful presence.

Peake ran to the spearheaded gates, through the overgrown courtyard and up the cracked marble staircase that led to the front door. Holding both babies under one arm he banged repeatedly with his fist, hoping he would be heard through the storm.

The lieutenant continued to pound on the door for a good five minutes, his eyes fixed on the deserted streets behind him, fearing he would catch sight of his pursuers at any moment. When the door finally yielded, Peake turned round and was blinded by the light of a candle. A voice he hadn't heard in five years whispered his name. He shaded his eyes with one hand and recognised the inscrutable face of Aryami Bose.

The woman read his expression and gazed down at the children, a shadow of pain passing over her face.

'She's dead, Aryami,' murmured Peake. 'She was already dead when I found her …'

Aryami closed her eyes and breathed deeply. Peake saw that the news cut deep into the lady's heart, her worst suspicions confirmed.

'Come in,' she said at last, letting him pass and closing the door behind him.

Peake hurried over to a table, where he laid down the babies and removed their wet clothes. Without saying a word, Aryami fetched some dry strips of cloth and wrapped the children in them while Peake stoked the fire.

'I'm being followed, Aryami,' said Peake. 'I can't stay here.'

'You're wounded,' said the woman, pointing to the gash from the nail.

'Just a scratch,' Peake lied. 'It doesn't hurt.'

Aryami moved closer to him and stretched out her hand to stroke his face.

'You always loved her ...'

Peake turned his head away and didn't reply.

'They could have been your children,' said Aryami. 'They might have had better luck.'

'I must go, Aryami,' the lieutenant insisted. 'If I stay here they'll find me. They won't give up.'

They exchanged defeated looks, both aware of the fate that awaited Peake as soon as he returned to the streets. Aryami took his hands in hers and pressed them tightly.

'I was never good to you,' she said. 'I feared for my

daughter, for the life she might have had with a British officer. But I was wrong. I suppose you'll never forgive me.'

'It doesn't matter any more,' replied Peake. 'I *must* go. Right now.'

He took one last look at the babies, who had settled quietly by the fire. They smiled as they looked at him, their eyes bright and filled with a playful curiosity. At last they were safe. The lieutenant walked to the door and took a deep breath. Exhaustion and the throbbing pain in his leg overwhelmed him after the few moments of rest. He had used the last reserves of his strength to bring the infants to this place, and now he wondered how he was going to face the inevitable. Outside, the rain was still lashing down but there was no sign of his pursuer or his henchmen.

'Michael ...' said Aryami behind him.

The young man stopped but didn't turn round.

'She knew,' lied Aryami. 'She knew from the start, and I'm sure that, in some way, she felt the same for you. It was my fault. Don't hold it against her.'

Peake replied with a nod and closed the door behind him. For a few seconds he stood there, under the rain, finally at peace with himself, then he set off to meet his pursuers. After retracing his steps back to the abandoned warehouse, he entered the dark building once more in search of a hiding place.

As he crouched in the shadows weariness and pain

fused slowly into a drunken sense of calm, and his lips betrayed a faint smile. He no longer had any reason, or hope, to go on living.

~

THE LONG TAPERED FINGERS in the black glove stroked the bloodstained tip of the nail poking through the broken plank near the entrance to the warehouse. Slowly, while the assassins waited in silence behind him, the slender figure, whose face was hidden under a black hood, raised the tip of one forefinger to his lips and licked the dark thick blood as if it were a drop of honey. A few seconds later the hooded figure turned towards the men he had hired a few hours earlier for a handful of coins and the promise of further pay when they'd finished the job. He pointed inside the building. The three henchmen scurried through the opening made by Lieutenant Peake a short while earlier. The hooded man smirked in the darkness.

'You've chosen a sad place to die, Peake,' he whispered to himself.

Hiding behind a column of empty crates in the depths of the warehouse, Peake watched the silhouettes of the three men as they entered the building. Although he couldn't see him from where he stood, he was certain that their master was waiting on the other side of the wall; he could sense his presence. Peake pulled out his revolver and rotated the cylinder until one of the two bullets was aligned with the barrel, muffling the sound under his tunic. He was no longer running away from death, but he was determined not to travel this road alone.

The adrenalin coursing through his veins had eased the pain in his knee until it was just a dull, distant throb. Surprised at how calm he felt, Peake smiled again and remained motionless in his hiding place. He watched the slow advance of the three men through the passage until his executioners came to a halt about ten metres away. One of the men lifted a hand to stop the others and pointed at some stains on the ground. Peake raised his weapon to his chest, cocked the hammer, and took aim.

At a new signal, the three men separated. Two of them went sideways while the third made straight for the pile of crates, and Peake. The lieutenant counted to five, then suddenly pushed the column of boxes forward. The crates crashed down on top of his attacker while Peake ran towards the opening through which they had entered the warehouse.

One of the killers surprised him at a junction in the corridor, wielding his knife close to the lieutenant's face. But before the thug could even blink, the barrel of Peake's revolver was thrust under his chin.

'Drop the knife,' spat the lieutenant.

Seeing the ice in the lieutenant's eyes, the man did as he was told. Peake grabbed him by his hair and, without removing his weapon, turned to the assassin's allies, shielding his body with that of his hostage. The other two thugs moved menacingly towards Peake.

'Lieutenant, spare us the drama and hand over what we're looking for,' a familiar voice murmured behind him. 'These are honest men. With families.'

Peake turned to see the hooded man leering at him in the dark, just a few metres from where he stood.

'I'm going to blow this man's head off, Jawahal,' Peake snarled.

His hostage closed his eyes, trembling.

The hooded man crossed his arms patiently and gave out a small sigh of annoyance.

'Do so if it pleases you, Lieutenant. But that won't get you out of here.'

'I'm serious,' Peake replied.

'Of course, Lieutenant,' said Jawahal in a conciliatory tone. 'Shoot if you have the courage required to kill a man in cold blood and without His Majesty's permission. Otherwise, drop the weapon, and that way we'll be able to reach an agreement that is satisfactory to both parties.'

The two armed henchmen were standing nearby, ready to jump on Peake at the first signal from the hooded man.

'Very well,' Peake said at last. 'What do you think of *this* agreement?'

He pushed his hostage onto the floor and, raising his revolver, turned towards the hooded man. The first shot echoed through the warehouse. Jawahal's gloved hand emerged from the cloud of gunpowder, his palm outstretched. Peake thought he could see the crushed bullet shining in the dark, then melting slowly into a thread of liquid metal that slid through Jawahal's fingers like a fistful of sand.

'Bad shot, Lieutenant. Try again, only this time come closer.'

Without giving him time to move, the hooded man leaned forward and grasped the hand with which Peake was holding his weapon. He then pulled the end of the gun towards his own face until it rested between his eyes.

'Didn't they teach you to do it like this at the academy?' he whispered.

'There was a time when we were friends,' said Peake.

Jawahal smiled with contempt.

'That time, Lieutenant, has passed.'

'May God forgive me,' muttered Peake, pulling the trigger again.

In an instant that seemed endless, Peake watched as the bullet pierced Jawahal's skull, tearing the hood off his head. For a few seconds light passed through the wound but gradually the smoking hole closed in on itself. Peake felt the revolver slipping from his fingers.

The blazing eyes of his opponent fixed themselves on his and a long black tongue flicked across the man's lips.

'You still don't understand, do you, Lieutenant? Where are the babies?'

It was not a question. It was an order.

Dumb with terror, Peake shook his head.

'As you wish.'

Jawahal squeezed Peake's hand. The lieutenant felt the bones in his fingers being crushed under his flesh. The spasm of pain made him fall to his knees, unable to breathe.

'Where are the babies?' Jawahal hissed.

Peake tried to say something, but the agony spreading from the bloody stump that had been his hand paralysed his speech.

'Are you trying to say something, Lieutenant?' Jawahal whispered, kneeling beside him.

Peake nodded.

'Good, good.' His enemy smiled. 'Frankly, I don't find your suffering amusing. So help me put an end to it.'

'The children are dead,' Peake groaned.

An expression of distaste crept over Jawahal's face.

'You were doing so well, Lieutenant. Don't ruin it now.'

'They're dead,' Peake repeated.

Jawahal shrugged and slowly nodded his head.

'All right,' he conceded. 'You leave me no choice. But before you go, let me remind you that, when Kylian's life was in your hands, you were incapable of saving her. She died because of men like you. But those men have gone. You are the last one. The future is mine.'

Peake raised his eyes to Jawahal, and as he did so, he noticed the man's pupils narrowing into thin slits, his golden irises blazing. With painstaking elegance, Jawahal started to remove the glove on his right hand.

'Unfortunately you won't live to see it,' Jawahal added. 'Don't think for a second that your heroic act has served any purpose. You're an idiot, Lieutenant Peake. You always gave me that impression, and now all you have done is confirm it. I hope there is a hell reserved especially for idiots, Peake, because that's where I'm sending you.'

Peake closed his eyes and listened to the hiss of fire just inches from his face. Then, after a moment that seemed eternal, he felt burning fingers closing round his throat, cutting off his very last breath. In the distance he could hear the sound of that accursed train and the ghostly voices of hundreds of children howling from the flames. After that, only darkness.

ONE BY ONE, ARYAMI Bose blew out the candles that lit up her sanctuary until only the hesitant glow of the fire remained, projecting fleeting haloes of light against the naked walls. The children were now asleep and the silence was broken only by the rain pattering against the closed shutters and the occasional crackling of the fire. Silent tears slid down Aryami's face as she took the photograph of her daughter Kylian from the small brass and ivory box where she kept her most prized possessions.

A travelling photographer from Bombay had taken that picture some time before the wedding and hadn't accepted any payment for it. It showed Kylian just as Aryami remembered her, with that uncanny luminosity that seemed to emanate from her. Kylian's radiance had mesmerised all who knew her, just as it had captivated the expert eye of the photographer who had given her the nickname by which she was still remembered: the Princess of Light.

Naturally, Kylian never became a true princess and had no kingdom other than the streets she grew up on. The day she left the Bose home to go and live with her husband, the people of Machuabazar had said farewell with tears in their eyes as they watched the white carriage carry away their Black Town princess for ever. She was scarcely more than a child at the time.

Aryami sat down next to the babies, facing the fireplace, and pressed the old photograph against her chest. Outside the storm raged on and Aryami drew on the force of its anger to help her decide what she should do next. Lieutenant Peake's pursuer would not be content simply with killing him. The young man's courage had earned her a few valuable minutes, which she could not waste, not even to mourn for her daughter. Experience had taught her that there would always be plenty of time to lament the errors of the past.

∽

SHE PUT THE PHOTOGRAPH back into the box and took out a pendant she'd had made for Kylian years ago, a jewel she never had the chance to wear. It consisted of two gold circles, a sun and a moon, that fitted into one another to make a single piece. She pressed the centre of the pendant and the two parts separated. Aryami strung each half on a separate gold chain and put one round each of the babies' necks.

As she did so, she considered the decisions she must make. There seemed to be only one way of ensuring the children's survival: she must separate them and keep them apart, erase their past and hide their identity from the world and from themselves, however painful that might be. It was not possible for them to remain together; sooner or later they would give themselves away, and she could not take that risk. Aryami knew she had to resolve the dilemma before daybreak.

She took the babies in her arms and kissed them gently on the forehead. Their tiny hands stroked her face and fingered the tears that rolled down her cheeks. Both babies gurgled cheerfully at her, not understanding. She hugged them tight in her arms once more then placed them back in the improvised cot she had made for them.

She then lit a candle and took paper and pen. The future of her grandchildren was now in her hands. Taking a deep breath she began to write. In the background she could hear the rain easing off and the roar of the storm fading towards the north as an endless blanket of stars unfurled over Calcutta.

∽

HAVING REACHED THE AGE of fifty, Thomas Carter thought that the city that had been his home for the last thirty-two years had no more surprises in store for him.

In the early hours of that morning in May 1916, after one of the fiercest monsoon storms he remembered, the surprise had arrived at the door of St Patrick's Orphanage in the form of a basket containing a baby and a sealed letter marked personal and addressed to him.

The surprise was two-fold. Firstly, nobody bothered to abandon a baby in Calcutta on the doorstep of an orphanage, for there were plenty of alleyways, rubbish dumps and wells all over the city where it could be done more easily. Secondly, nobody wrote letters of introduction like the one he received, signed and leaving no doubt as to its author.

Carter examined his spectacles against the light, breathed on them, then wiped them with an old cotton handkerchief he used for the same task at least a dozen times a day – twice as much during the Indian summer.

The baby boy was asleep downstairs, in Vendela's bedroom. The head nurse had been keeping a watchful eye on him since he'd been examined by Dr Woodward, who'd been dragged out of his bed shortly before dawn with no other explanation than a reminder of his Hippocratic oath.

The infant was essentially healthy. He showed some signs of dehydration but didn't seem to be suffering from any of the catalogue of ills that cut short the lives of thousands of children, denying them the right even to reach the age when they'd be able to say their mothers' name. The only things that had come with the child were the gold pendant in the shape of a sun that Carter held between his fingers, and the letter – a document which, were he to believe its content, placed him in a very awkward situation.

Carter put the pendant in the top drawer of his desk and turned the key. Then he picked up the letter and read it for at least the tenth time.

Dear Mr Carter,

I feel obliged to ask for your help in the most painful of circumstances, appealing to the friendship that I know united you and my late husband for over ten years. During that time my husband never ceased to praise your honesty and the extraordinary trust you inspired in him. That is why today I beg you to heed my plea with the greatest urgency, however strange it may seem, and if possible with the greatest secrecy.

The child I am obliged to hand over to you has lost both his parents. The murderer swore he would kill them and

*then wipe out their descendants. I cannot reveal the reasons
that led this man to commit such an act, nor do I think it
appropriate to do so. Suffice it to say that the discovery of the
child should be kept secret. Under no circumstance should
you inform the police or the British authorities, because the
murderer has connections in both that would soon lead him to
the boy.*

*For obvious reasons, I cannot raise the child myself
without exposing him to the same fate that befell his parents.
That is why I must beg you to take care of him, give him
a name and educate him according to the principles of
your institution, so that he grows up to be as honest and
honourable as his parents were. And it is vitally important
that the child should never learn the truth about his past.*

*I don't have time to give you any more details, but I will
remind you once more of the friendship and trust you shared
with my husband in order to justify my request.*

*When you finish reading this letter, I beg you to destroy it,
together with anything that might lead to the discovery of the
child. I am sorry I cannot undertake this request in person,
but the seriousness of the situation prevents me from doing so.*

*In the hope that you will make the right decision, please
accept my eternal gratitude.*

Aryami Bose

A knock on the door interrupted his reading. Carter
removed his spectacles, carefully folded the letter and
placed it in the drawer of his desk, which he then locked.

'Come in,' he said.

Vendela, the head nurse of St Patrick's, put her head round the door; as usual her expression was stern and efficient. She didn't seem to be the bearer of good news.

'There's a gentleman downstairs who wishes to speak to you,' she said briefly.

Carter frowned.

'What about?'

'He wouldn't give any details.' Her tone seemed to imply that any such details were bound to be vaguely suspicious.

Vendela hesitated, then stepped into the office and closed the door behind her.

'I think it's about the baby,' the nurse said anxiously. 'I didn't tell him anything.'

'Have you spoken to anyone else?' Carter enquired.

Vendela shook her head. He gave her a nod and put the key of the desk in his trouser pocket.

'I can tell him you're not in,' suggested Vendela.

For a moment Carter considered the option, but decided that if Vendela's suspicions were correct – and they usually were – it would only reinforce the impression that St Patrick's Orphanage had something to hide. That made up his mind.

'No. I'll receive him, Vendela. Ask him to come in and make sure none of the staff talk to him. Absolute secrecy on this matter. All right?'

'Understood.'

Carter heard Vendela's footsteps as she walked down the corridor. He wiped his glasses again. Outside the rain was hammering against the windowpanes once more.

THE MAN WORE A long cloak, and his head was wrapped in a turban, which was pinned with a dark brooch shaped like a snake. He had the affected manners of a prosperous North Calcutta merchant and his features seemed vaguely Hindu, although his skin was an unhealthy colour, as if it had never been touched by sunlight. The racial melting pot of Calcutta had filled its streets with a fusion of Bengalis, Armenians, Jews, Anglo-Saxons, Chinese, Muslims and numerous other groups who had come to the land of Kali in search of fortune or refuge. The man's face could have belonged to any of those races, or to none.

Carter could sense the stranger's eyes burning into his back, inspecting him carefully as he poured tea into two cups on the tray Vendela had provided.

'Do sit down,' said Carter to the man. 'Sugar?'

'I'll take it the way you take it.'

The stranger's voice betrayed no accent or emotion of any sort. Carter swallowed hard, then fixed a friendly smile on his lips and turned round to pass his visitor the cup. A gloved hand, with long fingers sharp as claws, closed round the scalding china without a moment's hesitation. Carter sat down in his armchair and stirred sugar into his tea.

'I'm sorry to bother you, Mr Carter. I suppose you must be very busy, so I'll be brief.'

Carter gave a polite nod.

'What is the reason for your visit, Mr ...?'

'My name is Jawahal, Mr Carter,' the stranger explained. 'I'll be frank. My question may seem odd to you, but have you found a child, a baby, just a few days old, either last night or today?'

Carter frowned and did his best to look surprised. Nothing too obvious, but not too subtle either.

'A baby? I'm not sure I understand ...'

Jawahal smiled broadly.

'I don't know where to begin. You see, it's rather an awkward story. I trust you'll be discreet, Mr Carter.'

'But of course, Mr Jawahal,' replied Carter, taking a sip of his tea.

The man, who had not tasted his cup, relaxed and launched into his tale.

'I own a large textile business in the north of the city,' he began. 'I am what might be described as comfortably off. There are those who would call me wealthy, and rightly so, I suppose. I'm responsible for a number of families and I'm privileged to be able to help them as much as I can.'

'With things the way they are, we all need to do what

29

we can,' said Carter, his gaze fixed on those two dark inscrutable eyes.

'Yes, of course,' the stranger continued. 'The matter that brings me to your worthy institution is a painful one, and I'd like to put an end to it as soon as possible. A week ago a young girl who works in one of my factories gave birth to a baby boy. It seems that the father of the child is an Anglo-Indian rogue who disappeared as soon as he heard of the girl's pregnancy. I'm told that the girl's family come from Delhi. They're Muslim, very strict, and they were not aware of the situation.'

Carter nodded gravely.

'A couple of days ago one of my foremen told me that, in a fit of madness, the girl fled from the house where she was living with some relatives. It seems she was intending to sell the child,' Jawahal went on. 'Don't get me wrong. She's a good girl, but she was under so much pressure that she became desperate. Which isn't so surprising – this country is just as intolerant of human weakness as yours is.'

'And you think the baby might be here, Mr Jahawal?' asked Carter, trying to bring him back to the subject.

'Jawahal,' the visitor corrected him. 'Let me explain. Once I became aware of the circumstances I felt responsible, in a way. After all, the girl worked for me. I combed the city with a couple of trusted foremen and discovered that she had sold the child to a loathsome criminal who sells babies to professional beggars –

a phenomenon that nowadays is as common as it is deplorable. We found the man, but, for reasons that are now irrelevant, he managed to escape. This happened last night, near your orphanage. I have reason to believe that, fearing what might happen to him, he may have abandoned the baby nearby.'

'I see,' said Carter. 'And have you informed the local authorities of this matter, Mr Jawahal? The trafficking of children is punished severely, as you must know.'

The stranger folded his hands together and gave a little sigh.

'I was hoping to solve this problem without having to go to those lengths,' he said. 'If I did that, I would implicate the young girl, and the child would be left without a father or a mother.'

Carter sized up the stranger's story, nodding slowly and repeatedly to show he understood although he didn't believe a single word.

'I'm sorry I can't be of help to you, Mr Jawahal. Unfortunately we haven't found a baby or heard of any child being found nearby,' Carter explained. 'Still, if you leave me your details I'll get in touch if I hear anything, although I'm afraid I would have to inform the authorities if the baby was abandoned outside this orphanage. That's the law, and I can't ignore it.'

The man stared silently at Carter for a few seconds without blinking. Carter held his gaze and didn't alter his expression, although he could feel his stomach shrinking and his pulse accelerating, as if he were facing a snake that was about to strike. Finally the stranger gave a pleasant smile and pointed in the direction of the Raj Bhawan, the palatial government building that rose in the distance.

'You British are admirable observers of the law, which is to your credit. Wasn't it Lord Wellesley who, in 1799, decided to move government headquarters to that magnificent site in order to lend its laws greater weight? Or was it in 1800?'

'I'm afraid I'm not an expert on local history,' Carter replied, disconcerted by the sudden twist Jawahal had given the conversation.

The visitor frowned, mutely signalling his disapproval of Carter's confessed ignorance.

'With only two hundred and fifty years to its name, Calcutta has so little history that the least we can do is learn about it, Mr Carter. But, returning to the subject, I'd say it was in 1799. Do you know why the move was made? Wellesley, the governor general, said that India must be ruled from a palace and not from an accountants' office; with the ideas of a prince, not those of a spice trader. Quite a vision, I'd say.'

'Indeed,' Carter agreed. He stood up, ready to see the visitor out.

'All the more so in an empire in which decadence is an art form and Calcutta its main showcase,' Jawahal added.

Carter nodded his head, not quite sure what he was agreeing with.

'I'm sorry I've wasted your time, Mr Carter,' concluded Jawahal.

'On the contrary,' replied Carter. 'I'm just sorry I haven't been of any assistance. In such circumstances we must all do what we can to help.'

'Absolutely,' Jawahal agreed, also standing up. 'Once again, I appreciate your kindness. I just wanted to ask you one more question.'

'With pleasure,' answered Carter, although he couldn't wait to get rid of this man.

Jawahal smiled maliciously, as if he'd read Carter's thoughts.

'At what age do the children you take in leave this place, Mr Carter?'

Carter couldn't hide his surprise.

'I hope you don't think I'm being tactless,' Jawahal added hurriedly. 'If that is the case, please ignore my question. I'm just curious.'

'No, not at all. It's no secret. The boarders at St Patrick's remain under our roof until the day they turn sixteen. That's when the guardianship period ends. At that point they are considered to be adults, or so the law says, ready to take charge of their own lives. As you can see, this is a privileged institution.'

Jawahal listened attentively and appeared to be considering the matter.

'I imagine it must be very painful for you to see them leave after having cared for them all those years,' Jawahal observed. 'In a way, you're like a father to all these children.'

'It's my job,' Carter lied.

'Of course. But – if you don't mind my asking – how do you know the real age of a child who has no parents or family? It's a technicality, I suppose ...'

'The age of our boarders is set from the day the child is taken in, or else the institution makes an approximate calculation,' Carter explained, feeling uncomfortable about discussing the orphanage's procedures with the stranger.

'Which makes you a little god, Mr Carter.'

'That is a view I do not share,' Carter replied dryly. Jawahal relished the displeasure on Carter's face.

'Forgive my audacity, Mr Carter,' Jawahal replied. 'It was a pleasure to meet you. I may visit in the future and make a donation to your noble institution. Perhaps I'll return in sixteen years' time; that way I'll be able to meet the youngsters who become part of your large family today ...'

'It will be a pleasure to receive you then, if that is your wish,' said Carter, leading the stranger to the door. 'It looks like the rain has got worse. Maybe you'd prefer to wait until it dies down?'

The man turned towards Carter and his pupils glowed like two black pearls. He seemed to have been weighing up every gesture, every expression from the moment he'd entered the office, sniffing out any cracks in the story and analysing every word. Carter regretted extending his offer of hospitality. At that precise moment the only thing Carter wanted was to see the back of this individual. He didn't care if a hurricane was laying waste to the city.

'The rain will stop soon, Mr Carter,' Jawahal replied. 'Thanks all the same.'

Right on cue, Vendela was waiting in the corridor as the meeting ended, and she escorted the visitor to the exit. From the window of his office Carter watched the black figure setting off into the rain then disappearing among the narrow streets at the foot of the hill. Carter stood there for a while, looking out of his window, his eyes fixed on the Raj Bhawan, the seat of the British government. A few minutes later, just as Jawahal had predicted, the rain stopped.

Thomas Carter poured himself another cup of tea and sat in his armchair gazing out at the city. He had grown up in a place similar to the home he now managed, in Liverpool. Within the walls of that institution he had learned three things that would always serve him well: not to overvalue material comforts, to appreciate the classics and, last but not least, to recognise a liar from a mile away.

He took a leisurely sip of his tea and, in view of the fact that Calcutta could still surprise him, decided to start celebrating his fiftieth birthday. He walked over to a glass cabinet and took out the box of cigars he reserved for special occasions. Striking a match, he lit the valuable item with due calm and ceremony. Then, putting the flame to good use, he pulled Aryami Bose's letter out of the drawer and set fire to it. While the parchment turned to ashes on a small tray with St Patrick's initials engraved on it, Carter savoured the cigar and, in honour of Benjamin Franklin, one of his childhood heroes, decided that their new tenant would be called Ben, and that he personally would put all his energy into making sure the orphanage provided the boy with the family fate had stolen from him.

BEFORE I CONTINUE WITH MY STORY AND START describing the events that took place sixteen years later, I must take a brief moment to introduce some of its protagonists. Of course, while all of this was taking place in the streets of Calcutta, some of us had not yet been born and others were only a few days old. Yet we had one thing in common, a circumstance that would bring us together under the roof of St Patrick's: none of us had a family or a home.

We learned to survive without either of those things. Better still, we invented our own family and created our home. It was a family and a home we had chosen freely, and neither lies nor chance had any place there. The only father the seven of us ever knew was Mr Thomas Carter, with his speeches about the wisdom to be found in the pages of Dante and Virgil; and our only mother was the city of Calcutta, whose mysteries were concealed in the streets that lay beneath the stars of the Bengali Peninsula.

The club we invented had a colourful name, the true origin of which was known only to Ben. He had christened the club at whim, although some of us had a sneaking suspicion that he'd borrowed the word from the old mail-order catalogue of some Bombay importer. Be that as it may, the Chowbar Society was set up at some point in our lives, after which the orphanage games seemed dull in comparison. By then we were cunning enough to slip out of the building in the small hours of the night, long after the venerable Vendela's curfew, and make straight for our society's headquarters – the top secret and supposedly haunted house which for decades had stood abandoned on the corner of Cotton Street and Brabourne Road, in the middle of the Black Town, just a few streets away from the Hooghly River.

I have to admit that the ramshackle house we proudly called the Midnight Palace (in consideration of the hour when we held our meetings) was never really haunted. The rumours about its supernatural powers arose because of our subterfuge. One of our founding members, Siraj, a full-time asthmatic and learned expert on Calcutta's tales of ghosts, apparitions and curses, hatched a convincingly sinister legend about an alleged former resident. This helped keep our secret hideaway free of intruders.

The story, in short, was about an old tradesman who floated through the house wrapped in a white cloak. He had blazing red eyes and long wolfish fangs that rested over his lips, and he hungered after unsuspecting curious souls. The bit about the eyes and the teeth was, of course, Ben's contribution, as he loved to concoct plots so gruesome they left Mr Carter's classics – Sophocles and the gory Homer included – in the dust.

Despite the humorous echoes of its name, the Chowbar Society was as select and strict as any of the clubs that filled the Edwardian buildings of central Calcutta, emulating their London namesakes; their elegant lounges, where members could vegetate, brandy in hand, were the birthright of the British male elite. Our surroundings may have been less splendid, but our aim was far nobler.

The Chowbar Society had been founded with two firm objectives. The first was to guarantee each of its seven members the help, protection and unconditional support of the others, in any circumstance, danger or adversity. The second was to share the knowledge each of us acquired, so that we could equip ourselves for the day when we would have to face the world alone.

Every member had sworn upon his own name and honour (we had no close relatives to swear by) to observe those two objectives and to keep the society a secret. During the seven years of its existence no new member was ever admitted. I lie. We made one exception, but to write about that now would be to get ahead of myself ...

Never was there a society whose members were more united, and whose oath carried such weight. The Chowbar Society was nothing like the clubs for wealthy gentlemen in the West End, for none of us had a home or a loved one to go to when we left the Midnight Palace. It was also very different from the ancient student societies in Cambridge, because it did admit women.

So I will begin with the first woman who pledged her oath as a founder member of the Chowbar Society, although when the ceremony took place none of us (including the person I'm alluding to, who was nine at the time) thought of her as a woman. Her name was Isobel and, as she said herself, she had been born for the stage. Isobel dreamed of becoming the successor to Sarah Bernhardt, seducing audiences from Broadway to Shaftesbury Avenue and leaving the divas of the newly formed cinema industry unemployed, both in Hollywood and Bombay. She collected newspaper cuttings and theatre programmes, wrote her own plays ('active monologues' she called them) and performed them for us with great success. Most outstanding were her sketches about a femme fatale on the brink of the abyss. But, beneath all the extravagance and melodrama, Isobel possessed – with the possible exception of Ben – the best brain in the group.

The best legs, however, belonged to Roshan. Nobody could run like Roshan, who had grown up in the streets of Calcutta under the tutelage of thieves, beggars and all kinds of other specimens from the jungle of poverty that flourished in the newly expanding areas to the south of the city. When the boy was eight, Thomas Carter brought him to St Patrick's and, after a few escapes and returns, Roshan decided to stay with us. Among his many talents was that of locksmith. There wasn't a lock on earth that wouldn't yield to his skill.

I've already spoken about Siraj, our specialist in haunted houses. Leaving aside his asthma, his pale complexion and poor health, Siraj possessed an encyclopedic memory, particularly when it came to sinister stories about the city, of which there were hundreds. For the ghost stories that enhanced our special evenings, Siraj was the researcher and Ben the narrator. From the ghostly rider of Hastings House to the spectral leader of the 1857 mutiny, including the spine-chilling episode of the so-called black hole of Calcutta (where over a hundred men suffocated, after being captured in a siege at the old Fort William), there wasn't a tall tale or gruesome incident that escaped Siraj's archives. Needless to say, for the rest of us his passion was a cause for great joy and celebration. Unfortunately, however, Siraj had an almost unhealthy adoration for Isobel. At least once every six months his proposals for a future marriage – which were invariably refused – triggered a romantic storm within the group that aggravated the spurned lover's asthma.

Isobel's affections belonged exclusively to Michael, a tall skinny boy who was quiet by nature and given to long inexplicable spells of melancholy. Michael had the dubious privilege of having known, and therefore of remembering, his parents. They had died during a flood of the Ganges Delta when an overloaded barge had capsized. Michael spoke little and was a good listener. There was only one way of deciphering his thoughts: by looking at the dozens of drawings he did during the day. Ben used to say that if there was more than one Michael in the world, he'd invest all his fortune – still to be made – in the paper business.

Michael's best friend was Seth, a strong Bengali boy with a serious expression who smiled about six times a year and even then with hesitation. Seth was a scholar of anything that came into his line of fire, a tireless devourer of Mr Carter's classics, and keen on astronomy. When he wasn't with us, he concentrated all his efforts on building a strange telescope, with which, according to Ben, you couldn't even see the tips of your toes. Seth never appreciated Ben's vaguely caustic sense of humour.

Only Ben remains, and, although I've left him until the end, I still find it hard to talk about him. There was a different Ben for every day. His mood changed every half-hour and he'd go from long stretches of silence, a sad expression on his face, to periods of hyperactivity that ended up exhausting us all. One day he wanted to be a writer; the following day an inventor and a mathematician; the day after that a sailor or a deep-sea diver; the rest of the time it was all of those things with a few more added. Ben invented mathematical theories that even he didn't manage to remember and wrote such bizarre tales of adventure that he ended up destroying them a week after they were finished, embarrassed at the thought that he had penned them. He machine-

gunned us constantly with elaborate ideas and complex puns which he always refused to repeat. Ben was like a bottomless trunk, full of surprises, also of mystery, light and shadow. He was, and I suppose he still is, even though we haven't seen one another in decades, my best friend.

As for me, there's not much to tell. Just call me Ian. I had only one dream, and it was a modest one: to study medicine and become a doctor. Fate was good to me and I was granted that wish. As Ben wrote in one of his stories, I 'just happened to be passing by and was a witness to those events'.

I remember that in the last days of that month, May 1932, all of us – all seven members of the Chowbar Society – were going to turn sixteen. It was a fateful age, both feared and keenly anticipated by us all.

Following its statutes, St Patrick's would return us to society when we reached sixteen so that we could grow into responsible men and women. That date held another meaning that we all understood only too well: it signified the dissolution of the Chowbar Society. From that summer onwards our paths would diverge, and despite our promises and all the kind lies we had told ourselves, we knew that it would not be long before the bond that had joined us was washed away like a sandcastle on the seashore.

I have so many memories of those years that even today I catch myself smiling at Ben's witty remarks and *the fantastic stories we shared in the Midnight Palace. But perhaps, of all the images that refuse to be swept away by the current of time, the one I recall most vividly is that of a figure I often thought I saw at night in the dormitory shared by most of the boys of St Patrick's – a long dark room with a high vaulted ceiling reminiscent of a hospital ward. I suppose that, due to the insomnia I suffered until two years after I moved to Europe, I found myself, yet again, a spectator of everything that was going on around me while the others slept …*

It was there, in that soulless dormitory, that night after night I thought I saw a pale light crossing the room. Not knowing how to react, I would try to sit up and follow the reflection until it reached the other end, and in that moment I would look at it again, just as I had dreamed I would look at it on so many other occasions. The evanescent silhouette of a woman swathed in spectral light slowly bent over the bed in which Ben was sleeping. Each time, I struggled to keep my eyes open and thought I could see the lady stroking my friend's face in a maternal way. I gazed at her translucent oval face surrounded by a halo of diaphanous light. The lady would raise her eyes and look at me. Far from being frightened, I embraced her sad wounded look. The Princess of Light would then smile at me and, after stroking Ben's face one more time, would dissolve into the night like a silver mist.

I always imagined that the vision I saw was the spirit of the mother Ben had never met and, somewhere in my heart, I maintained the childish hope that, if one day I managed to fall into a deep sleep, a similar apparition would also take care of me. That was the only secret I did not share with anyone, not even Ben.

© Jackie Freshfield

The Last Night of the Chowbar Society

Calcutta, 25 May 1932

FOR OVER THIRTY-FIVE YEARS, AS HEAD OF ST Patrick's, Thomas Carter had taught his pupils literature, history and arithmetic with the confidence of a jack of all trades and master of none. The only subject he was never able to deal with properly was the subject of their departure. Year after year, the boys and girls whom the law would soon place outside the influence and protection of his institution would file past him, their faces revealing a mixture of anticipation and fear. And as he watched them walk out of the orphanage, Thomas

Carter would think of their lives as the blank pages of a book in which he had written the initial chapters of a story he would never be allowed to finish.

Beneath the austere expression of a man not given to displays of emotion, nobody feared the date on which those blank books would leave his desk for ever more than Thomas Carter. They would pass into unknown hands, perhaps to more unscrupulous pens who would inscribe a sombre twist in the plot, a lifetime away from the dreams and the expectations with which his pupils undertook their solitary flight into the streets of Calcutta.

Experience had taught him to abandon any desire to find out how his students fared once he could no longer offer guidance and shelter. For Thomas Carter, saying goodbye usually went hand in hand with the bitter taste of disappointment – sooner or later he would discover that the young people who had been robbed of a past were also, it seemed, being robbed of a future.

That hot night in May, as he listened to the young people's voices in the courtyard, where they were having a small farewell party, Thomas Carter stared at the city lights from the darkness of his office. Flocks of black clouds fled across a canopy of stars towards the horizon.

Once again he had refused the invitation to the party and instead had remained in his armchair, sitting quietly with no light other than the multicoloured reflections from the paper lanterns with which Vendela and the pupils had decorated the trees in the courtyard and the facade of St Patrick's, as if it were a ship ready to be launched. There would be time enough to utter words of farewell in the few days remaining until he had to comply with the law and return the children to the streets from which he had rescued them.

As had become the custom in recent years, it wasn't long before Vendela knocked on his door. For once, she came in without waiting for a reply and closed the door behind her. Carter noticed the nurse's cheerful face and smiled in the dark.

'We're getting old, Vendela,' said the headmaster.

'You're getting old, Thomas,' she corrected him. 'I'm maturing. Aren't you coming down to the party? The kids would love to see you. I've reminded them you aren't exactly the life and soul of a party ... But if they haven't listened to me for the past few years then they're not going to start now.'

Carter lit a small lamp on his desk and gestured to Vendela to take a seat.

'How long have we been together, Vendela?' he asked.

'Twenty-seven years and eight months, Mr Carter. More than I endured with my dear late husband, God rest his soul.'

Carter laughed. 'How have you managed to put up with me all this time? Don't hold back. Today's a holiday and I'm in a good mood.'

Vendela shrugged and fiddled with a piece of scarlet streamer that was tangled in her hair.

49

'The pay isn't bad and I like the children. You're not coming down, are you?'

Carter shook his head slowly.

'I don't want to ruin the party,' he explained. 'And besides, I couldn't bear to hear another of Ben's jokes.'

'Ben's very calm tonight,' said Vendela. 'He's sad, I suppose. The boys have already given Ian his ticket.'

Carter's face lit up. The members of the Chowbar Society – whose clandestine existence had been known to Carter for some time – had for months been saving money to buy a ticket on a ship to Southampton, which they planned to give to their friend Ian as a goodbye present. For years Ian had been expressing his desire to study medicine, and Mr Carter, at Ben and Isobel's suggestion, had written to a number of English schools, supporting the boy and recommending him for a scholarship. The news of the scholarship had arrived a year ago, but the cost of the journey to London turned out to be far higher than anyone had expected.

Faced with this problem, Roshan suggested robbing the offices of a shipping company that was two blocks away from the orphanage. Siraj proposed they organise a raffle. Carter took out a sum from his meagre personal savings and Vendela did the same, but it was not enough.

So Ben decided to write a three-act play entitled *The Spectres of Calcutta* – a phantasmal piece of gibberish in which everyone died, including the stagehands. With

Isobel playing the lead as Lady Windmare, the rest of the group performing secondary roles and an over-the-top production courtesy of Ben, it enjoyed remarkable success with its audiences – though not with its critics – in various schools in the city. As a result, enough money was collected to pay for Ian's journey.

'Ian had tears in his eyes when he received the gift,' said Vendela.

'He is a wonderful lad, a little insecure but wonderful. He'll make good use of the ticket and the scholarship,' said Carter proudly.

'He asked after you. He wanted to thank you for your help.'

'You didn't tell him I contributed money from my own pocket, did you?' asked Carter in alarm.

'I did, but Ben denied it, saying you'd spent the year's entire budget on your gambling debts.'

The noise from the party echoed through the courtyard. Carter frowned.

'That boy is a devil. If he wasn't about to leave, I would throw him out.'

'You adore the boy, Thomas.' Vendela laughed as she stood up. 'And he knows it.'

The nurse made her way to the door, turning as she reached it. She didn't give up easily.

'Why don't you come down?'

'Goodnight, Vendela.'

'You're a boring old man.'

'And proud of it …'

Recognising the futility of her task, Vendela mumbled a few words and left Carter alone. The director of St Patrick's turned his desk lamp off and walked stealthily to the window to peer at the party through the slats of his blind. The garden was lit with flares, and lanterns cast a copper glow over the familiar smiling faces under the full moon. Although none of them knew it, they each had a one-way ticket to somewhere, but only Ian knew his destination.

'IN TWENTY MINUTES IT will be midnight,' Ben announced.

His eyes shone as he watched the firecrackers spreading a shower of golden sparks into the air.

'I hope Siraj has some good stories tonight,' said Isobel as she stared at the bottom of her glass, holding it up to the light as if she expected to find something in it.

'The best,' Roshan assured them. 'Tonight is our last night. The end of the Chowbar Society.'

'I wonder what will become of the Palace,' said Seth.

For years none of them had referred to the dilapidated old house by any other name.

'Guess,' Ben suggested. 'Most likely a bank. Isn't that what they always build when they knock something down in any city? It's the same the world over.'

Siraj had joined them and was considering Ben's prediction.

'They might turn it into a theatre,' the skinny boy proposed, gazing at Isobel, the impossible object of his affection.

Ben rolled his eyes and shook his head. When it came to flattering the girl, Siraj had no dignity.

'Maybe they won't touch it,' said Ian, who had been listening quietly to his friends, stealing a few quick glances at the picture Michael was drawing on a small sheet of paper.

'What are you doing there, master?' asked Ben.

Michael looked up from his drawing for the first time. He looked as if he had just stepped out of a faraway world. He smiled shyly and exhibited the sheet of paper.

'It's us,' the club's resident artist explained.

The six other members of the Chowbar Society examined the picture for five long seconds in silence. The first to look away from the drawing was Ben. Michael recognised the enigmatic expression that crossed his friend's face when he suffered one of his strange attacks of melancholy.

'Is that supposed to be my nose?' asked Siraj. 'I don't have a nose like that! It looks like a fish hook!'

'That's exactly what you've got,' Ben stated with a smile that did not fool Michael, although it may have fooled the others. 'Don't complain; if he'd drawn you in profile all you'd see is a straight line.'

'Let me have a look,' said Isobel, snatching the picture and studying it in the flickering light of a lantern. 'Is this how you see us?'

Michael shrugged.

'You've drawn yourself looking in a different direction from the rest of us,' observed Ian.

'Michael always looks at what others don't see,' said Roshan.

'And what have you seen in us that nobody else can, Michael?' asked Ben.

He joined Isobel and analysed the drawing. Thick pencil strokes depicted the group next to a pond in which their faces were all reflected. There was a large full moon in the sky and below it was a forest disappearing off into the distance. Ben examined the blurred faces on the water's surface and compared them to those of the figures by the edge of the pond. Not a single one of them carried the same expression as its reflection. Isobel's voice rescued him from his thoughts.

'May I keep it, Michael?' she asked.

'Why you?' Seth protested.

Ben placed a hand on the Bengali boy's broad shoulders and gave him a brief intense look.

'Let her keep it,' he murmured.

Seth nodded and Ben patted his back affectionately. As he did so, he caught sight of an elderly woman, elegantly dressed, and a young girl of about their age, crossing the orphanage courtyard and heading towards the front door of the building.

'Is anything the matter?' whispered Ian, next to him.

Ben shook his head slowly.

'We have visitors,' he said, without taking his eyes off the woman and the young girl. 'Or something like that ...'

WHEN BANKIM KNOCKED ON his door, Thomas Carter was already aware of the arrival of the woman and her companion. He had seen them through the window as he watched the party below. He turned on the desk lamp and told his assistant to come in.

Bankim was a young man with very marked Bengali features and lively, penetrating eyes. He had grown up in the orphanage and, after working for a few years in different schools around the province, had returned to St Patrick's as a physics and maths teacher. Bankim's happy ending was one of the few exceptions which, year after year, gave Carter hope. To see him there as an adult, helping educate other young people in the same classrooms he had once sat in, was the best possible reward.

'I'm sorry to bother you, Thomas,' said Bankim. 'But there's a lady downstairs who says she needs to speak to you. I've told her you aren't available, that we're having a party, but she won't listen and was most insistent, to say the least.'

Carter gave his assistant a puzzled look, then checked his watch.

'It's almost midnight. Who is she?'

Bankim shrugged his shoulders.

'I don't know, but I do know she won't leave until she sees you.'

'She didn't say what she wanted?'

'She only asked me to give you this,' Bankim replied, handing Carter a small shiny chain. 'She said you'd know what it was.'

Carter took the chain and examined it under his desktop lamp. Hanging from it was a gold pendant, a circle with the shape of a moon. It took a few seconds for the image to jog Carter's memory. He closed his eyes and felt his stomach knot. He had a very similar pendant hidden in the box he kept under lock and key in his glass cabinet. A pendant he had not seen in sixteen years.

'Is there a problem, Thomas?' asked Bankim, visibly worried by the change in Carter's expression.

The headmaster shook his head and smiled faintly as he put the gold chain into his shirt pocket.

'None at all,' he replied. 'Ask her to come up. I'll see her.'

Bankim eyed him with surprise, and for a moment Carter thought his former pupil was going to ask him a question he didn't want to hear. But in the end Bankim simply nodded and left the office, gently closing the door behind him. Two minutes later Aryami Bose entered Thomas Carter's private sanctuary, removing the veil that covered her face.

~

BEN LOOKED INTENTLY AT the girl as she waited under the arches of the main entrance to St Patrick's. Bankim had returned and, after being asked to follow him, the old lady had instructed the girl in no uncertain terms to remain by the door. It was obvious the woman had come to visit Carter, and considering how lacklustre the head of the orphanage's social life was, Ben assumed that any midnight visit from a mysterious beauty, whatever her age, must definitely be classed as unexpected. He smiled and concentrated once more on the girl. Tall and slim, she was dressed in simple though unusual clothes that looked as if they'd been made by someone with a unique personal style and obviously not bought in any old bazaar in the Black Town. Her features, which he couldn't see clearly from where he stood, seemed to be soft and her skin was pale and luminous.

'Anyone home?' Ian whispered in his ear.

Ben signalled towards the girl, his eyes still transfixed.

'It's almost midnight,' Ian added. 'We're meeting in

the Palace in a few minutes. Final session, may I remind you?'

Ben nodded absently.

'Wait a minute,' he added and started to walk resolutely towards the girl.

'Ben,' Ian called behind him. 'Not now, Ben ...' Ben ignored his friend. The curiosity he felt was stronger than all the ceremonial delights of the Chowbar Society. He adopted the saintly smile of a model pupil and walked on. The girl saw him approach and lowered her eyes.

'Hello. I'm Mr Carter's assistant – he's the head of St Patrick's,' said Ben. 'May I help you in any way?'

'Actually, no ... Your ... colleague has already taken my grandmother to see the headmaster,' said the girl.

'Your grandmother?' asked Ben. 'I see. I hope it's nothing serious. I mean it's midnight and I wondered whether there was something wrong.'

She gave a weak smile and shook her head. Ben smiled back. She was not such easy prey.

'My name is Ben,' he said politely.

'Sheere,' replied the girl, looking towards the door as if she expected her grandmother to emerge at any moment.

Ben rubbed his hands.

'Well, Sheere,' he said. 'While my colleague Bankim takes your grandmother to Mr Carter's office, perhaps I can offer you some hospitality. The head always insists we be polite to visitors.'

'Aren't you a bit young to be the headmaster's assistant?' asked Sheere, avoiding the boy's eyes.

'Young? You flatter me. I'm just blessed with an enviable complexion, but I'll be twenty-three soon.'

'I never would have guessed it,' replied Sheere.

'It runs in the family,' Ben explained. 'Our skin is resistant to aging. To this day people mistake my grandfather for an altar boy.'

'Really?' asked Sheere, suppressing a nervous laugh.

'So how about accepting St Patrick's hospitality?' Ben insisted. 'We're having a party for some of the kids who are about to leave us. It's sad, but a whole new life will open up before them. It's exciting too.'

Sheere fixed her eyes on Ben and her lips slowly formed a sceptical smile.

'My grandmother asked me to wait here.'

Ben pointed at the door. 'Here?' he asked. 'Just here?'

Sheere nodded.

'You see ...' Ben began, waving his hands about. 'I'm sorry to have to tell you this, but ... Well, I thought I might not have to. These things are not good for the image of the institution, but you leave me no option. There's a structural problem. With the walls.'

The young girl looked at him in astonishment.

'Structural?'

Ben adopted a serious expression and nodded.

'Exactly. It's regrettable, but here on the very spot where you're standing, not even a month ago, Mrs Potts, our old cook, God bless her, was hit by a piece of brick that fell from the second floor and for two weeks she thought she was Moll Flanders. Imagine the scandal.'

Sheere laughed.

'I don't think it's a laughing matter, if I may say so,' said Ben, his tone icy.

'I don't believe a single word you've said. You're not the headmaster's assistant, you're not twenty-three, and no cook was ever hit by a shower of bricks,' said Sheere defiantly.

'Are you suggesting I have provided you with inaccurate information?'

'To put it mildly.'

Ben weighed up the situation. The first part of his strategy was on the point of floundering, so he had to think of a change of direction, and it had to be clever.

'I may have been carried away by my imagination, but not everything I've said is untrue.'

'Oh?'

'I didn't lie about my name. I'm called Ben. And the bit about offering you our hospitality is also true.'

Sheere gave a winning grin.

'I'd love to accept, Ben. But I must wait here. Honestly.'

The boy adopted an expression of calm acceptance.

'All right. I'll wait with you,' he announced solemnly. 'If a brick falls, let it fall on me.'

Sheere shrugged and fixed her eyes on the door again.

A long minute of silence went by. Neither of them moved or uttered a word.

'It's a hot night,' said Ben at last.

Sheere turned her head. 'Are you going to stand there all night?'

'Let's make a deal,' Ben proposed. 'Come and have a glass of ice-cold lemonade with me and my friends and then I'll leave you in peace.'

'I can't, Ben. Really.'

'We'll only be twenty metres away,' said Ben. 'We could tie a little bell to the door.'

'Is it so important for you?' asked Sheere.

Ben nodded.

'It's my last week in this place. I've spent my whole life here and in five days' time I'll be alone again. Completely alone. I don't know if I'll ever be able to spend another night like this one, among friends. You don't know what it's like.'

Sheere looked at him for a long while.

'I do know,' she said at last. 'Take me to that lemonade.'

ONCE BANKIM HAD LEFT his office, Mr Carter poured himself a small glass of brandy and offered another to his visitor. Aryami declined and waited for Carter to sit in his armchair, with his back to the large window below which the young people were still celebrating, unaware of

61

the icy silence that filled the headmaster's room. Carter wet his lips and looked questioningly at the old woman. Time had not diminished the authority of her features in the slightest. Her eyes still blazed with the same fire he remembered in the woman who, so long ago, had been his best friend's wife. They gazed at one another for a long time.

'I'm listening,' said Carter finally.

'Sixteen years ago I was obliged to entrust you with a baby boy, Mr Carter,' Aryami began in a low but firm voice. 'It was one of the most difficult decisions of my life and I know for a fact that during these past years you have honoured the trust I put in you and haven't let me down. During this time I never interfered with the boy's life, for I was well aware that he wouldn't be better off anywhere else but here, under your protection. I've never had the opportunity to thank you for what you've done for him.'

'I was only doing my duty,' Carter replied. 'But I don't think that is why you've come here, at this late hour.'

'I wish I could say it was, but you're right,' said Aryami. 'I've come here because the boy's life is in danger.'

'Ben.'

'That's the name you gave him. He owes everything he knows and everything he is to you, Mr Carter,' said Aryami. 'But there is something that neither you nor I can protect him from any longer: the past.'

The hands on Thomas Carter's watch pointed towards

62

midnight. Carter downed his brandy, then turned to glance through the window at the courtyard below. Ben was talking to a girl Carter didn't recognise.

'As I said earlier, I'm listening,' Carter repeated.

Aryami sat up and, clasping her hands together in her lap, she began to tell her story ...

'FOR SIXTEEN YEARS I'VE travelled this country in search of refuge and somewhere to hide. Two weeks ago I was spending a month in the house of some relatives in Delhi, convalescing after an illness, when a letter arrived for me. Nobody could have known that my granddaughter and I were there. When I opened it, I found a blank sheet of paper inside, without a single letter written on it. I thought it might be a mistake or perhaps a joke, until I examined the envelope. It bore the postmark of Calcutta's main post office. The ink was blurred and some of it was hard to make out, but I was able to decipher the date: 25 May 1916.

'I put away the letter that had apparently taken sixteen years to cross India and reach the door of that house, a place to which only I had access, and I didn't look at it again until that evening. My eyesight hadn't played a trick on me: the date was the same, but something else had changed. The sheet of paper, which only a few hours earlier had been completely blank, now contained a single line written in red ink so fresh I smudged the writing with just a brush of my fingers. "They are no longer children, old woman. I've come back for what is mine. Stay out of my way." That is what I read in the letter before throwing it into the fire.

'I knew then who had sent it and I also knew that the moment had come when I must unearth the memories I had suppressed all these years. I don't know whether I ever spoke to you about my daughter Kylian, Mr Carter. I'm an old woman now, awaiting the end of my life, but there was a time when I was a mother too, the mother of the most marvellous creature that ever set foot in this city.

'I remember those days as the happiest of my life. Kylian had married one of the most brilliant men in the country and had gone to live with him in the house he had built himself in the north of the city, a house the like of which had never been seen. My daughter's husband, Lahawaj Chandra Chatterghee, was an engineer and a writer. He was one of the first to design the telegraph network for this country, Mr Carter, one of the first to design the electric power grid that will govern the future of our cities, one of the first to build a rail network in Calcutta ... One of the first in everything he decided to do.

'But their happiness was short-lived. Chandra Chatterghee died in the horrific fire that destroyed the old Jheeter's Gate Station, on the other side of

64

the Hooghly River. You must have seen that building at some time? It's completely abandoned now, but once it was one of the most glorious buildings in Calcutta – a landmark in steel construction, a labyrinth of tunnels, multiple storeys, systems for piping fresh air and for the hydraulics connecting to the rails. Engineers from the world over came to visit and admire the structure, all of it created by the engineer Chandra Chatterghee.

'Nobody knows how it happened, but the night of its official inauguration a fire broke out in Jheeter's Gate, and a train that was transporting over three hundred abandoned children to Bombay went up in flames and was buried in the dark tunnels dissecting the earth. Nobody came out alive. The train is still stranded somewhere deep in the shadows, in the underground network of passages on the western edge of Calcutta.

'The night the engineer and the children died in that train was one of the worst tragedies ever to hit this city. For many, it was a sign that perpetual darkness was descending over Calcutta. There were rumours that the fire had been started by a group of British financiers who viewed the new railway line as a threat, for it would prove that transport by sea, one of the largest businesses in Calcutta since the days of Lord Clive and the colonial company, was nearing its end. The train was the future. The railway tracks were the path by which this country and this city would one day arrive at a new age, free of British domination. The night Jheeter's Gate burnt down, those dreams turned to nightmares.

'A few days after Chandra's disappearance, my daughter Kylian, who was expecting her first child, was threatened by a strange character who emerged from the shadows of Calcutta, a murderer who swore he would kill the wife and descendants of the man he blamed for all his misfortunes. That man, that criminal, was responsible for the fire in which Chandra lost his life. A young officer from the British army, an ex-suitor of my daughter's called Lieutenant Michael Peake, tried to stop the madman, but the task proved more difficult than he expected.

'The night my daughter was due to give birth, some men broke into the house and took her away. Hired assassins. Men with no name or conscience who, for a few coins, can easily be found in the streets of this city. On the verge of despair, Lieutenant Peake spent a whole week combing Calcutta in search of my daughter. As the tense week came to a close Peake had a terrifying thought, which turned out to be true. The murderer had taken Kylian into the very bowels of the ruins of Jheeter's Gate. There, among the filth and the remains of the tragedy, my daughter had given birth to the boy you have turned into a young man, Mr Carter.

'She had given birth to him – to Ben – and also to his sister, whom I have tried to turn into a young woman. Just as you did with the boy, I gave the girl a name, the name her mother had always intended for her: Sheere.

'Risking his own life, Lieutenant Peake managed to snatch the two children from the murderer's hands. But the murderer, blind with anger, swore he'd follow their trail and kill them as soon as they reached adulthood, to wreak vengeance on their dead father, Chandra Chatterghee. That was his sole intention: to destroy every trace of the engineer's work and his life, at any cost.

'Kylian died promising that her soul would not rest until she knew that her children were safe. Lieutenant Peake, the man who had secretly loved her as much as her own husband, gave his life so that the promise that had sealed her lips would come true. On 25 May 1916 Lieutenant Peake managed to cross the Hooghly River and hand over the children to me. To this day I do not know what became of him.

'I decided that the only way of saving these children was to separate them and conceal their identity and their whereabouts. You know the rest of Ben's story better than I do. As for Sheere, I took her under my wing and set off on a long journey around the country. I raised the girl in remembrance of the great man her father was and of my daughter, the great woman who gave life to her. I never told her more than I thought was necessary. I was naive enough to think that time and space would eventually erase all traces of the past, but our footprints are never lost. When I received that letter I knew my flight had come to an end and I must return to Calcutta to warn you. I wasn't honest in the letter I wrote to you that night, Mr Carter, but I acted according to my heart, believing deep in my soul that I was doing the right thing.

'When I realised the murderer knew where we were, I couldn't leave my granddaughter alone, so I took her with me and together we travelled back to Calcutta. During the entire journey I was haunted by a thought that became increasingly obvious as we approached our destination. I was convinced that now Ben and Sheere had left their childhood and become adults, the murderer had awoken once more from the darkness and was intent on carrying out his ancient promise. And I knew, with the certainty that only comes when one is close to a tragedy, that this time he would stop at nothing ...'

FOR A LONG TIME Thomas Carter kept his eyes glued to his hands and didn't say a word. The only reasonable thing he could think to do at the moment was to pour himself another glass of brandy and drink a solitary toast to his health.

'You don't believe me ...'

'I didn't say that,' Carter pointed out.

'You didn't say anything,' said Aryami. 'That's what's worrying me.'

Carter savoured the brandy and wondered what had made him wait ten years to release the heady charms of the superb spirit. Why on earth had he kept it locked away in his cabinet like some useless relic?

'It's not easy to believe what you've just told me, Aryami,' replied Carter. 'Put yourself in my shoes.'

'And yet you took the boy into your care sixteen years ago.'

'I took charge of an abandoned child, not of an improbable story. This is my duty, my job. This building is an orphanage, and I'm the head of it. That's all there is to it.'

'There *is* more to it than that, Mr Carter,' replied Aryami. 'At the time I did a little investigating: you never informed the authorities of Ben's arrival. You never filed a report. There are no documents to prove that he was taken in by this institution. There must have been some reason why you acted in this way if you didn't believe what you call this "improbable story".'

'I'm sorry to have to contradict you, Aryami, but such documents do exist. I may have put down other dates and other circumstances as a precaution, but this is an official institution, not a travelling circus.'

'You haven't answered my question,' Aryami cut in. 'So I'll ask you again: what prompted you to fake Ben's records if you didn't believe the facts I set out in my letter?'

'With all due respect, I don't see why I need to reply to that question.'

Aryami looked straight into Mr Carter's eyes but he tried to look away. The old lady smiled bitterly.

'You've seen him,' said Aryami.

'Are we talking about a new character in the story?'

'Who is fooling who, Mr Carter?'

The conversation seemed to have reached deadlock. Carter stood up and paced round the office under the watchful eye of Aryami Bose.

'Supposing I believe your story,' he said, turning towards her. 'It's just a supposition. What would you expect me to do now?'

'Get Ben away from this place,' Aryami replied emphatically. 'Talk to him. Warn him. Help him. I'm not asking you to do anything for the boy that you haven't already been doing for years.'

'I need to consider this matter carefully,' said Carter.

'Don't take too long. This man has waited sixteen years; perhaps he won't mind waiting another day. Or perhaps he will.'

Carter collapsed into his armchair, defeated.

'I had a visit from a man named Jawahal the day we found Ben,' Carter explained. 'He asked about the boy and I told him we didn't know anything. Soon after, the man disappeared and was never seen again.'

'This man uses a lot of different names and identities, but he has only one objective, Mr Carter,' said Aryami, her steely eyes shining. 'I haven't crossed the whole of India to sit and watch my daughter's children die because of the indecision of a couple of old fools, if you'll forgive the expression.'

'Old fool or not, I need time to think. Perhaps we'd better talk to the police.'

Aryami sighed.

'There *is* no time, and it wouldn't do any good,' she replied harshly. 'Tomorrow afternoon I'm leaving Calcutta with my granddaughter. Tomorrow afternoon Ben must leave this place and get as far away as possible. You have a few hours to talk to the boy and prepare everything.'

'It's not that simple,' Carter objected.

'It's as simple as this: if you don't talk to him, I will,' Aryami stated, making her way to the door. 'And pray that this man doesn't find him before he sees the light of day.'

'I'll speak to Ben tomorrow,' said Carter. 'I can do no more.'

Aryami threw him a last glance from the doorway.

'Tomorrow, Mr Carter, is today.'

'A SECRET SOCIETY?' SHEERE asked, her eyes sparkling with curiosity. 'I thought secret societies only existed in penny dreadfuls.'

'Siraj here could spend hours contradicting you,' said Ian. 'He's our expert on the subject.'

Siraj nodded gravely, agreeing with the reference to his boundless wisdom.

'Have you heard about the Freemasons?' he asked.

'Please,' Ben butted in. 'Sheere is going to think we're a bunch of sorcerer apprentices.'

'And aren't you?' laughed the girl.

'No,' said Seth solemnly. 'The Chowbar Society is founded on two entirely worthy principles: to help one another, and to share our knowledge so we can build a better future.'

'Isn't that what all great enemies of humanity claim to do?' asked Sheere.

'Only for the last two or three thousand years,' said Ben, interrupting again. 'Anyway, this is a very special night for the Chowbar Society.'

'We're disbanding,' said Michael.

'Hark, the dead *do* speak,' remarked Roshan, surprised to hear him talk.

Sheere looked around the group, trying to hide her amusement at the crossfire between them.

'What Michael means is that today we're holding the last meeting of the Chowbar Society,' Ben explained. 'After seven years, the final curtain.'

'What a shame,' said Sheere. 'For the first time in my life I come across a real secret society, and it's about to disband. I won't have time to become a member.'

'Nobody said that new members were accepted,' said Isobel, quick as a flash. She'd been listening in to the conversation, her eyes never leaving the intruder. 'In fact, if it hadn't been for the resident bigmouths here who've already broken one of the oaths, you wouldn't even know it existed. All they need is a glimpse of skirt and they'd sell their souls.'

Sheere offered Isobel a conciliatory smile, struck by the slight hostility in her tone. It was not easy to accept not being the only girl.

'According to Voltaire, the worst misogynists are always women,' said Ben casually.

'And who the hell is Voltaire?' snapped Isobel. 'Only your twisted mind could come out with such rubbish.'

'Ignorance has spoken!' replied Ben. 'Although perhaps Voltaire didn't say exactly that …'

'Stop fighting,' Roshan intervened. 'Isobel is right. We shouldn't have said anything.'

Sheere watched nervously as the mood appeared to darken in a matter of seconds.

'I don't want to cause an argument. I'd better return to my grandmother. I'll forget everything you've said,' she stated, returning the lemonade glass to Ben.

'Not so fast, princess,' Isobel exclaimed behind her.

Sheere turned to face the girl.

'Now that you know something, you might as well know everything and then keep it secret,' she said, offering an embarrassed half-smile. 'I'm sorry about what I said earlier.'

'Good idea,' said Ben. 'Go on.'

Sheere raised her eyebrows.

'She'll have to pay the admission fee,' Siraj reminded Isobel.

'I haven't got any money ...'

'We're not a church – we don't want your money,' replied Seth. 'The price is something else.'

Sheere scanned each face in search of an answer. Ian smiled back at her.

'Don't worry, it's nothing bad,' the boy explained. 'The Chowbar Society holds its meetings in the dead of night at a secret location. We each pay the price of entry when we join.'

'Where's the secret location?'

'It's a palace,' replied Isobel. 'The Midnight Palace.'

'Never heard of it.'

'Nobody has except us,' Siraj said.

'And what is the price?'

'A story,' replied Ben. 'A personal, secret story you have never told anyone else. You share it with us and then your secret will never leave the Chowbar Society.'

'Do you have anything like that?' asked Isobel defiantly, biting her lower lip.

Once again Sheere looked at the six boys and the girl, who were watching her cautiously. In all her years of moving around with her grandmother she had never stayed in one place long enough to make a single true friend, much less seven of them willing to listen and to invite her to be a part of something.

'I have a story that I'm quite certain you've never heard,' she said at last.

'Right then,' said Ben rubbing his hands. 'Let's get going.'

～

WHILE ARYAMI BOSE WAS explaining the reasons that had brought her and her granddaughter back to Calcutta after so many years of exile, the seven members of the Chowbar Society were leading Sheere through the bushes that surrounded the Midnight Palace. To the newcomer's eyes, the palace was just a large abandoned house with a dilapidated roof through which you could see the star-studded sky. Gargoyles, columns and reliefs loomed through the sinuous shadows, the vestiges of what must once have been a stately mansion straight out of the pages of a fairy tale.

They crossed the garden via a narrow tunnel that had been hacked through the undergrowth and led straight to the main entrance of the house. A light breeze stirred the leaves and whistled through the stone arches of the Palace. Ben turned and looked at Sheere, grinning from ear to ear.

'What do you think of it?'

'It's ... different,' Sheere replied, not wishing to dampen his enthusiasm.

'Sublime,' Ben corrected her, marching on, oblivious to any other opinion regarding the charms of the Chowbar Society's headquarters.

Sheere smiled to herself and let him lead the way, thinking how much she would have liked to have known this group and this mansion during the years it had served as their refuge and sanctuary. The place exuded that aura of magic and dreams that rarely exists beyond the blurred memories of our early years. It didn't matter that it was only for one night; she was looking forward to paying the admission fee to the almost extinct Chowbar Society.

'My secret,' she began, 'is in fact the story of my father. The two are inseparable. I never met him, and I have no memory of him except what I learned from the lips of my grandmother and what I read in his books and notebooks. Yet, however strange this may seem to you, I've never felt closer to anyone in the world. Even though he died before I was born, I'm sure he will wait for me until I join him, and on that day I'll finally be able to see for myself that he is just as I imagined him: the best man who ever existed.

'I'm not so different from you. I didn't grow up in an orphanage, but I've never known what it's like to have a home or someone to talk to, apart from my grandmother, for longer than a month. We lived in trains, in strangers' houses, on the streets, never having a place we could call home or somewhere to return to. During all these years the only friend I've had is my father. And as I've said, although he was never there, I discovered everything I know about him from his books and the memories of my grandmother.

'My mother died giving birth to me, and I've had to live with the sorrow of having no memory of her. The only image I have is the reflection I've found in my father's writings. Of all his books, including the treatises on engineering and the thick tomes I never really understood, my favourite was always a slim volume of stories called *Shiva's Tears*. He wrote it just before his thirty-fifth birthday, when he was busy developing the idea of Calcutta's first railway line and a revolutionary station made of steel he dreamed of building in the city. A small publishing house in Bombay printed only six hundred copies of the book, but my father never saw a single rupee. I have a copy. It's a small black volume with the words "*Shiva's Tears* by L. Chandra Chatterghee" embossed in gold on the spine.

'The book is divided into three parts. The first focuses on his ideas for a new nation built on the spirit of progress, on technology, railways and electricity. He called it "My country". The second part describes a fabulous house he planned to build for himself and his family once he'd managed to amass the fortune he longed for. He describes every corner, every room, every colour and every object in such detail that no architect's plan could equal it. He called this part of the book "My house". The

77

third part, called "My mind", is a collection of the short stories and fables he'd been writing ever since he was a boy. My favourite is the one that gives the book its title. It's very short. Here it is...'

A long time ago Calcutta was struck down by a terrible plague that took the lives of its children, so that little by little, as the inhabitants grew older, they lost all hope for the future. To resolve the situation, Shiva set off on a long journey in search of a cure. During his travels he frequently had to confront danger. In fact, he met with so many difficulties that the journey kept him away for many years, and when he returned to Calcutta he discovered that everything had changed. In his absence, a sorcerer had come from the other end of the world bringing with him a strange remedy which he proceeded to sell to the people of Calcutta for a high price indeed: the soul of every healthy child born after that day.

This is what Shiva's eyes saw. Where once there had been a jungle of mud huts, there now rose a city so large that nobody could view it in a single glance and it faded into the horizon no matter which direction you looked. A city of palaces. Shiva was fascinated by the spectacle and decided to turn into a human being and walk through the streets of the city dressed as a beggar, so that he could get to know its new inhabitants, the children whom the sorcerer's remedy had made possible and whose souls now belonged to him. But a great disappointment awaited Shiva.

For seven days and seven nights the beggar walked through the streets of Calcutta, knocking on palace doors, but they were all slammed in his face. Nobody wanted to listen to him. People shunned him and poked fun at him. As he roamed the immense city in despair, he discovered that poverty, misery and darkness filled the hearts of its men. Such was Shiva's sadness that on the last night he decided to abandon his city for good.

As he did so, he began to weep and, without realising it, he left behind a trail of tears scattered through the jungle. At dawn Shiva's tears turned to ice. When the men realised what they had done, they tried to make amends for their mistake by storing Shiva's tears in a sanctuary. But, one by one, the tears melted in their hands and the city dwellers never saw ice again.

From that day onwards, the curse of a terrible heat fell upon the city and the gods turned their backs on it, leaving it at the mercy of the night spirits. The few remaining righteous men prayed that, one day, Shiva's tears might fall again from heaven and break the spell that had turned Calcutta into a doomed city.

'Of all my father's stories, this was always my favourite. It's probably the simplest, but it embodies the true essence of what my father meant to me – and still

79

does. Like the men of the doomed city, who had to pay the price for the mistakes of the past, I too await the day when Shiva's tears will fall on me and free me of my loneliness. Meanwhile, I dream of the house my father built, first in his mind and, years later, somewhere in the north of the city. I know it still exists, although my grandmother has always denied it. She doesn't know this, but I believe that in his book my father described the exact spot where he was planning to build it, here, in the Black Town. All these years I've lived with the hope of being able to walk into it one day and recognise everything I already know by heart: the library, the bedrooms, the armchair in the study …

'So that is my story. I've never told anyone because I had no one to tell it to. Until today.'

As SHEERE FINISHED HER tale, the darkness that reigned in the Midnight Palace helped conceal the tears of some of the members of the Chowbar Society. No one seemed ready to break the silence that infused the air following the end of her story. Sheere laughed nervously and looked at Ben.

'So do I qualify as a member?'

'As far as I'm concerned,' he replied, 'you deserve to be an honorary member.'

'Does the house really exist, Sheere?' asked Siraj, who was fascinated with the idea.

'I'm sure it does,' she replied. 'And I'm determined to find it. The clue is somewhere in my father's book.'

'When?' asked Seth. 'When shall we start looking?'

'Tomorrow,' Sheere said. 'You can help, if you want to ...'

'You'll need someone with brains,' Isobel remarked. 'You can count on me.'

'I'm an expert locksmith,' said Roshan.

'I can find maps in the Town Hall dating right back to the establishment of the government in 1859,' said Seth.

'I can find out if there's any mystery surrounding the house,' said Siraj. 'It might be haunted.'

'I can draw it exactly as it is,' said Michael. 'I can make plans. From the book, I mean.'

Sheere laughed and looked at Ben and Ian.

'Fine,' said Ben. 'Someone will have to be the director of operations: I accept the job. Ian can put antiseptic on anyone who gets a splinter.'

'I suppose you're not going to accept a no,' said Sheere.

'We deleted the word "no" from the dictionary in the orphanage library six months ago,' Ben declared. 'Now you're a member of the Chowbar Society, your problems are our problems. Company orders.'

'I thought we were disbanding the society,' Siraj reminded them.

'I decree an extension due to grievous circumstances

81

that cannot be ignored,' said Ben, throwing his friend a withering look.

Siraj melted into the shadows.

'All right,' Sheere conceded, 'but we have to go back now.'

∼

THE LOOK WITH WHICH Aryami greeted Sheere and the other members of the Chowbar Society could have frozen the surface of the Hooghly River. The elderly woman was waiting by the front of the building with Bankim, whose expression was so serious Ben immediately started dreaming up some improbable excuse to get his new friend out of the scolding that was clearly coming her way. He went ahead of the others and put on his best smile.

'It was my fault. We just wanted to show your granddaughter the courtyard behind the building,' he said.

Not even deigning to look at him, Aryami went straight over to Sheere.

'I told you to wait here and not move,' she said, her face flushed with anger.

'We've only been a few metres away,' said Ian.

Aryami looked daggers at him.

'I didn't ask *you*, young man,' she retorted, not bothering to be polite.

'We're sorry to have worried you, we didn't mean to—'
Ben insisted.

'Leave it, Ben,' Sheere interrupted. 'I can speak for myself.'

The woman's hostile expression softened for a moment. This didn't go unnoticed by any of the young people. Aryami pointed at Ben and her face grew pale in the faint light of the lanterns dotted around the garden.

'Are you Ben?' she asked, lowering her voice.

The boy nodded, concealing his surprise as he met the old woman's inscrutable gaze. There was no anger in her eyes, only sadness and anxiety. Aryami took her granddaughter by the arm.

'We must go,' she said. 'Say goodbye to your friends.'

The members of the Chowbar Society nodded farewell and Sheere gave a shy smile as she walked away, her arm still held tightly by Aryami Bose. They disappeared into the dark streets of Calcutta. Ian went over to Ben, who seemed lost in thought, his eyes fixed on the retreating figures of Sheere and Aryami as they ventured into the night.

'For a moment I thought that woman was frightened,' said Ian.

Ben nodded, still staring.

'Who isn't frightened on a night like this?'

'I think you'd all better go to bed,' said Bankim from the doorway.

'Is that a suggestion or an order?' Isobel asked.

83

'You know that my suggestions are always orders,' declared Bankim, pointing to the building. 'In.'

'Tyrant,' whispered Siraj to himself. 'Enjoy your last few days.'

'The ones who re-enlist are always the worst,' added Roshan.

Bankim nodded happily as he watched the six boys and the girl file past him, ignoring their mumbled protests. Ben was the last one through the door and he exchanged a look with Bankim.

'However much they complain,' he said, 'they'll miss you in five days' time.'

'So will you, Ben,' laughed Bankim.

'I already do,' he murmured to himself as he started up the staircase to the first-floor dormitories, aware that in less than a week he would no longer be counting the twenty-four steps he knew so well.

AT SOME POINT IN the early hours Ben woke up and thought he could feel a gust of icy air on his face. A beam of pale light flickered through the narrow pointed window. Ben reached out a hand towards his bedside table and turned the face of his watch to catch the moonlight. The hands were crossing the equator towards dawn: three o'clock in the morning.

He sighed, suspecting that sleep had deserted him,

evaporating like dew in the morning sun. Perhaps the spectre of Ian's insomnia was haunting him for a change. He closed his eyes again, conjuring up images of the party that had ended a few hours earlier, trusting they would soothe him to sleep. Just then he heard a strange sound that seemed to be whistling through the leaves of the courtyard garden.

He sat up, pulled back his sheets and walked slowly towards the window. From there he could hear the tinkling of the darkened lanterns in the branches of the trees and the distant echo of what sounded like children's voices, laughing and talking in unison, hundreds of them. Leaning his forehead against the windowpane and peering through the condensation made by his own breath, he thought he could make out the silhouette of a slender figure standing in the middle of the courtyard, wrapped in a black cloak. The figure was staring straight at him. He jumped back in alarm, and before his very eyes the windowpane slowly cracked, starting with a small fissure in the centre that spread like a spider's web gouged out by hundreds of invisible claws. The hairs on the back of Ben's neck stood on end and his breathing quickened.

He looked around him. All his friends were fast asleep. Ben heard the children's voices again and noticed that a thick mist was filtering through the cracks in the glass. He moved closer again and looked down into the courtyard. The figure was still standing there, but this time it stretched out an arm and pointed at him. Suddenly its long sharp fingers burst into flame. Ben stood there for a few seconds, gripped by the vision. Then the figure turned and began to walk away into the darkness. Ben rushed out of the dormitory.

The corridor was deserted, the only light coming from an ancient gas lamp that had survived renovation works at the orphanage a few years before. He hurtled down the stairs, across the dining halls, and emerged through the kitchen side door just in time to see the figure disappearing into the dark alleyway that led round the back of the building. The narrow alley was filled with a thick mist that seemed to rise from the sewer gratings.

Ben immersed himself in the tunnel of cold swirling fog, running for about a hundred metres until he came to a large open space to the north of St Patrick's – a wasteland that housed both a scrap-metal dump and a citadel of empty shacks once belonging to the most deprived inhabitants of North Calcutta. Dodging the muddy puddles that covered the path through the twisting maze of burnt-out adobe huts, he advanced into the place Thomas Carter had always warned them against. The children's voices came from somewhere deep inside that desolate swamp of poverty and filth.

Ben headed through a narrow gap between two derelict shacks, then suddenly stopped when he realised he'd found what he was looking for. Before him stretched an endless deserted plain filled with the remains of old huts enveloped by a blue mist wafting out of the darkness. The sound of the children seemed to be coming from the same spot, only this time it wasn't laughter or nursery rhymes that Ben heard, but the terrible panicked shrieks of hundreds of trapped children. A cold gust of wind hurled him against the wall of one of the shacks, as out of the mist came the furious roar of a huge steel machine that made the earth tremble beneath his feet.

He blinked then looked again, thinking he must be hallucinating. A train was emerging from the fog, its metal armour red hot and enveloped in flames. He could see the agony on the faces of dozens of children who were trapped inside it as burning fragments rained down in all directions in a cascade of sparks. The engine itself, a majestic steel sculpture, seemed to be melting. In the driver's cab, standing motionless amid the flames, was the same figure he had seen in the courtyard. The creature was watching Ben, with arms open wide as if to welcome him.

Ben could feel the heat of the fire on his face and he covered his ears to stifle the excruciating howls of the children. The blazing train tore across the deserted plain and Ben realised with horror that it was racing straight towards St Patrick's like a guided missile. He ran after it, dodging the shower of sparks and molten iron, but was not able to keep up with the train as it accelerated towards the orphanage, tinting the sky scarlet as it flew by. Gasping for breath, he screamed with all his might to alert those who were sleeping peacefully in the building, unaware of the tragedy that was about to befall them. He watched in despair as the train homed in on St Patrick's. Any moment now the engine would pulverise the orphanage and fling its inhabitants into the air. He fell to his knees and screamed one last time as he watched the train enter the rear courtyard and rush uncontrollably towards the large wall that formed the back of the building.

Ben prepared himself for the worst but could never have imagined what he would witness a fraction of a second later.

As the crazed locomotive, cloaked in a tornado of flames, crashed into the wall, it changed into an apparition of eerie lights, the entire train sinking into the red-brick wall like a shadowy serpent, disintegrating in the air and taking with it the dreadful howls of the children and the deafening roar of the engine.

Two seconds later total darkness returned, and the silhouette of the orphanage stood out, unscathed, against the distant lights of the White Town and the Maidan to the south. The last of the mist vanished into the cracks in the wall and soon there was no evidence of the phenomenon he had just witnessed. Slowly Ben walked up to the back of the building and placed his palm on the undamaged surface. An electric shock ran up his arm, throwing him to the ground. On the wall the imprint of his hand was black and smoking.

When he stood up his heart was racing and his hands shook. Breathing deeply, he dried the tears provoked by the fire. When he'd calmed down, at least partially, he walked round the building to the kitchen door. Using a trick Roshan had taught him for lifting the inside latch, Ben opened the door cautiously, then crossed the kitchen and the downstairs corridor until he reached the staircase. The orphanage was still sunk in the deepest of silences and Ben realised that nobody but he had heard the roar of the train.

He went back to the dormitory. His friends were still asleep and there was no sign of a cracked windowpane. He walked through the room and lay down on his bed, breathing heavily. Again he picked up his watch from the bedside table and checked the time. He could have sworn that he'd been out of the building for at least twenty minutes, but the watch showed the same time as when he'd woken earlier. He held it to his ear and heard the regular ticking of the mechanism. He set the watch back in its place, then tried to put some order to his thoughts. He was beginning to doubt what he had witnessed, or what he thought he'd seen. Perhaps he hadn't left the room and he'd dreamed the whole episode. The regular breathing around him and the unharmed windowpane seemed to confirm that explanation. Or perhaps he was a victim of his own imagination. Feeling confused, he closed his eyes and tried to doze off, hoping he might fool his body by pretending to sleep.

At daybreak, just as the sun was reaching the Grey Town – the Muslim sector in the east of Calcutta – he jumped out of bed and ran out to the rear courtyard to examine the back wall once more. There were still no traces of the train. Ben was about to conclude that it had indeed all been a dream, an unusually intense one but still a dream, when out of the corner of his eye he noticed a dark stain on the wall. He drew closer and recognised the shape of his palm clearly imprinted on the bricks. He gave a deep sigh and hurried back to the dormitory to wake Ian, who for the first time in weeks had managed to fall into the arms of Morpheus, free for once of his persistent insomnia.

IN THE DAYLIGHT THE Midnight Palace lost some of its magical aura and became just a sprawling old ruin of a house that had seen better times. Viewing their favourite setting without the embellishment and mystery of the Calcutta nights could have had a stark effect on the members of the Chowbar Society, but fortunately Ben's words softened the impact. They all listened to him in respectful silence, their expressions going from amazement to disbelief.

'And it vanished into the wall, as if it were air?' Seth asked.

Ben nodded.

'That's the strangest story you've told this month, Ben,' Isobel stated.

'It's not a story. It's what I saw.'

'Nobody is doubting you, Ben,' said Ian, 'but we were all asleep and didn't hear a thing. Not even me.'

'That really *is* incredible,' said Roshan. 'Perhaps Bankim put something in the lemonade.'

'Is nobody going to take me seriously?' said Ben. 'You've seen the handprint.'

No one replied. Ben focused on his small asthmatic comrade, the most gullible when it came to spooky stories.

'Siraj?'

The boy looked up and gazed at the rest of the group, assessing the situation.

'It wouldn't be the first time something like this has been seen in Calcutta ... There's the story of Hastings House, for example.'

'I don't see what one thing has to do with the other,' Isobel objected.

The story of Hastings House – formerly the governor's residence in the province south of Calcutta – was one of Siraj's favourite tales and probably the most emblematic of all the ghost stories that packed the annals of the city. According to local legend, on nights when there was a full moon the phantom of Warren Hastings, the first governor of Bengal, drove a ghostly carriage up to the porch of his old mansion in Alipore, where he would then search frantically for some documents that had disappeared during his chaotic rule of the city.

'The people of Calcutta have been seeing him for decades,' Siraj protested. 'It's as much a fact as the monsoon flooding the streets.'

The members of the Chowbar Society became embroiled in a heated discussion about what Ben had seen, during which only the person concerned did not intervene. A few minutes later, when all reason seemed to have flown out of the window, those taking part in the argument turned their heads to look at the figure in white that was standing in the doorway to the roofless hall, watching them in silence. One by one, they stopped talking.

'I don't want to interrupt …' said Sheere shyly.

'An interruption is most welcome,' said Ben. 'We were only arguing. For a change.'

'I heard the last bit,' Sheere admitted. 'Did you see something last night, Ben?'

'I don't know any more,' he admitted. 'How about you? Have you managed to escape from your grandmother? I think we got you into trouble last night.'

Sheere smiled and shook her head.

'My grandmother is a good woman, but sometimes she gets obsessed and thinks there's danger lurking round every corner,' Sheere explained. 'She doesn't know I'm here, so I can't stay long.'

'Why not? We were thinking of going down to the docks; you could come with us,' said Ben, much to the surprise of the others, as this was the first they'd heard of the plan.

'I can't go with you, Ben. I came to say goodbye.'

'What!' cried various voices at once.

'We're leaving for Bombay tomorrow. My grandmother says this city isn't safe and we must leave. She forbade me from seeing you again, but I didn't want to go without saying goodbye. You're the only friends I've had in ten years, even if that was just for a night.'

Ben looked at her in astonishment.

'You're going to Bombay?' he exploded. 'Why? Does your grandmother want to be a film star? This is absurd!'

'I'm afraid it isn't,' Sheere said sadly. 'I'll only be in Calcutta for a few more hours. I hope you don't mind if I spend some of that time with you.'

'We'd love you to stay, Sheere,' said Ian, speaking for all of them.

'Just a minute,' Ben protested. 'What's all this business about saying goodbye? A few more hours in Calcutta? That's nonsense. You could spend a hundred years in this city and not understand half of what goes on here. You can't just leave like that. Even less now that you're a full member of the Chowbar Society.'

'You'll have to talk to my grandmother,' Sheere sighed.

'That's exactly what I plan to do.'

'Great idea,' Roshan said. 'You made a wonderful impression on her yesterday.'

'Oh ye of little faith!' Ben retorted. 'What happened to our vow? As members of the society, we have to help Sheere find her father's house. Nobody leaves this city until we've found it and unravelled its mysteries. And that's that.'

'Count me in,' said Siraj. 'But how are you going to do it? Are you going to threaten Sheere's grandmother?'

'Sometimes the word is mightier than the sword,' Ben declared. 'I wonder, who said that?'

'Voltaire?' suggested Isobel.

Ben ignored her sarcasm.

'And which powerful words might you be using?' asked Ian.

'Not my own, that's for sure,' Ben explained. 'The words of Mr Carter. We'll get him to speak to your grandmother.'

Sheere looked down and shook her head despondently.

'It won't work, Ben. You don't know Aryami Bose. There's nobody as stubborn as her. It's in her blood.'

Ben gave a feline smile, his eyes shining.

'I'm even more stubborn. Wait till you see me in action, then you'll change your mind.'

'Ben, you're going to get us into trouble again,' said Seth.

Ben raised an eyebrow and looked at each of them in

turn, crushing any hint of rebellion.

'If anyone has anything else to say, speak now or for ever hold your peace,' he said solemnly.

Nobody protested.

'Good. Motion approved. Let's go.'

CARTER INSERTED HIS KEY in the hole and turned it twice. The lock clicked open and Carter entered the room, closing the door behind him. He didn't feel like seeing or speaking to anyone for at least an hour. He unbuttoned his waistcoat and walked over to his armchair. It was then that he noticed a figure seated in the chair opposite and realised he was not alone. The key slipped from Carter's fingers but didn't hit the floor; an agile hand, sheathed in a black glove, caught it as it fell. A sharp face peered around the wing of the armchair, its lips twisted in a dog-like snarl.

'Who are you and how did you get in here?' Carter demanded, unable to hide the tremor in his voice.

The intruder stood up and Carter felt the blood drain from his cheeks as he recognised the man who had paid him a visit sixteen years earlier. His face hadn't aged a single day and his eyes still blazed with the ferocity the headmaster remembered. Jawahal. Clutching the key in his hand, the visitor walked over to the door and locked it. Carter gulped. The warnings Aryami Bose had given him the night before raced through his mind. Jawahal squeezed the key between his fingers and the metal bent as if it were a hairpin.

'You don't seem very happy to see me, Mr Carter,' said Jawahal. 'Don't you remember the meeting we arranged sixteen years ago? I've come to make my donation.'

'Leave this place immediately or I'll call the police,' Carter threatened.

'Let's not worry about the police for the time being. I'll call them when I leave. Sit down and grant me the pleasure of your conversation.'

Carter sat in his armchair struggling to keep his emotions in check and appear calm and in control. Jawahal gave him a friendly smile.

'I imagine you know why I'm here.'

'I don't know what you're looking for, but you won't find it here,' replied Carter.

'Maybe I will, maybe I won't,' said Jawahal casually. 'I'm looking for a child who has now become a man. You know which child I mean. I'd hate to feel obliged to hurt you.'

'Are you threatening me?'

Jawahal laughed. 'Yes,' he replied coldly. 'And when I threaten someone, I mean it.'

For the first time, Carter considered the possibility of crying out for help.

'If you're thinking about screaming,' said Jawahal. 'Let me at least give you a reason to do so.'

As soon as he'd uttered those words, Jawahal spread his right hand in front of his face and calmly began to pull off the glove.

～

SHEERE AND THE OTHER members of the Chowbar Society had only just stepped into the courtyard when the windows of Thomas Carter's office on the first floor exploded with a thunderous blast, and fragments of glass, wood and brick cascaded over the garden. For a moment the young people froze in their tracks, then they immediately rushed towards the building, ignoring the smoke and the flames issuing from the gaping hole that had opened in the facade.

When the explosion took place, Bankim was at the other end of the corridor, looking through a pile of documents he was preparing to take to Carter for his signature. The shock wave knocked him down; when he looked up through the cloud of smoke that filled the corridor, he saw that the door of the headmaster's office had been blown off its hinges and smashed against the wall. Bankim jumped up and ran towards the source of the explosion, but as he approached he saw a black silhouette emerge, wreathed in flames. It spread its dark cloak and swooped down the corridor like a huge bat, moving at incredible speed, before it disappeared leaving behind it a trail of ash and with a sound that reminded Bankim of the furious hiss of a cobra.

Bankim found Carter lying on the floor inside the office. His face was covered in burns and his clothes were smouldering. Bankim crouched beside his mentor and tried to sit him up. The headmaster's hands were shaking and Bankim noticed with relief that he was still breathing, albeit with difficulty. Bankim shouted for help and soon the faces of some of the boys appeared round the doorway. Ben, Ian and Seth helped him lift Carter off the floor, while the others moved rubble out of the way and prepared a space in the corridor.

'What the hell happened?' asked Ben.

Bankim shook his head, unable to answer, clearly still in shock. Between them they managed to carry the wounded man into the corridor while Vendela, her face as white as porcelain and a desperate look in her eyes, ran to alert the nearest hospital.

Gradually the remaining members of St Patrick's began to appear. Nobody understood what had caused the blast and they did not recognise the body that lay scorched on the floor. Ian and Roshan formed a cordon round Mr Carter and told everyone who approached that they needed to keep the way clear.

The wait seemed infinite.

The ambulance from Calcutta General Hospital seemed to take for ever to negotiate the labyrinth of city streets and reach St Patrick's. For another half an hour everyone waited restlessly, but just as they were beginning to give up hope, one of the doctors from the medical team came over to Bankim and the group of friends while three other medics continued to assist the victim.

When they saw the doctor approaching, they all crowded round him anxiously. He was a young man with red hair and intense eyes, and seemed decidedly competent. Or maybe they just hoped, and prayed, he would be.

'Mr Carter has suffered serious burns and there seem to be a few broken bones, but he's out of danger. What worries me most now are his eyes. We can't guarantee that he'll recover his eyesight completely, although it's still too early to know for certain. He'll have to be taken to the hospital so that we can sedate him properly before treating his wounds. He'll certainly have to undergo surgery. I need someone who can authorise his admission papers.'

'Vendela can do that,' said Bankim.

The doctor nodded.

'Good. There's something else. Which of you is Ben?'

They all stared at him in surprise. Ben looked up, confused.

'I'm Ben,' he replied. 'Why?'

'He wants to speak to you,' said the doctor, his tone implying that he'd tried to dissuade Carter and that he disapproved of his request.

Ben nodded and hurried off towards the ambulance.

'Just one minute,' warned the doctor. 'Not a second longer.'

~

BEN WENT OVER TO the stretcher on which Thomas Carter was lying and tried to smile reassuringly, but when he saw the state the headmaster was in he felt his stomach shrink and the words just wouldn't come to his lips. One of the doctors standing behind him gave him a nudge. Ben took a deep breath and nodded.

'Hello, Mr Carter. It's Ben.' He wondered whether Mr Carter could hear him.

The wounded man tilted his head slightly and raised a trembling hand. Ben took it and pressed it gently.

'Tell that man to leave us alone,' Carter groaned, his eyes still shut.

The doctor gave Ben a look and waited a few seconds before leaving.

'The doctors say you're going to get better ...' said Ben.

Carter shook his head.

'Not now, Ben.' Each word seemed to require a titanic effort. 'You must listen to me carefully and not interrupt. Understood?'

Ben nodded. 'I'm listening, sir.'

Carter squeezed his hand.

'There's a man who is looking for you and wants to kill you, Ben. A murderer,' Carter said, struggling to articulate his words. 'You must believe me. This man calls himself Jawahal and he seems to think you have some connection to his past. I don't know why he's looking for you but I do know he's dangerous. What he's done to me is only a shadow of what he's capable of. You must speak to Aryami Bose, the woman who came to the orphanage yesterday. Tell her what I've told you, explain what has happened. She tried to warn me, but I didn't take her seriously. Don't make the same mistake. Find her and talk to her. Tell her Jawahal was here. She'll tell you what to do.'

The burnt lips of Thomas Carter closed once more and Ben felt as if the whole world was collapsing around him. What the head of St Patrick's had confided in him seemed utterly unreal. The shock of the explosion had obviously affected Carter's reasoning, making him imagine some kind of conspiracy and a whole host of other improbable dangers. At that moment Ben couldn't contemplate any other explanation, especially in view of what he had dreamed the night before. Imprisoned in the claustrophobic atmosphere of the ambulance, with its cold stench of ether, he wondered for a split second whether the inhabitants of St Patrick's were all beginning to lose their minds, himself included.

'Did you hear me, Ben?' Carter insisted, his voice failing. 'Have you understood what I said?'

'Yes, sir,' Ben mumbled. 'You mustn't worry.'

Finally Carter opened his eyes and Ben realised with horror what the flames had done to them.

'Ben, do as I said. *Now.*' He was trying to shout but his voice was consumed by pain. 'Go and see that woman. Swear to me you will.'

Ben heard footsteps behind him. The red-haired doctor grabbed his arm and began dragging him out of the ambulance. Carter's hand slipped from Ben's and was left suspended in mid-air.

'That's enough,' yelled the doctor. 'This man has suffered enough already.'

'*Swear* you will!' groaned Carter, reaching out to him.

The boy watched in dismay as the doctors injected another dose of sedative into the headmaster.

'I swear, sir,' said Ben, not knowing if Carter could still hear him. 'I swear.'

Bankim was waiting for Ben outside. A short distance away stood the members of the Chowbar Society and everyone else who had been present when the disaster occurred. They were all watching Ben and appeared anxious and distressed. Ben approached Bankim and looked straight into his eyes, which were bloodshot from the smoke and tears.

'Bankim, I need to know something,' said Ben. 'Did anyone called Jawahal visit Mr Carter?'

Bankim looked blank.

'Nobody came today,' replied the teacher. 'Mr Carter spent the morning at a meeting with the Town Council and came back around twelve o'clock. Then he said he wanted to go and work in his office and didn't want to be disturbed, not even for lunch.'

'Are you sure he was alone when the blast occurred?' asked Ben, praying that he'd get a positive reply.

'Yes … I think so,' answered Bankim, although there was a shadow of doubt in his eyes. 'Why do you ask? What did he say?'

'Are you completely sure, Bankim?' Ben insisted. 'Think carefully. It's important.'

The teacher looked down, rubbing his forehead, as if he were trying to find the words to describe what he was barely sure of remembering.

'About a second after the explosion I thought I saw something, or someone, come out of the office. It was all very confusing.'

'Something or someone?' asked Ben.

Bankim looked up and shrugged his shoulders.

'I don't know what it was,' he replied. 'Nothing I can think of can move that fast.'

'An animal?'

'I don't know. It was probably just my own imagination.'

Aware of Bankim's disdain for superstition and alleged supernatural phenomena, Ben knew the teacher would never admit to having seen something that was beyond his powers of analysis or understanding. If his mind couldn't explain it, his eyes couldn't see it. As simple as that.

'If that's the case,' Ben insisted one last time, 'what else did you imagine?'

Bankim looked up at the blackened gap that a few hours earlier had been Thomas Carter's office.

'I thought this thing was laughing,' Bankim admitted in a whisper. 'But I'm not going to repeat that to anyone.'

Ben nodded and, leaving Bankim by the ambulance, he walked over to his friends, who were desperate to hear about his conversation with Carter. Only Sheere observed him with visible concern, as if, deep in her heart, she alone was capable of understanding that Ben's news would steer events down a dark and fatal path from which none of them would be able to escape.

'We need to talk,' said Ben calmly. 'But not here.'

I RECALL THAT MAY MORNING AS THE FIRST SIGN OF a storm that was relentlessly closing in on us, shaping our destiny, building up behind our backs and swelling in the shadow of our complete innocence – that blessed ignorance which made us believe we were worthy of a special state of grace: because we had no past we felt we had nothing to fear from the future.

Little did we know that the jackals of misfortune were not pursuing poor Thomas Carter. Their fangs thirsted for younger blood, blood infused with the stain of a curse that could not be hidden, not even among the noisy street markets or in the depths of Calcutta's deserted palaces.

We followed Ben to the Midnight Palace, searching for a secret place where we could listen to what he had to say. That day none of us feared that behind the strange accident and the uncertain words uttered by the scorched lips of our headmaster there might be any threat greater than that of separation and the emptiness towards which the blank pages of our future seemed to be leading us. We had yet to learn that the Devil created youth so that we could make our mistakes, and that God established maturity and old age so that we could pay for them …

I also remember that as we listened to Ben's report of

his conversation with Thomas Carter, each one of us, without exception, knew he was keeping something from us, something the wounded headmaster had confided in him. And I remember the worried expression on the faces of my friends, mirrored on my own, as we realised that, for the first time in all those years, our friend Ben had chosen to keep us in the dark.

A few minutes later he asked to speak privately with Sheere, and I thought that my best friend had just delivered the final blow to the doomed Chowbar Society. But future events would prove that, once again, I had misjudged Ben and the loyalty which our club inspired in his soul.

At the time, however, watching my friend's face as he spoke to Sheere, I realised that the wheel of fortune had begun to turn backwards. Our opponent in the game was prepared to bet high and we didn't have the knowledge, or experience, to match him.

© Mark Rusher

City of Palaces

IN THE HAZY LIGHT OF THAT HUMID SCORCHING DAY the reliefs and gargoyles on the facade of the Chowbar Society's secret hideout resembled wax figures melting into the walls. The sun lay hidden behind a dense bank of clouds and a suffocating mist rose from the Hooghly River, sweeping through the streets of the Black Town like the fumes from a poisoned marsh.

Ben and Sheere were talking behind two fallen roof beams in the central hall of the old mansion, while the others waited about a dozen metres away, glancing occasionally at the pair with suspicion.

'I don't know whether I've done the right thing,

hiding this from my friends,' Ben confessed to Sheere. 'I know they'll be upset, and it goes against the oaths of the Chowbar Society, but if there's even the remotest possibility that there's a murderer out there who wants to kill me, I have no intention of getting them mixed up in it. I don't really want to involve you either, Sheere. I can't imagine how your grandmother could be connected to all this, and until I discover what that connection is, it's best to keep this secret to ourselves.'

Sheere nodded. It upset her to think that somehow the secret she shared with Ben would come between him and his friends, but she was also aware that things might turn out to be more serious than they imagined, and she was savouring the closeness to Ben this special link gave her.

'I need to tell you something too, Ben,' Sheere began. 'This morning, when I came to say goodbye to you, I didn't think it was important. But now things have changed. Last night, when we were returning to the house where we've been staying, my grandmother made me swear I would never speak to you again. She said I must forget you and that if I tried to get close to you it might end in tragedy.'

Ben sighed at the speed with which the torrent of threats against him was multiplying. Everyone, except himself, appeared to know some terrible secret that turned him into a target, the bearer of misfortune.

'What reason did she give for saying something like

that?' asked Ben. 'She'd never seen me before last night and I don't think my behaviour could justify anything like that.'

'I'm sure it has nothing to do with your behaviour,' Sheere said. 'She was scared. There was no anger in her words, only fear.'

'Well, we're going to have to find something else besides fear if we want to understand what's going on,' replied Ben. 'We'll go and see her straight away.'

He walked over to where the other members of the Chowbar Society were waiting. He could tell from their faces that they'd been discussing the matter and had come to a decision. Ben guessed who would be the spokesperson for the inevitable complaint. They all looked at Ian, who rolled his eyes and sighed.

'Ian has something to tell you,' Isobel stated. 'But we all feel the same way.'

Ben faced his friends and smiled.

'I'm listening.'

'Well,' Ian began. 'The essence of what we're trying to say—'

'Don't beat about the bush, Ian,' Seth interrupted.

Ian whisked round, with all the restrained fury his placid nature allowed.

'The term "spokesperson" means one person does the speaking, the others just shut up.'

Nobody else dared to make any more objections to his speech and Ian returned to his task.

'As I was saying: basically, we think there's something that doesn't add up. You said Mr Carter told you he was attacked by some criminal who is stalking the orphanage. A criminal nobody has seen and whose motives, from what you've said, we can't understand. We also don't understand why Mr Carter asked to speak to you specifically or why you've been talking to Bankim and haven't told us what it was about. You must have your reasons for keeping this secret and sharing it only with Sheere, or at least you think you do. But, to be honest, if you value our society and its aims, you should trust us and not hide anything from us.'

Ben considered Ian's words as the rest of his friends nodded in agreement.

'If I've kept anything from you it's because I think that otherwise I might be putting your lives in danger,' Ben explained.

'The founding principle of this society is to help one another no matter what, not just to listen to funny stories and disappear the moment things go wrong,' Seth protested angrily.

'This is a society, not some girlie orchestra,' added Siraj.

Isobel slapped the back of his head.

'Be quiet!' she snapped.

'All right,' Ben agreed. 'All for one, and one for all. Is that what you want? The Three Musketeers?'

All eyes were trained on him as slowly, one by one, they nodded their heads.

'OK. I'll tell you everything I know, which isn't much,' said Ben.

For the next ten minutes the Chowbar Society heard the unedited version of his tale, including his conversation with Bankim and what Sheere's grandmother had said. After his account, it was question time.

'Has anyone ever heard of this Jawahal?' asked Seth. 'Siraj?'

The walking encyclopedia's only answer was an unambiguous 'No.'

'Do we know whether Mr Carter could have been doing business with someone like that? Would there be anything about it in his files?' asked Isobel.

'We can find out,' replied Ian. 'Right now, the main thing is to speak to your grandmother, Sheere.'

'I agree,' said Roshan. 'Let's go and see her and then we can decide on a plan of action.'

'Any objections to Roshan's proposal?' asked Ian.

A 'no' resounded through the ruins of the Midnight Palace.

'Fine, let's go.'

'Just a minute,' said Michael.

The friends turned to listen to the quiet pencil virtuoso who chronicled the adventures of the Chowbar Society.

'Has it occurred to you that all this might be connected to the story you told us this morning, Ben?'

Ben gulped. He had been asking himself that same

question, but hadn't been able to find a link between the two events.

'I don't see a connection, Michael,' said Seth.

The others thought about it for a while, but none of them seemed inclined to disagree with Seth.

'I don't think there's a connection either,' agreed Ben at last. 'It must have been a dream.'

Michael looked him straight in the eye, something he hardly ever did, and held out a small drawing. Ben examined it and saw the shape of a train crossing a desolate plain dotted with run-down shacks. At the front a majestic wedge-shaped engine crowned with tall chimneys spat out steam and smoke into a sky filled with black stars. The train was swathed in flames and hundreds of ghostly faces peered through the carriage windows, their arms outstretched, howling amid the blaze. Michael had faithfully translated Ben's words onto paper. Ben felt a shiver down his spine.

'I don't see, Michael …' Ben murmured. 'What are you driving at?'

Sheere went over to them and her face grew pale when she saw the drawing and realised the link Michael had identified between Ben's vision and the incident at St Patrick's.

'The fire,' she said softly. 'It's the fire.'

ARYAMI BOSE'S HOME HAD been closed up for years, inhabited only by books and paintings, but the spectre of thousands of memories imprisoned between its walls still permeated the house.

On the way there they had agreed that the best plan would be for Sheere to go into the house first, so that she could tell Aryami what had happened and explain that the friends wanted to speak to her. Once this first phase had been completed, the members of the Chowbar Society thought it would also be better to limit the number of representatives at the meeting. The sight of seven strange youths was bound to slow her tongue. It was therefore decided that only Ian, Sheere and Ben would be present at the conversation. Once again Ian agreed to act as ambassador for the society, although he was beginning to suspect that the frequency with which he was chosen for the job had less to do with his friends' trust in his intelligence and moderation than with his harmless appearance, which was perfect for winning over adults and authority figures. After walking through the streets of the Black Town and waiting a few minutes in the jungle-like courtyard surrounding Aryami Bose's home, Ian and Ben entered the house at a signal from Sheere, while the others waited for their return.

Sheere led them to a room that was poorly lit by about a dozen candles floating on water inside glass containers. Drops of melted wax formed petals around the candles, dulling the reflection of the flames. The three friends sat down in front of the old lady, who gazed at them in silence from her armchair. In the darkness around them they glimpsed hangings covering the walls and shelves buried under years of dust.

Aryami waited for their eyes to meet hers and then she leaned in towards them.

'My granddaughter told me what happened,' said Aryami. 'But I can't say I'm surprised. For years I've lived with the fear that something like this might occur, although I never imagined it would happen in this way. First of all, you must realise that what you've witnessed today is only the beginning and that, after hearing me out, it will be up to you either to let these events continue or to put a stop to them. I'm old and I don't have the courage or the strength to fight against forces that are far stronger than me and that with each passing day I find harder to understand.'

Sheere took her grandmother's wrinkled hand and stroked it gently. Ian noticed Ben biting his nails and gave him a discreet nudge.

'There was a time when I thought that nothing could be more powerful than love. And it's true, love is powerful, but that power pales into insignificance next to the fire of hatred. I know these revelations aren't exactly the best present for your sixteenth birthday – normally young people are allowed to live in blissful ignorance of the real nature of the world until they are much older – but I'm afraid you're not going to have that privilege. I also know that you'll doubt my words and my judgement, simply because they are those of an old woman. In recent years I've come to recognise that look in the eyes of my own granddaughter. The fact is that nothing is more difficult to believe than the truth; conversely, nothing seduces like the power of lies, the greater the better. It's only natural, and you will have to find the right balance. Having said that, let me add that this particular old woman hasn't been collecting only years; she has also collected stories, and none sadder or more terrible than the one she's about to tell you. You have been at the heart of this story without knowing it, until today ...'

'THERE WAS A TIME when I too was young and did all the things young people are expected to do: marry, have children, get into debt, become disappointed and give up the dreams and principles you have always sworn to uphold. In a word, I became old. Even so, fate was generous to me, or at least that's what I thought at the beginning: it joined my life to that of a man about whom the best and worst you could say was that he was a good person. I can't deny it, he wasn't exactly suave. I remember my sisters sniggering at him when he came to the house. He was rather clumsy and shy and looked as if he'd spent the last ten years of his life locked up in a library – hardly the kind of man any girl your age dreams of, Sheere.

'My suitor was a teacher at a state school in South Calcutta. His pay was miserable and his clothes were in line with his pay. Every Saturday he would come and pick me up wearing the same suit, the only one he had, which he reserved for school meetings and for going out with me. It took six years before he could afford another one, although he never looked good in suits: he didn't have the right frame.

'My two sisters married smart good-looking young men who treated your grandfather with disdain and, behind his back, would throw me suggestive looks which I was supposed to interpret as invitations to enjoy the pleasures of a real man.

'Years later, those lazy good-for-nothings ended up living off the charity of my husband, but that's another story. Although he could see right through them – he was always able to look into the soul of anyone he dealt with – he didn't refuse to support the bloodsuckers and pretended to have forgotten how they had mocked and scorned him when he was young. I wouldn't have helped them but, as I said, my husband was a good person. Perhaps too good.

'Unfortunately his health was fragile, and he left me early on, one year after the birth of our only daughter, Kylian. I had to bring her up on my own and try to teach her everything her father would have wanted her to learn. Kylian was the light that illuminated my life after the death of your grandfather. She inherited her kind nature from him, and her instinct for seeing into the hearts of others. But where your grandfather was forever clumsy and shy, Kylian radiated brightness and elegance. Her beauty began in her gestures, in her voice, in the way she moved. As a child, her words enchanted visitors and passers-by as if they were a magic spell. I remember watching her charm the merchants in the bazaar when she was only ten. It seemed to me that my girl was like a swan that had somehow emerged from the ugly duckling that was my husband. His spirit lived within her, in the most insignificant of her gestures and in the way she would sometimes stand in the porch of this house and stare quietly at the people going by, then look at me, her face deadly serious, and ask me why there were so many unfortunates in the world.

'Soon everyone in the Black Town began to refer to her by the nickname she'd been given by a Bombay photographer: the Princess of Light. And it wasn't long before would-be princes began to crawl out of the woodwork. Those were wonderful days, when she shared with me the absurd secrets her elegantly attired suitors confided in her, the dreadful poems they wrote to her and a whole collection of anecdotes which, had the situation gone on much longer, might have led us to believe that this city was full of nothing but halfwits. But soon a man appeared on the scene who was destined to change everything: your father, Sheere, the most intelligent, and also the strangest, man I have ever known.

'In those days, as today, the vast majority of marriages were arranged between families, like a contract in which the wishes of the future spouses carry no weight at all. Most traditions reflect the ills of a society. All my life I had sworn that the day Kylian got married she would do so to someone she had chosen freely.

'The first time your father came through this door, he seemed the complete opposite of the dozens of swaggering peacocks that were forever hanging around your mother. He didn't speak much, but when he did, his words were razor-sharp and did not invite a reply. He was kind and, when he wanted, he could display a strange charm that seduced slowly but surely. Even so, your father was always distant and cold with everyone. Everyone, that is, except your mother. In her company he became a different person, vulnerable and almost childlike. I never discovered which of the two he really was, and I suppose your mother took the secret to her grave.

'On the few occasions when he deigned to speak to me, he didn't say much. At last he decided to ask for my consent to marry your mother, and I enquired how he intended to provide for her and what his situation was. My years on the brink of poverty with your grandfather had taught me to protect Kylian against it. I was convinced that there's nothing like an empty stomach for destroying the myth that hunger is a noble condition.

'Your father looked at me – keeping his real thoughts to himself, as he always did – and replied that he was an engineer and a writer. He said he was trying to obtain a post with a British construction company and that a Delhi publisher had paid him an advance on a manuscript he'd sent. All of which, once you cleared away the long words with which your father laced his talk when it suited him, smelled to me of deprivation and hardship. I told him so. He smiled, and taking my hand gently in his, he whispered these words I'll never forget: "Mother, this is the first and last time I'll say this. From now on, your daughter and I are in charge of our own future, and that includes providing for her and carving out a life for myself. Nobody, alive or dead, will ever be allowed to interfere. On that matter you must rest assured and trust in the love I have for her. But if worry still gives you sleepless nights, don't let a single word, gesture or action sully the bond which, with or without your consent, will unite us for ever, because eternity would not be long enough for you to regret it."

'Three months later they were married, and I never spoke to your father in private again. The future proved him right, and soon he began to make a name for himself as an engineer, without abandoning his passion for literature. They moved into a house not far from here – which was demolished years ago – while he conceived what was going to be their dream home, a real palace which he designed down to the minutest detail. He planned to retire there with your mother. Nobody could imagine then what was about to happen.

'I never really got to know him. He didn't give me the chance, nor did he seem to be interested in opening up to anyone but your mother. He intimidated me, and when I was with him I felt quite incapable of approaching him or trying to win him over. It was impossible to know what he was thinking. I used to read his books, which your mother would bring when she came to see me, and I'd study them carefully in an effort to discover clues that might allow me to penetrate the maze of his mind. I never succeeded.

'Your father was a mysterious man who never talked about his family or his past. Maybe that's why I was never able to foresee the threat that hovered over him and my daughter, a threat born of that dark and unfathomable past. He never let me help him and, when disaster struck, he was as alone as he'd always been, locked in the fortress of solitude he'd made for himself. Only one person ever held the keys, during the time she shared with him: Kylian.

'But your father, like all of us, had a past, and from that past a figure emerged who would bring darkness and tragedy upon our family.

'When your father was young and roamed the streets of Calcutta, dreaming about numbers and mathematical formulae, he met a lonely orphan boy of his own age. At the time your father lived in the most abject poverty and, like so many children in this city, he caught one of the fevers that claim thousands of lives every year. During the rainy season the monsoon unleashed powerful storms over the Bengali Peninsula, flooding the entire Ganges Delta and the surrounding area. Year after year the salt lake that still lies to the east of the city would overflow; and when the rain ceased and the water level subsided, all the dead fish were exposed to the sun, producing a cloud of poisonous fumes which winds from the mountains in the north would then blow over Calcutta, spreading illness and death like some infernal plague.

'That year your father was a victim of the deadly winds and he would have died had it not been for his friend Jawahal, who looked after him for twenty days in a hovel made of mud and burnt wood on the banks of the Hooghly River. When he recovered, your father swore he would always protect Jawahal and would share with him whatever the future might bring, because now his life also belonged to his friend. It was a child's oath. A pact of blood and honour. But there was something your father didn't know: Jawahal, his guardian angel, who was barely nine years old at the time, carried in his veins an illness far more terrible than the one that had almost taken your father's life. An illness that would manifest itself much later, at first imperceptibly, then as surely as a death sentence: madness.

'Years later your father was told that Jawahal's mother had set fire to herself in front of her son as a sacrificial act to the goddess Kali, and that his mother's mother had ended her days in a miserable cell in a lunatic asylum in Bombay. Those two events were only links in the long chain of horrors and misfortunes that characterised the history of the family. But your father was a strong person, even as a boy, and he took on the responsibility of protecting his friend, whatever the outcome of his terrible inheritance.

'It all went well until Jawahal turned eighteen, when he cold-bloodedly murdered a wealthy trader in the bazaar, just because the man refused to sell him a large medallion on the grounds that Jawahal's appearance made the trader doubt his solvency. Your father kept Jawahal hidden in his home for months and put his own life and future at risk by protecting him from the police, who were searching for him all over town. He succeeded, but that incident was only the start of it. A year later, on the night of the Hindu new year celebrations, Jawahal set fire to a house where about a dozen old women lived, then sat outside watching the flames until the beams collapsed and the building turned to ash. This time not even your father's cunning was able to save Jawahal from the hands of justice.

'There was a trial – long and terrible – at the end of which Jawahal was given a life sentence for his crimes. Your father did what he could to help him, spending all his savings on lawyers, sending clean clothes to the prison where his friend was being held, bribing the guards so they wouldn't torment him. But the only thanks he got from Jawahal were words of hatred. He accused your father of having denounced him, of abandoning him and wanting to get rid of him. He reproached him for breaking the oath they had made years earlier and swore revenge because, as he shouted from the dock when his sentence was read out, half your father's life belonged to him.

'Your father hid this secret in the depths of his heart and never wanted your mother to find out about it. Time erased all trace of those events. After the wedding, the first years of married life and your father's early success, it became just a memory, a remote episode buried in the past.

'I remember when your mother became pregnant. Your father turned into a different person, a stranger. He bought a puppy and said he was going to train it to become a watchdog, turn it into the best nanny for his future son. And he didn't stop talking about the house he was going to build, the plans he had for the future, a new book …

'A month later Lieutenant Michael Peake, one of your mother's former suitors, knocked on the door with news that would sow terror in their lives: Jawahal had set fire to the secure prison block where he was being held, and had escaped. Before fleeing he'd slit his cellmate's throat and had used his blood to write a single word on the wall: REVENGE.

'Peake promised that he would personally look for Jawahal and protect the couple from any possible threat. Two months went by with no sign of the escaped prisoner. Until your father's birthday.

'Just before sunrise a parcel was delivered to him by a beggar. It contained a large medallion – the piece that had led Jawahal to commit his first murder – and a note. In it Jawahal explained that after spying on them for a few weeks and discovering that your father was now a successful man with a dazzling wife, he wished them well and would perhaps soon pay them a visit, so that they could "share what belonged to them both, like brothers".

'The following days were strewn with panic. One of the sentries Peake had employed to guard the house at night was found dead. Your father's dog was discovered at the bottom of the well in the courtyard. And every morning the walls of the house were daubed with new threats, written in blood, which Peake and his men were powerless to prevent.

'Those were difficult days for your father. His finest work had just been built, the Jheeter's Gate Station on the western bank of the Hooghly. It was an impressive, revolutionary steel structure, the culmination of his project to establish a railway network throughout the entire country, to encourage development of local trade and modernise the provinces so that they could eventually overcome domination by the British. That was always one of his obsessions, and he could spend hours speaking passionately about it, as if it were some divine mission he'd been entrusted with. The official opening of Jheeter's Gate was taking place at the end of the week, and to mark the occasion it was decided to charter a train that would transport three hundred and sixty-five orphans to their new home in western India. They came from the most deprived backgrounds, and your father's project would mean a whole new life for them. It was something he had pledged to do from the very start, his life's dream.

'Your mother was desperate to attend the ceremony for a few hours, and she assured your father that the protection offered by Lieutenant Peake and his men would be sufficient to keep her safe.

'When your father climbed into the train and got the engine going that was supposed to take the children to their new home, something unexpected happened. The fire. A terrible blaze spread through the various levels of the station, fanning out along the train's carriages so that as it entered the tunnel, the train was transformed into a rolling inferno, a molten tomb for the children who travelled inside. Your father died that night, trying to save the orphans, while his dreams vanished for ever amid the flames.

'When your mother heard the news she almost lost you. But fate grew weary of sending misfortune to your family, and you were saved. Three days later, when she was only a few days from giving birth, Jawahal and his men burst into the house and after proclaiming that the Jheeter's Gate tragedy had been their doing, they took your mother away.

'Lieutenant Peake managed to survive the assault and followed them to the very bowels of the station, which by then was an accursed place nobody had set foot in since the night of the tragedy. Jawahal had left a note in the house swearing he'd kill your mother and the child she was about to deliver. But something happened that not even Jawahal had expected. It was not one child, but two. Twins. A boy and a girl. You two …'

ARYAMI BOSE TOLD THEM how Peake had managed to rescue them and bring them to her home, and how she had decided to separate them and hide them from their parents' murderer … but neither Sheere nor Ben was listening to her any longer. Ian stared at the white faces of his best friend and the girl. They hardly blinked; the revelations they had heard from the old woman's lips seemed to have turned them into statues. Ian heaved a deep sigh and wished he'd not been the one selected to attend this strange family reunion. He felt extremely uncomfortable, an intruder in the drama that was unfolding around his friends.

All the same, Ian swallowed his dismay and focused his thoughts on Ben. He tried to imagine the storm Aryami's account must have unleashed inside him and he cursed the abruptness with which fear and exhaustion had made the old lady reveal events that could potentially have consequences far greater than they imagined. For the moment he tried not to think of what Ben had told him that morning about his vision of a blazing train. The pieces of the jigsaw puzzle were multiplying with terrifying speed.

He recalled the dozens of times Ben had asserted that they, the members of the Chowbar Society, were people without a past. Ian was afraid that Ben's encounter with his own history in the gloom of that derelict house might cause him irreparable damage. They had known each other since they were small, and Ian was familiar with Ben's episodes of melancholy and realised it was always better to support him without asking any questions or trying to read his mind. Judging from what he knew of his friend, the impressive front behind which Ben usually hid his feelings must have suffered a tremendous blow. And he was sure Ben would never want to speak about it.

Ian placed a hand gently on Ben's shoulder, but his friend didn't seem to notice.

Ben and Sheere, who only a few hours earlier had felt a strong bond growing between them, now seemed incapable of looking at one another, as if the new cards dealt in the game had given them an unfamiliar modesty, a primal fear of exchanging even the simplest glance.

Aryami looked anxiously at Ian. In the room silence reigned. The old woman's eyes seemed to be begging them for forgiveness, the pardon granted the bearer of bad news. Ian tilted his head slightly, signalling to Aryami that they should leave the room. The old lady hesitated for a few seconds, but Ian stood up and offered her his hand. She accepted his help and followed him to the adjoining room, leaving Ben and Sheere alone. Ian stopped in the doorway and turned towards his friend.

'We'll be outside,' he murmured.

Without looking up Ben nodded.

THE MEMBERS OF THE Chowbar Society were wilting in the crushing heat of the courtyard when they saw Ian appear through the front door, together with the old woman. The two exchanged a few words. Aryami nodded wearily and then sought the shade of an old carved-stone veranda. Ian, his expression severe, which his friends took to be a bad sign, walked over to the group and stood in the shady spot they had left for him. Aryami watched them from a few metres away, a doleful expression on her face.

'Well?' asked Isobel.

'I don't know where to begin,' replied Ian.

'Try the worst part,' Seth suggested.

'Everything is the worst part,' said Ian.

The others went quiet and looked at him expectantly. Ian contemplated his friends and gave a weak smile.

'Ten ears are listening,' said Isobel.

Ian repeated what Aryami had just revealed inside the house, not omitting a single detail. The end of his narrative was dedicated exclusively to Ben and Sheere – who were still inside – and the fateful sword they had just discovered dangling over their heads.

By the time he finished, the entire membership of the Chowbar Society had forgotten the stifling heat that pressed down from the sky like some infernal punishment.

'How did Ben take it?' asked Roshan.

Ian frowned. 'How would you have felt if you were him?'

'What are we going to do now?' asked Siraj.

'What can we do?' asked Ian.

'A lot,' Isobel stated. 'Anything rather than sit here roasting our behinds when there's a murderer out there trying to kill Ben. And Sheere.'

'Anyone against?' asked Seth.

They all answered, 'No.'

'Very well, Colonel,' said Ian, looking pointedly at Isobel. 'What are your orders?'

'First, somebody should find out everything there is to know about this accident at Jheeter's Gate and the engineer,' said Isobel.

'I can do that,' offered Seth. 'There must be newspaper cuttings from the time in the library of the Indian Museum. And books, probably.'

'Seth is right,' said Siraj. 'The fire at Jheeter's Gate caused a great scandal in its day, and a lot of people still remember it. There must be records on the subject. Goodness knows where, but they must exist.'

'Then we'll have to search for them,' Isobel said. 'They could be a good starting point.'

'I'll help Seth,' said Michael.

Isobel nodded vigorously. 'We must find out everything we can about this man, his life, and also the amazing house which is supposed to be somewhere near here. Tracing it might lead us to the murderer.'

'We'll look for the house,' suggested Siraj, pointing at himself and Roshan.

'If it exists, we'll find it,' Roshan added.

'Fine, but don't go inside,' warned Isobel.

'We didn't intend to,' Roshan reassured her.

'What about me? What am I supposed to do?' asked Ian. He couldn't think of a task that would suit his particular skills as easily.

'You stay here with Ben and Sheere,' said Isobel. 'For all we know, Ben might start getting crazy ideas into his head before we even realise it. Stay by his side and make sure he doesn't do anything stupid. It's not a good idea for him to be seen out on the streets with Sheere.'

Ian agreed, aware that his was the most difficult task of the whole lot.

'We'll meet in the Midnight Palace before it turns dark,' Isobel concluded. 'Any questions?'

The friends looked at one another and quickly shook their heads.

'Good, let's get going.'

Seth, Michael, Roshan and Siraj set off at once to carry out their respective tasks. Isobel stayed behind with Ian, quietly watching them leave through the heat haze rising from the scorched dusty streets.

'What are *you* planning to do, Isobel?' asked Ian.

Isobel turned to him and smiled mysteriously.

'I have a hunch,' she said.

'I trust your hunches as much as I trust earthquakes,' Ian replied. 'What are you plotting?'

'You mustn't worry, Ian.'

'When you say that, I worry even more.'

'I might not get to the Palace by this evening,' said Isobel. 'If I haven't appeared, do what you have to do. You always know what has to be done, Ian.'

He sighed. He was worried. He hated all this mystery and the strange glint he noticed in his friend's eyes.

'Look at me, Isobel,' he ordered. She obeyed. 'Whatever your plan is, forget it.'

'I know how to take care of myself, Ian,' she said with a smile.

Ian, however, could not return the smile.

'Don't do anything I wouldn't do,' he begged.

Isobel laughed.

'I'll do one thing you would never dare to do,' she whispered.

Ian stared at her, mystified. Then, her eyes still shining enigmatically, she moved closer to him and brushed his lips gently with a kiss.

'Take care, Ian,' she said softly. 'And don't go dreaming …'

That was the first time Isobel had kissed him, and

as he watched her disappear through the wilderness of the courtyard, Ian couldn't help feeling a sudden and inexplicable fear that it might also be the last.

∾

ALMOST AN HOUR LATER Ben and Sheere emerged, their faces inscrutable but strangely calm. Sheere walked over to Aryami, who had spent all the time alone on the veranda, away from the discussions of Ian and his friends, and sat down next to her. Ben made straight for Ian.

'Where is everybody?' he asked.

'We thought it would be useful to investigate this individual Jawahal,' Ian replied.

'So you've been left to babysit?' Ben's forced humour didn't fool either of them.

'Something like that. Are you all right?' Ian motioned towards Sheere.

His friend nodded.

'Confused, I suppose,' Ben said at last. 'I hate surprises.'

'Isobel says it's not a good idea for you two to go out and about together, and I think she's right.'

'Isobel is always right, except when she argues with me,' replied Ben. 'But I don't think this is a safe place for us either. Even if it's been shut up for over fifteen years, it's still the family home. And St Patrick's isn't any safer, that's fairly obvious.'

'I think the best thing would be to go to the Palace and

wait for the others there,' said Ian.

'Is that Isobel's plan?' Ben smiled.

'Guess.'

'Where has she gone?'

'She wouldn't tell me.'

'One of her hunches?' asked Ben, alarmed.

Ian nodded.

'God help us.' Ben sighed and patted his friend's back. 'I'm going to talk to the ladies.'

Ian turned to look at Sheere and Aryami Bose. The old lady seemed to be having a heated discussion with her granddaughter. Ben and Ian exchanged glances.

'I suspect the grandmother is sticking to her plan of leaving for Bombay tomorrow,' said Ben.

'Will you go with them?'

'I don't intend to leave this city – ever. Even less so now.'

The two friends observed the development of the argument between grandmother and granddaughter for a few more minutes, then Ben whispered, 'Wait for me here,' and headed over towards them.

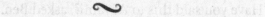

ARYAMI BOSE WENT BACK into the house, leaving Ben and Sheere alone by the entrance. Sheere's face was flushed with anger and Ben gave her a few moments until she was ready to speak. When she did, her voice shook with fury and her hands were clenched in a rigid knot.

'She says we're leaving tomorrow and she doesn't want to discuss the matter any further,' she explained. 'She also says you should come with us, but she can't make you.'

'I suppose she thinks it's for the best.'

'That's not what you think, is it?'

'I'd be lying if I said I did,' Ben admitted.

'I've spent my whole life running from town to town, taking trains, ships, carts ... I've never had my own home, my own friends or a place I could think of as mine,' said Sheere. 'I'm tired, Ben. I can't keep hiding from somebody I don't even know.'

Ben and Sheere looked at one another. After a while she spoke again.

'She's an old woman, Ben. She's frightened because her life is coming to an end and she knows she won't be able to protect us much longer. Her heart is in the right place, but running away again just isn't an option. What use would it be to take that train to Bombay tomorrow? To get off at some random station and change our names? To beg for a roof in any old village, knowing that the following day we might have to move again?'

'Have you said this to Aryami?' asked Ben.

'She won't listen. But this time I refuse to run away. This is my home, this is my father's city and this is where I plan to stay. And if that man comes for me I'll stand up to him. If he wants to kill me, let him try. But if I'm to go on living, I'm not prepared to do so like some fugitive who has to give thanks every day simply for being alive. Will you help me, Ben?'

'Of course,' he replied.

Sheere hugged him and dried her tears with the tip of her shawl.

'Do you know, Ben,' she said, 'last night, with your friends in that old house, your Midnight Palace, while I was telling you my story I kept thinking that I'd never had the opportunity to be a child. I grew up surrounded by old people, by fear and lies. The only company I had was beggars and people I met on our travels. I remember I used to invent imaginary friends and spend hours talking to them in station waiting rooms or on the long journeys we made in covered carts. Adults would look at me and smile. To them a little girl who spoke to herself seemed adorable. But it isn't adorable, Ben. It's not adorable to be alone, as a child or as an adult. For years I've wondered what other children were like, whether they had the same nightmares I had, whether they felt as miserable as I did. Whoever said that childhood is the happiest time of your life is a liar, or a fool.'

Ben observed his sister and smiled.

'Or both,' he joked. 'They usually go hand in hand.'

Sheere blushed.

'I'm sorry. I'm a chatterbox, aren't I?'

'No,' said Ben. 'I like listening to you. Besides, I'm sure we have more in common than you think.'

'We're brother and sister.' Sheere laughed nervously. 'What more do you want? Twins! It sounds so strange!'

'Well, you can only choose your friends,' Ben said, 'so having family is a bonus.'

'I'd rather you were my friend,' said Sheere.

Ian had come over to them and was relieved to see they both seemed in good spirits. They were even cracking jokes, which, given the circumstances, was no small achievement.

'As long as you know what you're letting yourself in for. Ian, this young lady wants to be my friend.'

'I wouldn't recommend it,' said Ian. 'I've been his friend for years and look at me. Have you come to a decision?'

Ben nodded.

'Is it what I think?'

Ben nodded again and this time Sheere joined in.

'What is it you've decided?' came Aryami Bose's embittered voice behind them.

The three youngsters turned to see her standing motionless, half-hidden in the shadows beyond the doorway. The silence was tense.

'We're not taking that train tomorrow, Grandmother,' Sheere replied eventually. 'Not me, not Ben.'

The old woman looked at each one in turn, her eyes ablaze.

'So the words of a few senseless children have made you forget, in just a few minutes, what I've been teaching you for years?'

'No, Grandmother. It's my own decision. And nothing in the world is going to make me change my mind.'

'You'll do as I say,' retorted Aryami, although the pain

of defeat could be heard in every word.

'Please—' Ian began politely.

'Be quiet, child,' snapped Aryami, her voice cold.

Ian suppressed his desire to answer back and lowered his eyes.

'Grandmother, none of us is a child any more. That's why I'm *not* taking that train,' said Sheere. 'And you know it.'

Aryami glared at her granddaughter but said nothing.

After a long pause she finally spoke again. 'I'll be waiting for both of you tomorrow at dawn, in Howrah Station.'

Sheere sighed and Ben noticed her face going red again. He touched her arm and motioned for her to drop the argument. Aryami turned away and her footsteps disappeared inside the house.

'I can't leave things like this,' Sheere murmured.

Ben let go of his sister's arm and she followed Aryami into the candlelit living room, where the old lady had sat down once more. Aryami didn't turn her head when she came in, ignoring her granddaughter's presence. Sheere drew closer and put her arms around her.

'Whatever happens, Grandmother,' she said, 'I'll always love you.'

Silently Aryami nodded, and her eyes filled with tears as her granddaughter walked back to the courtyard. Ben and Ian, who were waiting outside, greeted Sheere with the most optimistic expressions they could manage.

'Where will we go?' asked Sheere, trying to hold back her tears, her hands trembling.

'To the best place in Calcutta,' replied Ben. 'The Midnight Palace.'

❧

THE LAST LIGHT OF day was beginning to fade as Isobel caught sight of the ghostly angular structure of Jheeter's Gate Station emerging from the mist by the river. Holding her breath she stopped to gaze at the eerie sight before her: a thick framework of hundreds of steel beams, arches and domes, a vast labyrinth of metal and glass shattered by the fire. Spanning the river to the station's entrance on the opposite bank was an old ruined bridge.

Isobel approached the bridge and began to negotiate the rails that traversed it, a siding that led into the heart of the monumental carcass the station had become. The sleepers were rotten and black, with wild vegetation creeping over them. The rusty structure of the bridge groaned beneath her feet and Isobel noticed signs forbidding trespassers and warning of an impending demolition order. No train had crossed that bridge since the fire, and judging from its condition nobody had bothered to repair it, or even walk over it, she thought.

As the east bank of the Hooghly receded behind her and Jheeter's Gate loomed in front of her, silhouetted against the scarlet canopy of sunset, Isobel began to toy with the idea that perhaps her decision to come to this place had not been so sensible after all. From the dark tunnels hidden in the bowels of the station came a breath of wind impregnated with ash and soot, accompanied by an acrid stench. She focused on the distant lights of the barges that ploughed the Hooghly River and tried to conjure up the company of their anonymous crews as she covered the final stretch of the bridge separating her from the station. When she reached the end she stood and looked up at the huge steel pediment before her. There, obscured by the damage from the fire but still visible, were the carved letters announcing the station's name, like the entrance to a grandiose mausoleum: JHEETER'S GATE.

Isobel took a deep breath and readied herself to do the thing she had least wanted to do in her sixteen years of life: enter that place.

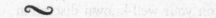

SETH AND MICHAEL WORE the saintly smiles of model students as they faced the merciless scrutiny of Mr de Rozio, head librarian of the Indian Museum.

'That's the most ridiculous request I've heard in my life,' de Rozio concluded. 'At least since the last time you were here, Seth.'

'Let me explain, Mr de Rozio,' Seth improvised. 'We know that normally you're only open in the morning, and what my friend and I are asking you might seem a little extravagant—'

'Coming from you, nothing is extravagant,' de Rozio interrupted.

Seth suppressed a smile. Mr de Rozio's caustic sarcasm was always a sign that he was interested. There was not a person on earth who knew his first name, except perhaps his mother and his wife, if in fact there was a woman in India brave enough to marry such a specimen. Beneath his Cerberus-like appearance, de Rozio had a renowned Achilles heel: his curiosity and love of gossip, albeit with an academic slant, made even the loud-mouthed women in the bazaar look like rank amateurs.

Seth and Michael eyed one another and decided to offer him some bait.

'Mr de Rozio,' Seth began in a melodramatic tone, 'I shouldn't tell you this, but I feel obliged and must rely on your well-known discretion ... There are a number of crimes connected with this matter, and we very much fear there'll be more unless we put a stop to it.'

For a few seconds the librarian's penetrating eyes seemed to grow.

'Are you sure Thomas Carter is aware of this?' he enquired.

'He's the one who sent us here,' replied Seth.

De Rozio observed them once more, searching their faces for clues that might betray some skulduggery.

'And your friend ...' de Rozio retorted, pointing at Michael. 'Why is he so quiet?'

'He was born a mute, sir. A very sad story,' Seth explained.

Michael gave a tiny nod as if he wished to confirm this statement. De Rozio cleared his throat tentatively.

'You mentioned this had something to do with some crimes?' he said with studied indifference.

'Murders, sir,' Seth confirmed. 'Quite a few.'

De Rozio checked his watch and, after a few moments' reflection, he shrugged.

'All right,' he conceded. 'But let this be the last time. What's the name of the man you want to investigate?'

'Lahawaj Chandra Chatterghee, sir,' Seth replied quickly.

'The engineer? Didn't he die in the Jheeter's Gate fire?'

'Yes, sir, but there was someone with him who didn't die. Someone who is very dangerous and who started the fire. That person is still out there, ready to commit new crimes.'

De Rozio smiled. 'Sounds vaguely interesting,' he murmured.

Suddenly a shadow crossed the librarian's face. De Rozio leaned his considerable bulk towards the boys and pointed at them sternly.

'This isn't some invention of that friend of yours?' he asked. 'What's his name?'

'Ben doesn't know anything about this, Mr de Rozio,' Seth reassured him. 'We haven't seen him for months.'

'Just as well,' de Rozio declared. 'Follow me.'

143

WITH TREPIDATION ISOBEL STEPPED inside the station, allowing her eyes to adapt to the darkness. Tens of metres above her was the main dome, with its great arches of steel and glass. Most of the panes had melted in the flames or had simply burst, shattering into red-hot fragments that had rained down over the entire station. Dusky light filtered through cracks in the darkened metal. The platforms faded into the shadows, forming a gentle curve beneath the huge vaulted ceiling, their surface covered with the remains of burnt benches and collapsed beams.

The large station clock, which once had presided over the central platform, was now just a sombre mute sentry standing by. As she walked under its dial, Isobel noticed that the hands had dropped down towards the ground like tongues of melted wax.

Nothing seemed to have changed in that place, were it not for the traces left by years of dirt and the impact of the rainwater torrential monsoons had swept through ventilation shafts and gaps in the roof.

Isobel stopped in the centre of the grand station and gazed around her.

A fresh gust of hot humid air blew through the building, ruffling her hair and scattering specks of dust over the platforms. Isobel shivered as she scanned the black mouths of the tunnels that went underground at the far end of each platform. She wished the other members of the Chowbar Society were with her, now that the situation was beginning to look far too similar to the stories Ben liked to invent for his evenings at the Midnight Palace. Isobel felt in her pocket and pulled out the drawing Michael had made of the Chowbar Society members standing by a pond in which their faces were reflected. She smiled when she saw the picture Michael had drawn of her and wondered if this was really how he saw her. She missed her friends.

Then she heard it for the first time, far away and muffled by the murmur of the breezes that blew through those tunnels. It was the sound of distant voices, rather like the rumble of the crowds she remembered hearing years ago after she dived into the Hooghly River, the day Ben taught her how to swim underwater, only this time Isobel was sure that these were not the voices of pilgrims approaching from the depths of the tunnels. What she heard were the voices of children, hundreds of them. And they were howling in terror.

DE ROZIO METICULOUSLY STROKED the three rolls of his regal chin and once again examined the pile of documents, cuttings and papers he had collected during various expeditions to the digestive tract of the Indian Museum's labyrinthine library. Seth and Michael watched him with a mixture of impatience and hope.

'Well,' the librarian began. 'This matter is rather more complicated than it seems. There's quite a bit of information about this Lahawaj Chandra Chatterghee. Most of the documentation I've seen is not that significant, but I'd need at least a week to get the papers on this person into some sort of order.'

'What have you found, sir?' asked Seth.

'A bit of everything, really,' de Rozio explained. 'Mr Chandra was a brilliant engineer, ahead of his time, an idealist obsessed with the idea of leaving this country with a legacy that would somehow compensate the poor for the suffering he attributed to British rule. Not very original, frankly. In short, he had all the requirements for becoming a miserable wretch. Even so, it seems he was able to navigate a sea of jealousy, conspiracy and subterfuge and even managed to convince the government to finance his golden dream: the building of a railway network that would link the main cities of the nation with the rest of the continent.

'Chandra believed that this would mark the end of the commercial and political monopoly that had begun in the days of Lord Clive and the Company, when trade was limited to using river and maritime transport. It would allow the people of India slowly to regain control over their country's wealth. But you didn't have to be an engineer to realise that things would never turn out that way.'

'Is there anything about a character called Jawahal?' asked Seth. 'He was a childhood friend of the engineer. He went on trial a few times. I think the cases were quite notorious.'

'There must be something somewhere, but there's a mountain of documents to sort through. Why don't you come back in a couple of weeks? By then I'll have had a chance to put this mess into some kind of order.'

'We can't wait two weeks, sir,' said Michael.

De Rozio stared at them severely.

'Wasn't your friend supposed to be a mute?'

Michael stepped forward, his expression dead serious and worth at least a thousand words.

'This is a matter of life and death, sir,' said Michael. 'The lives of two people are in danger.'

De Rozio saw the intensity in Michael's eyes and nodded, vaguely bewildered. Seth didn't lose a second.

'We'll help you search through the material,' he offered.

'You two? I don't know … When?'

'Right now,' replied Michael.

'Do you know the codes for the library index cards?' de Rozio asked.

'Like the alphabet,' lied Seth.

THE SUN DIPPED BEHIND the broken glass panes on the western side of Jheeter's Gate. A few seconds later Isobel watched, hypnotised, as hundreds of horizontal blades of light sliced through the shadows of the station. The howling voices grew in intensity and soon Isobel could hear them echoing round the dome. The ground began to shake under her feet and she noticed shards of glass falling from above. A sudden pain seared along her left forearm. When she touched the spot warm blood slid through her fingers. She ran towards one end of the station, covering her face with her hands.

As she took shelter under a staircase that led to the upper levels she noticed a large waiting room in front of her. Burnt wooden benches were strewn across the floor and the walls were covered with strange crudely drawn pictures. They seemed to represent deformed human shapes, demonic figures with long wolfish claws and eyes that popped out of their heads. The shaking beneath her feet was now intense, and Isobel approached the mouth of one of the tunnels. A blast of burning air scorched her face and she rubbed her eyes, unable to believe what she was seeing.

From the very depths of the tunnel emerged a glowing train covered in flames. Isobel flung herself to the ground as the train crossed the station with a deafening roar, metal grating against metal, accompanied by the yells of hundreds of children trapped in the flames. She lay there, her eyes closed, paralysed with terror, until the sound of the train died away.

Isobel raised her head and looked around her. The station was empty except for a cloud of steam that slowly lifted, tinted dark red by the afterglow of the sun. In front of her, barely half a metre away, was a puddle of some dark sticky substance. For a moment Isobel thought she could see the reflection of a face on its surface, the luminous sad face of a woman enveloped in light who was calling to her. She stretched out a hand towards the image and found the tips of her fingers soaked in the thick warm fluid. Blood. Isobel jerked her hand away and wiped her fingers on her dress as the vision slowly vanished. Gasping for breath, she dragged herself as far as the wall and leaned against it to recover.

After a minute she stood up again and looked around the station. The evening light was fading fast and soon night would be upon her. A single thought took hold of her: she didn't want to wait for that moment inside Jheeter's Gate. She started to walk nervously towards the exit and only then did she spy a ghostly silhouette advancing towards her through the mist. The figure raised a hand, and Isobel saw its fingers burst into flames to light up its path. By then she had realised that she wouldn't be able to get out of that place as easily as she had entered.

THROUGH THE COLLAPSED ROOF of the Midnight Palace shone a starry sky. Evening had taken with it some of the sweltering heat that had been pounding the city since dawn, but the breeze that blew timidly through the streets of the Black Town seemed little more than a warm moist sigh from the Hooghly River.

While they waited for the remaining members of the

Chowbar Society to arrive, Ian, Ben and Sheere were listlessly killing time among the ruins of the old mansion, each lost in their own thoughts.

Ben had opted to clamber up to his favourite corner, a naked beam that ran across the front pediment of the Palace. Sitting exactly in the middle, his legs dangling, Ben would often perch on his solitary lookout post to gaze out at the city lights and the silhouettes of the palaces and cemeteries that bordered the sinuous course of the Hooghly through Calcutta. He could spend hours up there without speaking, not even bothering to look down at solid ground.

From the Palace courtyard Ian kept an eye on his friend and decided to let him enjoy one of his last spiritual retreats; meanwhile, he returned to the task with which he had been occupied the last hour: trying to explain to Sheere the rudiments of chess, using a board which the Chowbar Society kept in its headquarters. The chess pieces were reserved for the annual championships that took place in December – something Isobel invariably won with a superiority that bordered on insult.

'There are two theories regarding the strategy of chess,' Ian explained. 'In fact there are dozens, but only a couple really count. The first is that the key to the game lies in the second row: king, knight, castle, queen, etc. According to this theory, the pawns are just pieces to be sacrificed while you develop your tactics. The second theory, on the other hand, supports the idea that pawns can and should be the most lethal pieces you use in your attack, and it is an intelligent strategy to treat them as such. To be frank, neither of these theories has worked for me, but Isobel is a passionate defender of the second one.'

In mentioning his friend's name, Ian was reminded of how worried he was about her. Sheere noticed his distant expression and rescued him with a new question about the game.

'What is the difference between tactics and strategy?' she asked. 'Is it purely technical?'

Ian weighed up Sheere's question although he doubted there was an answer to it.

'It's a linguistic difference, not a real one,' came Ben's voice from on high. 'Tactics are the collection of small steps you take to reach a position; strategy, the steps you take when there's nowhere left to go.'

Sheere looked up and smiled at Ben.

'Do you play chess?' she asked.

Ben didn't reply.

'Ben deplores chess,' Ian explained. 'According to him, it's the second most useless way of wasting your intelligence.'

'And what is the first?'

'Philosophy,' answered Ben from his lookout post.

'Ben *dixit*,' Ian proclaimed. 'Why don't you come down? The others should be arriving soon.'

'I'll wait,' Ben replied, returning to his place in the clouds.

In fact he didn't come down until half an hour later. Ian was engrossed in an explanation of the knight's ability to jump over other pieces when Roshan and Siraj appeared at the entrance to the Midnight Palace. After a while Seth and Michael also returned, and they all gathered round a small bonfire that Ian had built with the remaining bits of dry wood, which they kept in a part of the building to the rear of the Palace that was protected from the rain. The faces of the seven friends were tinted copper by the glow of the fire as they drank from the bottle of water Ben passed round. It wasn't cold, but at least it wasn't potentially deadly.

'Shouldn't we wait for Isobel?' asked Siraj, visibly anxious about his unrequited love.

'She might not come,' said Ian.

They all looked at him in bewilderment. Ian told them briefly about his conversation with Isobel that afternoon, his friends' expressions becoming markedly gloomy. When he'd finished, he reminded them that she had wanted them to share their discoveries with or without her being present, and he offered the first turn to whoever wished to take it.

'All right,' said Siraj nervously. 'I'll tell you what we found out, but then I'm going straight in search of Isobel. Only someone as stubborn as her would have decided to go off on an expedition tonight, alone and without telling us where she was going. How could you let her do that, Ian?'

Roshan came to Ian's rescue, placing his hand on Siraj's shoulder.

'You can't argue with Isobel,' he reminded Siraj. 'You can only listen. Tell them about the hieroglyphics and then we'll both go and look for her.'

'Hieroglyphics?' asked Sheere.

Roshan nodded.

'We found the house, Sheere,' Siraj explained. 'Or rather, we know where it is.'

Sheere's face suddenly lit up, her heart racing. The boys drew closer to the fire and Siraj pulled out a sheet of paper with a few lines of a poem copied out in his unmistakable handwriting.

'What's this?' asked Seth.

'A poem,' Siraj replied.

'Read it aloud,' said Roshan.

'*The city I love is a dark, deep*
house of misery, a home to evil spirits
in which no one will open a door, nor a heart.
The city I love lives in the twilight,
shadow of wickedness and forgotten glories,
of fortunes sold and souls in torment.
The city I love loves no one, it never rests; it is a
tower erected to the uncertain hell of our destiny,
of the enchantment of a curse that was written in blood,
the dance of deceit and infamy,
bazaar of my sadness ...'

153

The friends remained silent after Siraj had finished reading the poem, and for a moment there was only the whisper of the fire and the distant voice of the city whistling in the wind.

'I know those lines,' Sheere murmured. 'They come from one of my father's books. They're at the end of my favourite story, the tale of Shiva's tears.'

'Exactly,' Siraj agreed. 'We've spent the whole afternoon in the Bengali Institute of Industry. It's an incredible building, almost completely run-down, with floor after floor of archives and rooms buried in dust and rubbish. There were rats, and I bet that if we went there at night we'd find something lurking—'

'Let's stick to the point, Siraj,' Ben cut in. 'Please.'

'All right,' said Siraj, setting aside his enthusiasm for the mysterious building. 'The point is that, after hours of research – which I'm not going to go into, don't worry – we came across a file with documents that belonged to your father. It has been in the safekeeping of the Institute since 1916, the year of the accident at Jheeter's Gate. Among the papers is a book signed by him, and although we weren't allowed to take it away, we were able to examine it. And we were lucky.'

'I don't imagine how,' Ben objected.

'You should be the first to see it. Next to the poem someone, I suppose Sheere's father, did an ink drawing of a house,' Siraj explained, smiling mysteriously as he handed Ben the sheet of paper.

Ben examined the lines of the poem and shrugged his shoulders.

'All I can see is words.'

'You're losing your mental powers, Ben. It's a pity Isobel isn't here to see it,' Siraj joked. 'Read it again. Pay attention.'

Ben followed Siraj's instructions and frowned.

'I give up. The lines have no order or structure. It's just prose, cut up any which way.'

'Exactly,' Siraj agreed. 'But what is the rule guiding this division? In other words, why does he cut the line at the point he does when he could choose any other option?'

'To separate the words?' Sheere ventured.

'Or to join them…' murmured Ben.

'Take the first word of each line and make a sentence with them,' said Roshan.

Ben looked at the poem again and then at his friends.

'Read only the first word,' said Siraj.

'The house in the shadow of the tower of the bazaar,' read Ben.

'There are at least six bazaars in North Calcutta alone,' Ian pointed out.

'How many of them have a tower tall enough to project a shadow over the neighbouring houses?' asked Siraj.

'I don't know.'

'I do,' said Siraj. 'Two: the Shyambazar and the Machuabazar, to the north of the Black Town.'

'Even so, the shadow a tower can cast during the day would spread across a minimum range of a hundred and eighty degrees, changing every minute,' said Ben. 'That house could be anywhere in North Calcutta, which is like saying anywhere in India.'

'Just a moment,' Sheere interrupted them. 'The poem speaks of the twilight. It says, "the city I love lives in the twilight".'

'Have you checked that?' asked Ben.

'Of course we have,' replied Roshan. 'Siraj went to the Shyambazar and I went to the Machuabazar just a few minutes before sunset.'

'And?' they all pressed him.

'The shadow of the tower at the Machuabazar falls on an abandoned warehouse,' Siraj explained.

'Roshan?' asked Ian.

Roshan smiled. He plucked a half-burnt stick from the fire and drew the shape of a tower on the ashes.

'Like the hand of a clock, the shadow of Shyambazar's tower points to some gates flanked by tall iron railings. Behind them there's a courtyard full of palm trees and weeds. And above the palm trees I could just make out a house with a watchtower.'

'That's fantastic!' cried Sheere.

But Ben couldn't help noticing the anxious look on Roshan's face.

'What's the problem, Roshan?' he asked.

Roshan slowly shook his head.

'I don't know. There was something about the house I didn't like.'

'Did you see anything?' asked Seth.

Roshan shook his head again. Ian and Ben exchanged glances, but didn't say a word.

'Has it occurred to anyone that this might all be a trap?' asked Roshan.

Again Ian and Ben gave each other a meaningful look. They were both thinking the same thing.

'We'll have to take that risk,' said Ben, feigning as much conviction as possible.

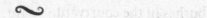

WITH TREMBLING HANDS ARYAMI Bose lit another match and reached forward to light the wick of the white candle that stood in front of her. The flickering flame cast hazy shadows across the dark room. A gentle draught caressed her hair and the back of her neck. Aryami turned round. A sudden gust of cold air, infused with an acrid stench, tugged at her shawl and blew out the candle. Darkness enveloped her again and the old lady heard two sharp knocks on the front door. She clenched her fists; a faint reddish light was filtering through the doorway. The banging was repeated, this time louder. The old woman felt a cold sweat rising through the pores on her forehead.

'Sheere?' she called out weakly.

Her voice echoed in the gloom of the house. There was no answer. A few seconds later the two knocks sounded again.

In the dark Aryami fumbled around on the mantelpiece. The only source of light came from the dying remains of a few coals in the fireplace below. She knocked over several objects before her fingers found the long metal sheath of the dagger she kept there, and as she drew out the weapon, the curved blade shone in the glow. A razor-sharp streak of light appeared beneath the front door. Aryami held her breath and slowly walked towards it. She stopped when she reached the door and heard the sound of the wind through the leaves of the bushes in the courtyard.

'Sheere?' she whispered again. There was no reply.

Holding the dagger firmly, she placed her left hand on the door handle and gently pulled it down. The rusty mechanism groaned after years of disuse. Gradually the door opened and the bluish brightness of the night sky cast a fan of light into the interior of the house. There was nobody there. The undergrowth stirred, the murmur of an ocean of small dry leaves. Aryami peered round the door and looked, first to one side, then to the other, but the courtyard was deserted. Just then, the old woman's leg bumped against something and she looked down to discover a small basket at her feet. It was covered with a thick veil which did not block the light coming from within the basket. Aryami knelt down and cautiously removed the cloth.

Inside she found two small wax figures shaped like naked babies. From each head emerged a lit cotton wick and the two effigies were melting, like candles in a temple. A shudder ran through Aryami's body. She threw the basket down the broken stone steps, stood up and was about to return indoors when she noticed something coming towards her along the corridor that led to the other end of her house: footsteps, invisible but aflame. The old woman felt the dagger slipping from her fingers as she slammed the front door shut.

As she stumbled down the steps, not daring to turn her back on the front door, Aryami tripped over the basket she'd thrown there a few seconds earlier. Lying helpless on the ground, she watched in astonishment as a tongue of flame licked at the base of the doorway and the old wood caught fire. She crawled a few metres until she reached the bushes, then pulled herself up and stared impotently as flames burst through the windows.

Aryami ran out into the street, and she didn't stop to look back until she was at least a hundred metres away from what had once been her home. Now it was a blazing pyre spitting red-hot sparks and ash into the sky. Neighbours began to lean out of their windows and come into the streets to gaze in alarm at the huge fire that had spread through the house in a matter of seconds. Aryami heard the crash of the roof as it collapsed and fell, engulfed in flames. A dazzling flash, like scarlet lightning, illuminated the faces of the crowd which had gathered to watch, and people looked at one another, bemused, unable to comprehend what had happened.

Aryami Bose wept bitterly for what had once been her childhood home, the home where she had given birth to her daughter. And as she melted into the confusion of Calcutta's streets, she bade goodbye to it for ever.

∾

IT WASN'T DIFFICULT TO determine the exact location of the engineer's house, following the cryptogram Siraj had decoded. According to the instructions, duly checked against the fieldwork Roshan had carried out, Chandra Chatterghee's house stood in a quiet street that led from Jatindra Mohan Avenue to Acharya Profullya Road, about a kilometre and a half north of the Midnight Palace.

As soon as Siraj was satisfied that the fruits of his research had been properly digested by his friends, he expressed his urgent desire to go in search of Isobel. All his friends' attempts at reassuring him and suggesting he should wait for her as she was certain to return fell on deaf ears, and in the end, true to his promise, Roshan offered to accompany him. The two set off into the night after agreeing they would meet the others at Chandra Chatterghee's house as soon as they had any news of Isobel.

'What have you two managed to find out?' asked Ian, turning to Seth and Michael.

'I wish our results were as spectacular as Siraj's, but to be honest the only thing we've discovered is a mass of loose ends,' Seth replied. He went on to tell them about their visit to Mr de Rozio, whom they'd left in the museum, continuing the research. They'd promised they would return in a couple of hours to help him.

'What we've discovered until now only goes to confirm what Sheere's grandmother – sorry, your grandmother – told us. At least in part.'

'There are some gaps in the engineer's story it won't be easy to fill in,' said Michael.

'Exactly,' Seth agreed. 'In fact, I think that what we *haven't* discovered is far more interesting than what we have ...'

'What do you mean?' Ben asked.

'Well,' Seth went on, warming his hands by the fire, 'Chandra's story is documented from the moment he became a member of the official Institute of Industry. There are papers confirming that he refused a number of offers from the British government to work for the army building military bridges, as well as a railway line that was to join Bombay and Delhi, for the exclusive use of the navy.'

'Aryami told us how much he loathed the British,' Ben commented. 'He blamed them for many of the things that have gone wrong in this country.'

'That's right,' Seth continued. 'But the curious thing is that, despite his open dislike of the British, of which there were many public displays, Chandra Chatterghee participated in a strange project for the British military between 1914 and 1915, a year before he died in the Jheeter's Gate tragedy. It was a mysterious business with a peculiar name: the Firebird.'

Sheere raised her eyebrows and drew closer to Seth, looking concerned.

'What was the Firebird?'

'It's hard to tell,' Seth replied. 'Mr de Rozio thinks that it might have had something to do with a military experiment. Some of the official correspondence that turned up among the engineer's papers was signed by a colonel called Sir Arthur Llewelyn. According to de Rozio, Llewelyn held the dubious honour of heading the forces that were responsible for repressing the peaceful demonstrations for independence that took place between 1905 and 1915.'

'Held?' asked Ben.

'That's what's so intriguing,' Seth explained. 'Sir Arthur Llewelyn, His Majesty's official butcher, died in the Jheeter's Gate fire. What he was doing there is a mystery.'

The five friends looked at one another, confused.

'Let's try to put some order to this,' Ben suggested. 'On the one hand we have a brilliant engineer who repeatedly refuses generous offers of employment from the British government due to his dislike of colonial rule. Up to there everything makes sense. But suddenly this mysterious colonel appears on the scene and involves him in an operation which, whatever way you look at it, must have made Chandra Chatterghee's stomach turn: a secret weapon, an experimental way of controlling crowds. And he accepts. It doesn't make sense. Unless ...'

'Unless Llewelyn had uncanny powers of persuasion,' said Ian.

Sheere raised her hands in protest.

'My father would never have taken part in any kind of military project, it's impossible. Certainly not for the British, and not for the Bengalis either. My father despised the military – he thought they were nothing but brutes blindly carrying out the dirty work of corrupt governments and colonial companies. He would never have allowed his skills to be used to invent something that would massacre his own people.'

Seth watched her quietly, weighing her words.

'And yet, Sheere, there are documents to prove that he *did* take part, in some way,' he said.

'There has to be some other reason,' she replied. 'My father built things and wrote books. He wasn't a murderer.'

'Leaving aside his ideals, there must be some other explanation,' Ben remarked. 'And that's what we're trying to discover. Let's go back to Llewelyn and his powers of persuasion. What could he have done to force Chandra to collaborate?'

'Perhaps his power didn't lie in what he could do,' Seth stated, 'but in what he could choose *not* to do.'

'I don't understand,' said Ian.

'This is my theory,' Seth continued. 'In all the engineer's records we haven't found a single mention of Jawahal, this childhood friend, except in a letter from Colonel Llewelyn addressed to Chandra and postmarked November 1911. In it our friend the colonel adds a postscript in which he briefly suggests that, if Chandra refuses to take part in the project, he will be forced to offer the post to his old friend Jawahal. What I think is this: Chandra had managed to conceal his relationship with Jawahal, who was by then in prison, and had developed his career without anybody knowing that he had once covered up for the man. But let's suppose that this Llewelyn had come across Jawahal in prison and Jawahal had revealed the true nature of their relationship. This would put Llewelyn in an excellent position for blackmailing the engineer and forcing him to collaborate.'

'How do we know that Llewelyn and Jawahal met one another?' Ian asked.

'It's only a supposition,' Seth replied. 'Sir Arthur Llewelyn, a colonel in the British army, decides to ask for the help of an exceptional engineer. The engineer refuses. Llewelyn investigates him and discovers a murky past, a trial to which the engineer is linked. He decides to pay a visit to Jawahal, and Jawahal tells him what he wants to hear. Simple.'

'I can't believe it,' said Sheere.

'Sometimes the truth is the hardest thing to believe. Remember what Aryami told us,' Ben said. 'But let's not rush into anything. Is de Rozio still investigating this?'

'He is, yes,' replied Seth. 'The number of documents is so vast that he'd need an army of library rats to make sense of anything.'

'You've made quite a good job of it,' remarked Ian.

'We weren't expecting anything less,' said Ben. 'Why don't you go back to the librarian, and don't lose sight of him for a moment. I'm sure we're missing something ...'

'What are you going to do?' asked Michael, although he already knew the answer.

'We'll go to the engineer's house,' Ben replied. 'Perhaps what we're looking for is there.'

'Or something else ...' Michael pointed out.

Ben smiled.

'As I said, we'll take that risk.'

SHEERE, IAN AND BEN arrived outside the gates that guarded Chandra Chatterghee's house shortly before midnight. To the east, the narrow tower of the Shyambazar was silhouetted against the moon's sphere, projecting its shadow over the garden of palm trees and bushes that hid the building.

Ben leaned on the gate of metal spears and examined their threatening sharp points.

'We'll have to climb over,' he remarked. 'It doesn't look easy.'

'We won't have to,' said Sheere next to him. 'Our father described every inch of this house in his book before he built it, and I've spent years memorising every detail. If what he wrote is correct, and I have no doubt that it is, there's a small lake behind these shrubs and the house stands further back.'

'What about these spears?' asked Ben. 'Did he write about them too? I'd rather not end up skewered like a roast chicken.'

'There's another way of getting into the house without having to jump over them,' said Sheere.

'Then what are we waiting for?' Ben and Ian asked together.

Sheere led them through what was barely an alleyway, a small gap between the railings surrounding the property and the walls of an adjacent building with Moorish features. Soon they reached a circular opening that looked as if it served as the main sewer for all the drains in the house. From it came a sour biting stench.

'In here?' asked Ben sceptically.

'What did you expect?' snapped Sheere. 'A Persian carpet?'

Ben scanned the inside of the sewage tunnel and sniffed.

'Divine,' he concluded, turning to Sheere. 'You first.'

© Jackie Freshfield

The Firebird

THEY EMERGED FROM THE TUNNEL BENEATH A small wooden bridge that arched over the lake, a dark velvety mantle of murky water stretching in front of Chandra Chatterghee's house. Sheere led the two boys along a narrow bank, their feet sinking into the clay, until they reached the other end of the lake. There she stopped to gaze at the building she had dreamed about all her life. Ian and Ben stood quietly by her side.

The two-storey building was flanked by two towers, one on either side. It featured a mix of architectural styles, from Edwardian lines to Palladian extravaganzas and features that looked as if they belonged to some castle tucked away in the mountains of Bavaria. The overall effect, however, was elegant and serene, challenging the critical eye of the spectator. The house seemed to possess a bewitching charm, so that although the first impression was one of bewilderment you then had the feeling that the impossible jumble of styles and forms had been chosen on purpose to create a harmonious whole.

'Is this how your father described it?' asked Ian.

Sheere nodded in amazement and walked towards the steps leading to the front door. Ben and Ian watched her hesitantly, wondering how she thought she was going to enter such a fortress. But Sheere seemed to move about the mysterious surroundings as if they had been her childhood home. The ease with which she dodged obstacles, almost invisible in the dark, made the two boys feel like trespassers in the dream Sheere had nurtured during her nomadic years. As they watched her walk up the steps, Ben and Ian realised that this deserted place was the only real home the girl had ever had.

'Are you going to stay there all night?' Sheere called from the top of the stairs.

'We were wondering how to get in,' Ben pointed out. Ian nodded in agreement.

'I have the key.'

'The key?' asked Ben. 'Where?'

'Here,' Sheere replied, pointing to her head with her

forefinger. 'You don't open the locks in this house with a normal key. There's a code.'

Intrigued, Ben and Ian came up the steps to join her. When they reached the door, they saw that at its centre was a set of four wheels on a single axle. Each wheel was smaller than the one behind it, and different symbols were carved on the metal rim of each, like the hours on the face of a clock.

'What do these symbols mean?' asked Ian, trying to decipher them in the dark.

Ben pulled a match from the box he always carried with him and struck it in front of the lock mechanism. The metal shone in the light of the flame.

'Alphabets!' cried Ben. 'Each wheel has an alphabet carved on it. Greek, Latin, Arab and Sanskrit.'

'Fantastic,' sighed Ian. 'Piece of cake ...'

'Don't worry,' said Sheere. 'The code is simple. All you have to do is make a four-letter word using the different alphabets.'

Ben looked at her intently.

'What is the word?'

'Dido,' replied Sheere.

'Dido?' asked Ian. 'What does that mean?'

'It's the name of a mythological Phoenician queen,' Ben explained.

Sheere smiled approvingly and Ian was momentarily jealous of the spark that seemed to exist between the two siblings.

'I still don't understand,' Ian objected. 'What have the Phoenicians got to do with Calcutta?'

'Queen Dido threw herself on a funeral pyre to appease the anger of the gods in Carthage,' Sheere explained. 'It's the purifying power of fire. The Egyptians also had their own myth, about the phoenix.'

'The myth of the firebird,' Ben added.

'Isn't that the name of the military project Seth told us about?' asked Ian.

His friend nodded.

'This whole thing is starting to give me goosebumps,' said Ian. 'You aren't seriously thinking of going inside? What are we going to do?'

Ben and Sheere exchanged a determined glance.

'It's very simple,' Ben replied. 'We're going to open this door.'

THE LIBRARIAN'S EYELIDS WERE beginning to feel like slabs of marble as he faced the hundreds of documents in front of him. The vast sea of words and figures he had retrieved from Chandra Chatterghee's files seemed to be performing a sinuous dance and murmuring a lullaby that was sending him to sleep.

'I think we'd better leave this until tomorrow morning, lads,' Mr de Rozio began.

Seth, who had been afraid he would say this for some

time, surfaced immediately from his jumble of folders and gave him a pious smile.

'Leave it, Mr de Rozio?' he objected in a light-hearted tone. 'Impossible! We can't abandon this now.'

'I'm only a few seconds away from collapsing over this table, son,' replied Mr de Rozio. 'And Shiva, in his infinite goodness, has granted me a weight, which, the last time I checked it, in February, was somewhere between two hundred and fifty and two hundred and sixty pounds. Do you know how much that is?'

Seth smiled jovially.

'About a hundred and twenty kilos,' he calculated.

'Exactly,' de Rozio confirmed. 'Have you ever tried moving an adult who weighs a hundred and twenty kilos?'

Seth thought about it.

'I have no recollection of such a thing, but—'

'Just a minute!' cried Michael from some invisible point behind the ring binders, boxes and piles of yellowing paper that filled the room. 'I've found something.'

'I hope it's a pillow,' protested de Rozio, raising his bulk.

Michael appeared from behind a column of dusty shelves carrying a box full of papers and stamped documents that had been discoloured by time. Seth raised his eyebrows, praying that the discovery would be worthwhile.

'I think these are the court records for a murder

trial,' said Michael. 'They were underneath a summons addressed to Chandra Chatterghee, the engineer.'

'Jawahal's trial?' cried Seth excitedly.

'Let me have a look,' said de Rozio.

Michael deposited the box on the librarian's desk, raising a cloud of dust that choked the cone of golden light projected by the electric lamp. The librarian's plump fingers carefully flicked through the documents, his tiny eyes examining their contents. Seth watched de Rozio's face, his heart in his mouth, waiting for some word or sign. De Rozio paused at a page that seemed to have a number of stamps on it and brought it closer to the light.

'Well, well,' he mumbled to himself.

'What is it?' begged Seth.

De Rozio looked up and gave a broad feline smile.

'I have in my hands a document signed by Colonel Sir Arthur Llewelyn. In it, citing reasons of state security and military secrecy, he is ordering the discontinuance of trial number 089861/A in court number four of the Calcutta High Court, in which a citizen named Lahawaj Chandra Chatterghee, an engineer by profession, is charged with alleged involvement and withholding and/or concealment of evidence in a murder investigation, and he instructs the transfer of the case to the Supreme Military Court of His Majesty's Armed Forces. All previous rulings are therefore overturned and all evidence provided by the defence and the prosecution during the hearing is declared null and void. It's dated 14 September 1911.'

Michael and Seth stared at Mr de Rozio in amazement, unable to utter a single word.

'So, you two,' the librarian concluded, 'which of you knows how to make coffee? This could be a very long night ...'

~

THE FOUR-WHEELED LOCK gave an almost inaudible click, and a few seconds later the two sides of the heavy iron door swung open, letting out a breath of air that had been trapped inside the house for years. Standing in the dark, Ian's face went pale.

'It opened,' he said in a whisper.

'How observant of you,' Ben remarked.

'This is no time for jokes,' Ian replied. 'We don't know what's in there yet.'

Ben pulled out his matchbox and rattled it in the air.

'That's only a matter of time. Would you like to go first?'

'I'll leave that honour to you,' Ian said, smiling.

'I'll go,' said Sheere, entering the house without waiting for a reply.

Ben quickly struck another match and followed her. Ian took one last look at the night sky, as if he feared this might be his last chance to see it, and after taking a deep breath plunged into the engineer's house. A moment later the large door closed behind them, as gently as it had opened to let them in.

The three friends huddled together as Ben held the match up high. The spectacle that unfolded before their eyes far exceeded any of their expectations.

They were standing in a hall supported by thick Byzantine columns and crowned with a concave dome covered with a huge fresco. This depicted hundreds of figures from Hindu mythology, forming an endless illustrated chronicle set in concentric rings around a central figure sculpted in relief on top of the painting: the goddess Kali.

The walls of the hall were lined with bookshelves forming two semicircles over three metres high. The floor was covered by a mosaic of brilliant black tiles and pieces of rock crystal, creating the illusion of a night sky studded with stars and constellations. Ian looked carefully at the design and recognised various celestial figures Bankim had told them about at St Patrick's.

'Seth should see this,' whispered Ben.

At the far end of the room, beyond the carpet of stars, was a spiral staircase leading up to the first floor.

Before Ben had time to react, the match had burnt down to his fingers and gone out, leaving the three in total darkness. The constellations at their feet, however, continued to shine.

'This is incredible,' Ian murmured to himself.

'Wait till you see upstairs,' said Sheere a few metres beyond him.

Ben lit another match. Sheere was already waiting for them by the spiral staircase, and without a word Ben and Ian followed her.

The spiral staircase rose in the middle of a lantern-shaped shaft, similar to structures they had studied in drawings of castles built on the banks of the Loire River. Looking up, the friends felt as if they were inside a huge kaleidoscope crowned with a cathedral-like rose window that fractured the moonlight into dozens of beams – blue, scarlet, yellow, green and amber.

When they reached the first floor, they realised that the needles of light issuing from the lantern's crown projected moving drawings and shapes against the walls of a large hall.

'Look at this,' said Ben, pointing at a rectangular surface about forty metres square that stood one metre above the ground.

All three walked over to it and discovered what appeared to be an immense model of Calcutta, reproduced with such precision and detail that when you looked at it closely you felt as if you were flying over the real city. They recognised the course of the Hooghly, the Maidan, Fort William, the White Town, the temple of Kali to the south, the Black Town, and even the bazaars. For a long time Sheere, Ian and Ben stood spellbound by the extraordinary miniature, captivated by its beauty.

'There's the house,' said Ben, pointing.

The other two drew closer and saw, right in the heart of the Black Town, a faithful reproduction of the house they were standing in. The multicoloured beams from the ceiling swept across the miniature streets, revealing the hidden secrets of Calcutta as they passed.

'What is that behind the house?' asked Sheere.

'It looks like a railway track,' said Ian.

'It is.' Ben followed the outline of the track until it came to the sharp, majestic silhouette of Jheeter's Gate, on the other side of a metal bridge spanning the Hooghly.

'This track leads to the station where the fire happened,' said Ben. 'It's a siding.'

'There's a train on the bridge,' Sheere observed.

Ben walked round the model to get closer to the reproduction of the train. As he examined it, an uncomfortable tingling ran down his spine. He recognised the train. He'd seen it the previous night, although he'd thought it was only the product of a nightmare. Sheere walked over to him and Ben saw there were tears in her eyes.

'This is our father's house, Ben,' she murmured. 'He built it for us.'

Ben put his arms round Sheere and hugged her. At

the other end of the room Ian looked away. Ben stroked Sheere's face and kissed her on the forehead.

'From now on,' he said, 'it will always be our home.'

At that moment the lights on the little train standing on the bridge lit up and, slowly, its wheels began to roll along the rails.

~

SILENT AS THE GRAVE, Mr de Rozio was devoting all his archivist's cunning to the reports on the trial which Colonel Llewelyn had been so determined to bury. Seth and Michael were doing the same with a folder full of plans and notes in Chandra's handwriting. Seth had found it at the bottom of one of the boxes containing the engineer's personal effects. After his death, because no relative or institution had claimed them and he had been an important public figure, they had ended up lost in the museum's archives. The library was shared by various scientific and academic institutions, among them the Higher Institute of Engineering, of which Chandra Chatterghee had been one of the most illustrious and controversial members. The folder was plainly bound and its cover bore a single inscription, handwritten in blue ink: *The Firebird*.

Seth and Michael had hidden their discovery so as not to distract the plump librarian from his task and had moved over to the other end of the room.

'These drawings are fantastic,' whispered Michael, admiring various illustrations of mechanical objects whose specific function he couldn't quite fathom.

'Let's concentrate,' Seth reminded him. 'What does it say about the Firebird?'

'Science isn't my forte,' Michael began, 'but if I'm right, this is a plan for an enormous flame-thrower.'

Seth examined the plans without understanding them in the slightest. Michael anticipated his queries.

'This is a tank for oil or some sort of fuel,' Michael said, pointing to the document. 'This suction mechanism is joined to it. It's a feeding pump, like the pump in a well, and it provides the fuel to keep this circle of flames alight. A sort of pilot light.'

'But the flames can't be more than a few centimetres high,' Seth objected. 'I don't see how there can be any real power there.'

'Look at this pipe.'

Seth saw what his friend was referring to: a sort of tube, rather like the barrel of a cannon or rifle.

'The flames emerge round the rim of the cannon.'

'And?'

'Look at this other end,' said Michael. 'It's a tank, an oxygen tank.'

'Simple chemistry,' murmured Seth, putting two and two together.

'Imagine what would happen if this oxygen were ejected under pressure through the pipe and passed through the circle of flames.'

'A flame-thrower,' Seth agreed.

Michael closed the folder and looked at his friend.

'What kind of secret could make Chandra design a toy like this for a butcher like Llewelyn? It's like giving the Emperor Nero a shipment of gunpowder …'

'That's what we need to find out,' said Seth, 'and quickly.'

SHEERE, BEN AND IAN followed the train's journey through the model until the tiny locomotive came to a halt just behind the miniature reproduction of the engineer's house. Slowly the lights went out and the three friends stood there, motionless and expectant.

'How the hell does the train move?' asked Ben. 'It must get its power supply from somewhere. Is there an electricity generator in the house, Sheere?'

'Not that I know of.'

'There must be,' said Ian. 'Let's look for it.'

Ben shook his head.

'That's not what's bothering me,' he said. 'Even supposing there is one, I've never heard of a generator that starts up by itself. Much less after years of not working.'

'Perhaps this model works on some other sort of mechanism,' Sheere suggested, although she didn't sound convinced.

'Perhaps there's someone else in the house,' replied Ben.

Ian cursed his luck.

'I knew it,' he murmured.

'Wait!' cried Ben.

Ian looked at his friend: he was pointing at the model. The train was moving again, this time in the opposite direction.

'It's going back to the station,' Sheere observed.

Slowly, Ben drew closer to the model, stopping by the section of railway track along which the train had started to roll.

'What's the plan?' asked Ian.

His friend didn't reply. Taking great care, Ben stretched out an arm towards the track. The engine was approaching fast, and as it passed in front of him he snatched it, unhooking it from the carriages. Little by little, the rest of the train reduced speed until it came to a halt. Ben held the engine up to the light from the rose window and examined it. Its minute wheels were gradually slowing down.

'Someone has a strange sense of humour,' he remarked.

'Why?' asked Sheere.

'There are three lead figures inside the engine, and they look too much like us for it to be a coincidence.'

Sheere moved over to where Ben was standing and took the little engine in her hands. The dancing lines of light cast a rainbow over her face and she gave a resigned smile.

'He knows we're here,' she said. 'There's no point in hiding any more.'

'Who knows?' asked Ian.

'Jawahal,' answered Ben. 'He's waiting. But I don't know what he's waiting for.'

WHEN THEY REACHED THE bridge that seemed to vanish into the haze over the Hooghly, Siraj and Roshan collapsed against a wall, exhausted after combing the city in search of Isobel. Far ahead the tips of Jheeter's Gate's towers peeped over the mist like the crest of a sleeping dragon.

'It will soon be dawn,' said Roshan. 'We should go back. Maybe Isobel has been waiting for us there.'

'I don't think so,' replied Siraj.

Roshan could tell from his friend's voice that their nocturnal adventure had taken its toll on him, but for the first time in years he hadn't heard Siraj complain once about his asthma.

'We've looked everywhere,' Roshan replied. 'We can't do any more. Let's at least go and get help.'

'There's one place we haven't visited ...'

Roshan gazed through the mist at the sinister structure of Jheeter's Gate.

'Isobel wouldn't be crazy enough to go in there.' He sighed. 'Nor would I.'

'I'll go by myself then,' said Siraj, standing up.

Roshan heard him wheezing. He closed his eyes despondently.

'Sit down,' he said, but he could already hear Siraj heading towards the bridge.

When he opened his eyes, the boy's skinny silhouette was plunging into the mist.

'Damn it,' Roshan muttered to himself, but he got up to follow his friend.

Siraj paused when he reached the end of the bridge and stared at the entrance to Jheeter's Gate looming ahead. Roshan joined him and they both stood there, examining the building. A gust of cold air issued from the station's tunnels carrying the stench of burnt wood and filth. The two friends tried to discern what might lie beyond the well of blackness that opened up inside the entrance.

'It looks like the gateway to hell,' said Roshan. 'Let's get out of here while we still can.'

'It's all in the mind,' said Siraj. 'Don't forget, it's only an abandoned station. There's nobody there. Only us.'

'If there isn't anyone there, why do we have to go in?'

'You don't have to go in if you don't want to,' replied Siraj. There was no reproach in his voice.

'Of course,' snapped Roshan. 'And leave you to go in alone? Forget it. Let's go.'

The two members of the Chowbar Society entered the station, following the track that led in from the bridge towards the central platform. The darkness inside the building was much denser that it had seemed from the outside and they could only make out a few shapes in the watery grey light. Roshan and Siraj walked slowly, barely a metre apart. Their footsteps seemed to form a repetitive litany against the sighing of the breeze that echoed from somewhere deep inside the tunnels.

'We'd better climb onto the platform,' said Roshan.

'No train has come through here for years – what does it matter?'

'It matters to me, all right?' Roshan replied. He couldn't get out of his mind the image of a train appearing through the mouth of the tunnel and crushing them under its wheels.

Siraj muttered something unintelligible but placatory, and was about to walk back to the platform end and clamber onto it when something drifted from the tunnels towards the two boys.

'What's that?' said Roshan in alarm.

'It looks like a piece of paper,' Siraj guessed. 'A bit of rubbish blown by the wind, that's all.'

The white paper twirled along the ground and stopped by Roshan's feet. The boy knelt down and picked it up. Siraj saw his friend's face crumble.

'What's the matter?' he asked. Roshan's fear was starting to feel contagious.

Without replying his friend handed him the sheet of paper. Siraj recognised it instantly. It was the picture

Michael had drawn of them by the pond, which Isobel had taken with her. Siraj gave it back, and, for the first time since they'd begun their search, he considered the very real possibility that Isobel might be in danger.

'Isobel …' Siraj called into the tunnels.

The echo of his voice faded into the depths of the station. He tried to concentrate on controlling his breathing, which was becoming more difficult by the moment. He waited for the echo to die away and, steadying his nerves, called again: 'Isobel?'

A loud metallic crash resounded from some distant corner of the station. Roshan gave a start and looked around him. The wind from the tunnels now whipped at their faces and the two boys took a few steps back.

'There's something in there,' whispered Siraj, pointing towards one of the tunnels. He seemed strangely calm.

Roshan stared at the black mouth of the tunnel and then he too could see it. The faraway lights of a train were approaching. He could feel the rails vibrating beneath his feet and he looked at Siraj in panic. Siraj seemed to be smiling.

'I'm not going to be able to run as fast as you, Roshan,' he said. 'We both know that. Don't wait for me. Go for help.'

'What on earth are you talking about?' cried Roshan, perfectly aware of what his friend was implying.

The train's headlights pierced the station like a burst of lightning in a storm.

'Run,' Siraj ordered him. '*Now*.'

Roshan looked frantically into his friend's eyes as he heard the thunderous roar of the engine. Siraj gave a nod. Then Roshan gathered all his strength and ran desperately towards the platform end, looking for a place where he could jump up, out of the train's path. He ran as fast as he could, not stopping to look behind him. He was sure that if he dared to look, he would be confronted with the metal front of the engine centimetres from his face. The fifteen metres that separated him from the end of the platform seemed like a hundred and fifty, and in his panic he thought he could see the railway tracks receding before his eyes at a dizzying speed. He threw himself to the ground, rolling over the rubble, and the train sped past him only a hair's breadth away. He heard the deafening screams of the children and felt the flames tearing at his skin for ten terrible seconds, during which he imagined that the whole structure of the station was going to collapse on top of him.

Then, all of a sudden, there was silence. Roshan stood up and opened his eyes. The station was deserted once more and the only trace of the train was two rows of flames gradually disappearing along the rails. He ran back to the point where he'd last seen Siraj. Cursing his cowardice, he cried out in anger – he realised he was alone.

In the distance dawn pointed the way to the exit.

THE FIRST LIGHT OF day seeped through the closed shutters of the library in the Indian Museum. Seth and Michael were dozing, their heads resting on the table, exhausted. Mr de Rozio heaved a deep sigh and pushed his chair away from the desk, rubbing his eyes. He had spent hours engrossed in the mountain of documents, trying to unravel those lengthy court records. His stomach was now begging for attention, and he had placed a moratorium on his consumption of coffee, which was necessary if he was to go on performing his duties with any degree of dignity.

'I give up, sleeping beauties,' he thundered.

Seth and Michael looked up with a start and noticed that the day had begun without them.

'Did you find anything?' asked Seth, suppressing a yawn.

His stomach was rumbling and his head felt as if it was full of purée.

'Is that a joke?' asked the librarian. 'I think you've been pulling my leg all along.'

'I don't understand, sir,' said Michael.

De Rozio gave a vast yawn, revealing cavernous jaws, which reminded the boys of a hippopotamus wallowing in a river.

'It's very simple,' he said. 'You came here with a tale of murder and crime and that absurd business about someone called Jawahal.'

'But it's all true. We have first-hand information.'

De Rozio laughed, his tone mocking.

'Maybe you're the ones who've been tricked,' he replied. 'In this entire pile of papers I haven't found a single mention of your friend Jawahal. Not one word. Zero.'

Seth felt his stomach fall to his feet.

'But that's impossible. Jawahal was sentenced and went to prison and then escaped years later. Perhaps we could start again from that point. From the escape. It must be documented somewhere ...'

De Rozio's astute eyes gave him a sceptical look. His expression clearly indicated that there would be no second chance.

'If I were you, boys, I'd return to the person who gave me this information and this time I'd make quite sure I was told the whole story. As for this Jawahal, who according to your mysterious informer was in prison, I think he's far more slippery than either you or I can handle.'

De Rozio studied the two boys. They were as pale as marble. The plump scholar smiled in commiseration.

'My condolences,' he murmured. 'You've been sniffing down the wrong hole ...'

Shortly afterwards, Seth and Michael were sitting on the stairs of the main entrance to the Indian Museum, watching the sunrise. A light rain had glazed the streets and they shone like sheets of liquid gold. Seth looked at his companion and showed him a coin.

189

'Heads, I go and visit Aryami and you go to the prison. Tails, it's the other way round.'

Michael nodded, his eyes half-closed. Seth tossed the coin and the circle of bronze spun in the air, catching the light, until it landed on the boy's hand. Michael leaned over to check the result.

'Give my regards to Aryami,' Seth mumbled.

THE NIGHT HAD SEEMED endless but finally daylight arrived at the engineer's house. For once in his life Ian blessed the Calcutta sun, as its rays erased the shroud of darkness that had enveloped them for hours. In the dawn the house seemed less threatening. Ben and Sheere were also visibly relieved to see the morning come.

'If there's one good thing about this house, it's that it's safe,' said Ben. 'If our friend Jawahal had been able to get in, he would have done so already. Our father might have had some strange inclinations, but he knew how to protect a home. I suggest we try to get some sleep. The way things are looking right now, I'd rather sleep during the day and stay awake at night.'

'I couldn't agree with you more,' said Ian. 'Where shall we sleep?'

'There are several bedrooms in the towers,' Sheere explained. 'We can choose.'

'I suggest we find rooms next to each other,' said Ben.

'Fine,' said Ian. 'And it wouldn't be a bad idea to eat something either.'

'That can wait,' Ben replied. 'Later on we'll go out and find something.'

'How can you two be hungry?' asked Sheere.

Ben and Ian shrugged their shoulders.

'Elemental physiology,' replied Ben. 'Ask Ian. He's the doctor.'

'As the teacher in a Bombay school once told me,' said Sheere, 'the main difference between a man and a woman is that the man always puts his stomach before his heart and a woman does the opposite.'

Ben considered the theory.

'Let me quote our favourite misogynist and professional bachelor, Mr Thomas Carter: "The real difference is that, while men's stomachs are much larger than their brains and their hearts, women's hearts are so small they keep leaping out of their mouths."'

Ian seemed bemused by the exchange of such illustrious quotes.

'Cheap philosophy,' pronounced Sheere.

'The cheap sort, my dear Sheere, is the only philosophy worth having,' declared Ben.

Ian raised a hand to signal a truce.

'Goodnight to both of you,' he said, then headed straight for one of the towers.

Ten minutes later all three had fallen into a deep sleep

from which nobody could have roused them. In the end tiredness conquered fear.

~

SETTING OFF FROM THE Indian Museum in Chowringhee Road, Seth walked south almost a kilometre downhill. He then turned east along Park Street, heading for the Beniapukur area, where the ruins of the old Curzon Fort prison stood next to the Scottish cemetery. The dilapidated graveyard had been built on what was once the official limit of the city. In those days a high mortality rate and the speed with which bodies decomposed meant that all burial grounds had to be situated outside Calcutta for reasons of public health. Ironically, although the Scots had been in control of Calcutta's commercial activity for decades, they discovered that they couldn't afford a place among the graves of their English neighbours, and were therefore forced to build their own cemetery. In Calcutta the wealthy refused to yield their land to anyone poorer, even after death.

As he approached what remained of the Curzon Fort prison, Seth understood why the building had not yet become another victim of the city's cruel demolition programme. There was no need – its structure already seemed to be hanging by an invisible string, ready to topple over the crowds at the slightest attempt to alter its balance. A fire had devoured the building, carving out gaps and destroying beams and props in its fury.

Seth approached the prison entrance, wondering how on earth he was going to discover anything among the heap of charred timber and bricks. Surely the only mementos of its past would be the metal bars and cells that had been transformed in their final hours into lethal ovens from which there was no escape.

'Have you come on a visit, boy?' whispered a voice behind him.

Seth spun around in alarm and realised that the words had come from the lips of a ragged old man whose feet and hands were covered in large infected sores. Dark eyes watched him nervously, and the man's face was caked in grime, his sparse white beard evidently trimmed with a knife.

'Is this the Curzon Fort prison, sir?' asked Seth.

The beggar's eyes widened when he heard the polite way the boy was addressing him, and his leathery lips broke into a toothless smile.

'What's left of it,' he replied. 'Looking for accommodation?'

'I'm looking for information,' replied Seth, trying to smile back at the beggar in a friendly manner.

'This world is full of ignoramuses: nobody is looking for information. Except you. So what do you want to find out, young man?'

'Do you know this place?'

'I live in it,' answered the beggar. 'Once it was my prison; today it's my home. Providence has been generous to me.'

'You were imprisoned in Curzon Fort?' asked Seth, incredulous.

'Once upon a time I made some big mistakes ... and I had to pay for them.'

'How long were you in prison, sir?' asked Seth.

'Right to the end.'

'So you were here the night of the fire?'

The beggar drew aside the rags draped over his body and Seth stared in horror at the purple scars covering his chest and neck.

'Maybe you could help me,' continued Seth. 'Two friends of mine are in danger. Do you remember a prisoner called Jawahal?'

The beggar closed his eyes and slowly shook his head.

'None of us called each other by our real names,' he explained. 'Our name, like our freedom, was something we left by the entrance when we came here. We hoped that if we managed to keep our name separate from the horror of this place, we might be able to recover it when we left, clean and untouched by memories. It didn't turn out that way of course ...'

'The man I'm referring to was convicted of murder,' Seth replied. 'He was young. He was the one who started the fire that destroyed the prison and then escaped.'

The beggar stared at him in surprise.

'The one who started the fire? The fire started in the boiler room. An oil valve exploded. I was outside my cell, doing my work shift. That was what saved me.'

'But he set it all up,' Seth insisted. 'And now he's trying to kill my friends.'

The beggar tilted his head to one side but then nodded.

'That may be so, son. But what does it matter any more? I wouldn't worry about your friends. There's not much this man, Jawahal, can do to them now.'

Seth frowned. 'Why do you say that?'

The beggar laughed.

'The night of the fire I was even younger than you are now. In fact, I was the youngest in the prison. This man, whoever he was, must be well over a hundred by now.'

Seth rubbed his temples, totally confused.

'Just a moment,' he said. 'Didn't the prison burn down in 1916?'

'1916?' The beggar laughed again. 'Dear boy, what are you going on about? Curzon Fort burnt down in the early hours of 26 April 1857. Seventy-five years ago.'

Seth stared open-mouthed at the beggar, who was studying him with curiosity and some concern at his evident dismay.

'What's your name?' the man asked.

'Seth, sir,' replied the boy, whose face had gone pale.

'I'm sorry I haven't been able to help you, Seth.'

'You have,' replied Seth. 'Now how can I help you?'

The beggar's eyes shone and he smiled bitterly.

195

'Can you make time go backwards, Seth?' The beggar stared at the palms of his hands.

Seth shook his head.

'Then you can't help me ... Go back to your friends, Seth. But don't forget me.'

'I won't, sir.'

MICHAEL STOPPED BY THE entrance to the street that led to Aryami Bose's house and stared in shock at the smoking ruins of what had once been the old lady's home. People had drifted in from the streets and were standing in the courtyard, watching in silence as the police searched the debris and questioned the neighbours. Michael hurried over and pushed through the circle of onlookers. A police officer stopped him.

'I'm sorry, lad. You can't come through.'

Michael looked over the policeman's shoulder and saw two of the man's colleagues lifting a fallen beam that was still glowing.

'What about the woman who lives in the house?' asked Michael.

The policeman seemed suspicious. 'You knew her?'

'She's my friends' grandmother,' Michael replied. 'Where is she? Is she dead?'

The officer observed him impassively for a few seconds then shook his head.

'We can't find any trace of her,' he said. 'One of the neighbours says he saw someone running down the street shortly after the flames burst through the roof. But I've already told you more than I should. Off you go now.'

'Thank you, sir,' said Michael. He made his way back through the mass that was gathering in the hope of some gruesome discovery.

Once he was free of the crowd, Michael examined the adjacent buildings, trying to guess where the old lady might have fled. Both ends of the street merged into the Black Town, with its tangle of buildings, bazaars and palaces. Aryami Bose could be anywhere.

For a few moments Michael considered the options, then finally decided to head for the banks of the Hooghly River, to the west. There thousands of pilgrims immersed themselves in the sacred waters of the Ganges, hoping heaven might purify them, although mostly they received only fevers and diseases in return.

With the sun beating down on him, Michael wove his way through the throng that flooded the streets, a constant gabble of merchants, quarrels and unheeded prayers. The voice of Calcutta. Some twenty metres behind him a figure wrapped in a dark shawl peered out from an alleyway and began to follow him through the crowd.

~

IAN OPENED HIS EYES with the absolute certainty that his persistent insomnia would allow him no more than a few hours' respite, despite the exhaustion brought about by recent events. Judging from the quality of the light bathing the room in the western tower of the engineer's house, he calculated that it must be somewhere around mid-afternoon. The hunger pangs that had assaulted him at dawn had returned with a vengeance, making him grit his teeth. As Ben used to joke, parodying the words of the writer Tagore, whose castle was only a short distance away: when the stomach speaks, the wise man listens.

As Ian slipped quietly from the room, he noticed with some envy that Ben and Sheere were still enjoying the sleep of the righteous. He suspected that when they woke up even Sheere would be prepared to swallow the first edible object within reach, and as far as Ben was concerned, there was no doubt whatsoever. Ian imagined his best friend was probably busy dreaming about a tray of gastronomic delights and a sumptuous dessert of *chhena* sweets – a mixture of lime juice and boiled milk that all sweet-toothed Bengalis adored.

Aware that he had already been granted more sleep than expected, he decided to venture out in search of provisions with which to placate his hunger and that of his friends. With a bit of luck he'd be back before either of them had even had time to yawn.

As he crossed the large hall containing the model town and made for the spiral staircase, he was pleased to see that in daylight the house looked considerably less menacing and that nothing else had changed. Ian noticed that the building was remarkably efficient at insulating them from the soaring temperatures outside. It wasn't hard to imagine the stifling heat beyond those walls, yet the engineer's house felt almost spring-like. Downstairs, he walked through some of the galaxies on the floor mosaic then opened the door to the outside world, hoping he wouldn't forget the combination of the eccentric lock that sealed Chandra Chatterghee's sanctuary.

The sun beat down mercilessly on the dense vegetation of the garden. The lake, which the night before had resembled a sheet of polished ebony, now threw bright reflections against the front of the house. Ian walked towards the secret tunnel beneath the wooden bridge and entered the passageway. Before its pungent stench could fill his lungs, he was out again, passing through the entry that led to the street. There, he threw an imaginary coin in the air and decided to begin his search for food by heading west.

As he walked along, humming to himself, he could never have imagined that behind him the four circles of the combination lock had slowly started to turn again, and that this time the four-letter word they would form when set in a vertical line was not Dido, but the name of a goddess much closer to home: Kali.

❧

IN HIS DREAMS BEN thought he heard a crash. He woke to find the room in total darkness. His first thought, in his initial daze after waking abruptly from a long deep sleep, was that night must have fallen and they had slept for over twelve hours. But a moment later he heard the dry thud again and realised that the room wasn't dark because it was night-time; something was happening in the house. The shutters were slamming shut like the tightly sealed sluice gates of a canal. Ben jumped out of bed and ran to the door in search of his friends.

'Ben!' he heard Sheere yelling.

He raced over to her room and opened the door. His sister was standing behind it, trembling and unable to move. Ben hugged her and led her out of the room, watching in horror as, one by one, the windows of the house were blocked out.

'Ben,' Sheere whispered. 'Something came into my room while I was sleeping and touched me.'

Ben felt a shudder run through his body. He led Sheere to the middle of the room containing the model of the city. Seconds later they were surrounded by nothing but darkness. Ben put his arms round Sheere and told her to remain silent as he scanned the room for any hint of movement. He couldn't make anything out in the dark, but they could both hear a murmur that seemed to be invading the structure of the house, a sound like tiny animals scuttling under the floors and between the walls.

'What's that, Ben?' whispered Sheere.

Before her brother could find an answer, something else stole the words from his lips. Little by little the lights in the model city were coming on, and the two siblings witnessed the birth of a nocturnal Calcutta. Ben gulped and Sheere clung on to him tightly. In the middle of the model the headlights of the little train flashed and its wheels slowly began to turn.

'Let's get out of here,' hissed Ben, guiding Sheere frantically towards the staircase that led to the ground floor. 'Now!'

They had only taken a few steps when they saw a circle of fire boring a hole through the door of the room where Sheere had been sleeping. In an instant the flames had consumed the wood, like a red-hot coal passing through a sheet of paper. Ben's feet were rooted to the floor as he watched blazing footsteps coming towards them from the doorway.

'Run!' he shouted, pushing his sister towards the staircase. 'Go on!'

Sheere hurled herself down the stairs while Ben

remained glued to the spot, right in the path of the fiery footsteps. He felt a breath of hot air impregnated with the stench of burnt paraffin against his face as a footstep fell only centimetres from his feet. Two red pupils glowed in the dark like red-hot irons, and Ben felt a fiery claw clamping his right arm. In an instant it had burnt right through his shirt-sleeve and scorched his skin.

'It is not yet time for us to meet,' whispered a piercing cavernous voice. 'Get out of my way.'

Before Ben could react, the iron grip had shoved him aside and sent him sprawling to the floor. Ben touched his wounded arm then looked up to see an incandescent vision descending the spiral staircase, destroying it as it went.

Sheere's screams of terror gave Ben the strength to get back on his feet again. He ran towards the staircase, which was now scarcely more than a skeleton of metal bars cloaked in flames. Realising that the steps had disappeared, Ben threw himself through the gap. His body struck the mosaic on the ground floor and a wave of pain raced up his burnt arm.

'Ben!' shouted Sheere. 'Help me!'

Ben looked up and saw Sheere being dragged across the floor of shining stars, cocooned in fire, like the chrysalis of some infernal butterfly. He jumped up and ran after her, following her abductor's trail towards the rear of the house and trying to dodge the furious impact of hundreds of books that were cascading off the shelves of the circular library. Suddenly he felt a blow to the head and fell flat on his face.

His sight began to cloud over but he could see the fiery visitor stop and turn to look at him. Sheere's face was distorted by panic, though her screams were no longer audible. Ben tried to claw his way along the floor, which was now covered in glowing coals, fighting against the drowsiness that was urging him to give up. A cruel wolfish smile appeared before him, and through his blurred vision he recognised the man he had seen in the ghostly train that travelled through the night. Jawahal.

'When you're ready, come and find me,' the fiery spirit whispered. 'You know where I am …'

A second later Jawahal grabbed Sheere again, pulling her through the wall of the house as if it were merely a curtain of smoke. Before he passed out, Ben heard the echo of the train as it rode away into the distance.

'HE'S COMING ROUND,' murmured a voice hundreds of miles away.

Ben tried to make out the fuzzy shapes moving in front of him and soon recognised some familiar faces. Hands made him comfortable and placed a soft object under his head. Ben blinked repeatedly. Ian's eyes were red and despairing – he was watching his friend anxiously. Next to him were Seth and Roshan.

'Ben, can you hear us?' asked Seth. He looked as if he hadn't slept in a week.

Ben suddenly remembered and abruptly tried to sit up. The three boys made him lie down again.

'Where's Sheere?'

Ian, Seth and Roshan looked at one another.

'She's not here, Ben,' Ian replied at last.

Ben felt the sky falling on top of him and closed his eyes.

'What happened?' he asked after a moment.

'I woke up before you two,' Ian explained, 'so I decided to go out and find something to eat. On the way I met Seth, who was coming over to the house. When we returned we saw that all the windows were closed and there was smoke coming from inside. We found you unconscious. Sheere wasn't here.'

'Jawahal has taken her.'

Ian and Seth exchanged a look.

'What's the matter? What have you found out?'

Seth ran both hands through his thick shock of hair, pushing it away from his forehead.

'I'm not sure that this Jawahal exists, Ben,' he declared. 'I think Aryami lied to us.'

'What are you talking about? Why would she lie to us?'

Seth summarised the discoveries they'd made at the museum and explained that there was no mention of Jawahal in any of the documents relating to the trial, except for that one letter addressed to the engineer and

204

signed by Colonel Llewelyn, who had covered up the matter for some reason. Ben listened to their revelations in amazement.

'That doesn't prove a thing,' he objected. 'Jawahal was sentenced and imprisoned. He escaped sixteen years ago and that was when his crimes began.'

Seth sighed, shaking his head.

'I went to the Curzon Fort prison, Ben,' he said glumly. 'There was no escape and no fire sixteen years ago. The jail burnt down in 1857. Jawahal could never have escaped from a prison that had ceased to exist for decades before his trial took place. A trial in which he isn't even mentioned. It just doesn't add up.'

Ben stared at him open-mouthed.

'She lied to us, Ben,' said Seth. 'Your grandmother lied to us.'

'Where is she now?'

'Michael is out looking for her,' Ian explained. 'When he finds her he'll bring her here.'

'And where are the others?'

Roshan looked hesitantly at Ian. Ian nodded gravely.

'Tell him,' he said.

MICHAEL STOPPED TO WATCH the evening haze spread over the eastern bank of the Hooghly. Dozens of human figures, partly covered in white threadbare robes, were dipping into the river, the sum of their voices lost in the murmur of the current. The sound of doves flapping their wings, rising above the jungle of palaces and faded domes along the luminous river, made him think of a shadowy Venice.

'Are you looking for me?' said the old woman. She was sitting a few metres away, her face hidden by a veil.

Michael looked at her and she lifted the veil. Aryami Bose's deep eyes were pale in the evening light.

'We don't have much time,' said Michael. 'Not any more.'

Aryami nodded and slowly rose to her feet. Michael offered her his arm and the two set off under cover of dusk towards the house of Chandra Chatterghee.

THE FIVE FRIENDS GATHERED around Aryami Bose. Patiently, they waited for the old lady to get comfortable and to honour the debt she owed them by offering up the truth. Nobody dared speak before she did. The dreadful urgency that was gnawing at their insides became a momentary calm as they began to worry that the secret Aryami had hidden from them so carefully might prove to be insurmountable.

Aryami looked at the faces of the youngsters with deep sadness and gave them a faint smile. She cast her eyes down and sighed, examining the palms of her small nervous hands as she began to speak. This time her voice seemed to lack the authority and determination they had learned to expect from her. At the end of her journey fear had undermined her resilience; she was now just an old woman, frail and frightened, a girl who had lived too long.

~

'BEFORE I BEGIN, LET me tell you that if I have lied, and I have been obliged to do so on numerous occasions, it has always been in order to protect someone. And if I lied to you, it was because I was certain that in doing so I would protect you, Ben, and your sister Sheere from something that might hurt you even more than the actions of a maddened criminal. Nobody can know how much I've suffered, having to carry this burden on my own from the day you were born. Listen carefully and rest assured that whatever I say will be the truth, as far as I know it, although there is nothing as terrible and difficult to believe as the stark reality of facts.

'It feels like years have passed since I told you the story of my daughter Kylian. I told you about her, about her extraordinary radiance and how, among all her suitors, the one she chose to be her husband was a man of humble origins and great talent, a young engineer with a promising future. But I also told you that since childhood this man had borne a heavy load on his shoulders, a secret that would lead to his death and to the death of many others. Although this may seem contradictory, let me start this tale at the end, not the beginning, in response to the findings you have so cleverly disentangled.

'Chandra Chatterghee was always a dreamer, a man possessed by a vision of a better and fairer future for his people, whom he could see dying in poverty in the streets. Meanwhile, behind the walls of their sumptuous homes, those whom he considered to be invaders, exploiters of our people's natural legacy, were living a life of luxury at the expense of the millions of wretched souls inhabiting the great roofless orphanage that is India.

'His dream was to provide the nation with an instrument for progress and the creation of wealth, as he believed this would eventually break the oppressive yoke of the Crown. It would be an instrument that would open up new routes between cities, new enclaves, ensuring a future for Indian families. He dreamed of an invention made of iron and fire: the railway. For Chandra, railway tracks were the arteries that would carry the new blood of progress throughout the land, and he conceived a heart from which all this energy would flow: his masterpiece, Jheeter's Gate Station.

'But the line separating dreams from nightmares is as fine as a needle, and very soon the shadows of the past returned. A high-ranking officer in the British army, Colonel Arthur Llewelyn, had enjoyed a meteoric career built on his exploits and the slaughter of innocent people – old and young, unarmed men and terrified women – in towns and villages throughout the whole Bengali Peninsula. Wherever the message of peace and a united India arrived, so too did his rifles and bayonets. A very gifted man with a promising future, as his superiors claimed with pride, but also a murderer hiding behind the Crown's flag and the power of its army.

'It didn't take long for Llewelyn to notice Chandra's talent and, without too many problems, he managed to draw a black ring around him, blocking his projects. A few weeks later not a single door in Calcutta, indeed in the entire province, was open to him. Except, of course, Llewelyn's. He proposed a series of jobs for the army – bridges, railway lines ... Every offer he made was rejected by your father; he preferred to support himself with the paltry sums he received from Bombay publishers in exchange for his manuscripts. In time, Llewelyn's noose slackened and Chandra began to work once more on his grand plan.

'After some years had gone by, Llewelyn's anger was rekindled. His own career was floundering and he urgently needed some dramatic incident, a new bloodbath, with which to recapture the attention of the London authorities and restore his reputation as the panther of Bengal. His solution was clear: to put pressure on Chandra but this time using different weapons.

'For years Llewelyn had been investigating the engineer, and finally his henchmen sniffed out the series of crimes linked to Jawahal. Llewelyn almost let the case come to light. Then, just at the point when your father was more enmeshed than ever in his Jheeter's Gate project, he intervened, closing down the case but threatening to reveal the truth unless your father created a new weapon for him, a deadly instrument of repression that would put an end to the riots that the pacifists and pro-independence campaigners kept strewing in Llewelyn's path. Chandra had to comply, therefore the Firebird was born, a machine that could turn a city or a village into an ocean of flames in a matter of seconds.

'Chandra developed the railway and the Firebird side by side, under constant pressure from Llewelyn, whose greed, together with the suspicions he was starting to arouse among his superiors, threatened to expose him. A man who until then had been considered calm, even-tempered and dutiful was now showing himself to be an obsessive maniac whose desire for success and recognition blocked his own chances of survival.

'Chandra realised that Llewelyn's downfall was only a matter of time, so he played along with him and made him believe that he would hand over the finished project sooner than planned. This only increased Llewelyn's mania and tore apart what little sanity he had left.

'In 1915, a year before the opening of Jheeter's Gate

and the railway line extending from it, Llewelyn ordered the slaughter of a defenceless crowd, with no possible justification, and was thrown out of the British army in a scandal that even reached the House of Commons. His star would never shine again.

'His madness now took on new dimensions. Llewelyn gathered a group of officers who were loyal to him – like Llewelyn, they had been stripped of their rank and instructed to give up their weapons. With this horde of butchers he set up a sinister paramilitary squad that operated in secret. They sported their old uniforms and medals in a grotesque parody, congregating in Llewelyn's former residence so that they could maintain the fiction that they were a secret elite unit and that it would not be long before they would force out the very men who had signed their expulsion orders. Needless to say, Llewelyn never admitted that he'd been downgraded and disciplined. According to him and his collaborators, they had all resigned in order to found a new military order.

'Soon your father received death threats against himself and his pregnant wife if he did not deliver the Firebird. As the project was clandestine, Chandra had to handle it with great care. If he asked the army for help, his past would eventually come out. His only option was to make a pact with Llewelyn and his men.

'Amid all that tension, two days before the projected opening of Jheeter's Gate – and not afterwards, as I told you before – Kylian gave birth to twins. A boy and a girl. Your sister Sheere and you, Ben.

'A symbolic journey had been planned for the inauguration of Jheeter's Gate. The first train would transport three hundred and sixty-five orphaned children – one for each day of the year – from Calcutta to the orphanages of Bombay. What Chandra proposed to Llewelyn and his men was this: he would load the Firebird onto the train and, taking advantage of a technical stop that he would arrange about a hundred and fifty kilometres after departure, in the vicinity of Bishnupur, the soldiers would be able to unload the device and make off with it. Llewelyn accepted. Chandra was planning to disable the machine and get rid of Llewelyn and his men before the train had even sounded its whistle. But Llewelyn was secretly suspicious of the arrangement and ordered his men to get to the station early.

'Your father had arranged to meet the soldiers inside Jheeter's Gate, a labyrinth that only he knew, and under the pretext of showing them the Firebird, he led them into the tunnels. Llewelyn, however, had taken his own precautions, and before going to meet the engineer he had kidnapped your mother, and both of you with her. Just as Chandra was about to eliminate his blackmailers, Llewelyn revealed that he was holding you and your mother, and he threatened to kill all of you unless your father handed over the Firebird. Chandra was forced to surrender. But this wasn't enough for Llewelyn. He ordered his men to chain your father to the engine, planning to cut him to pieces when the train began its journey, and then, right in front of your father, he cold-bloodedly plunged a knife into Kylian's throat. He let her bleed to death slowly, hanging her from a noose in the central vault of the station. He told her he would leave you, Ben and Sheere, in the tunnels to be devoured by rats.

'Leaving Chandra chained to the engine, Llewelyn ordered his men to start the train and take the Firebird with them. Meanwhile he was going to hide the babies in a tunnel where nobody would ever be able to find you. But things did not go according to plan. That idiot Llewelyn was overconfident and had supposed that Chandra Chatterghee would simply hand over a machine with the exterminating capability of the Firebird to an assassin like him. But Chandra had taken every precaution imaginable and had fitted the Firebird with a secret timer, known only to himself, that would release all the destructive power of the machine after a few seconds if anybody but him tried to use it.

'As Llewelyn and his cohort of thugs boarded the train, the gang leader made a decision: as a parting gift and a prelude to the revenge he was planning to exact on the city once he had mastered the deadly invention, he would destroy the station, letting the fire raze Chandra's work and the lives of all those who had gathered to witness its launch. However the moment Llewelyn ignited the Firebird, he also signed the death sentence of every single person on that train, including himself. Five minutes later an inferno was unleashed, taking with it the bodies and souls of both the innocent and the guilty.

'You will be wondering why I lied to you about the prison where Jawahal was held or why his name was never mentioned in the records. Before I continue, and this is the most important thing, I want you to understand that, whatever you may hear, Chandra was a great man. A man who loved his wife and who would have loved his children if he'd had the opportunity to be a father to them. Now that I've said that, I will reveal the truth ...

'When your father was young and fell ill with fever, he did not end up in a shack by the river where a boy looked after him until he was better, as I told you. Your father was brought up in an institution called Grant House that still exists in South Calcutta. You're too young to have heard the name, but there was a time when it was infamous. Your father arrived at Grant House after witnessing a terrible event when he was barely six years old. His mother, who was unwell and earned her living by selling her body for a pittance, set fire to herself in front of him, offering herself up as a sacrifice to the goddess Kali. Grant House, where Chandra grew up, was a home for the mentally ill – what you'd call a lunatic asylum.

'For years he was confined to the corridors of that place, with no parents or friends other than people whose lives were defined by delirium and suffering. People who cried out that they were devils, gods or angels only to forget their own names the following day. By the time he was old enough to leave the institution, Chandra's entire childhood had been coloured by the most profound horror and human misery Calcutta had ever witnessed.

'I don't need to tell you that there never was a sinister friend who committed those crimes. The only shadow in your father's life was that of the parasite that had penetrated his mind. His own hands committed the crimes, and the guilt and shame of it pursued him like a curse.

'Only Kylian's kindness and her radiant nature cured him, giving him back the ability to shape his destiny. At her side he wrote the books you've heard about, he planned the works that would make him immortal and dispelled the ghost of his double life. But human greed denied him his chance, and what could have been a happy and prosperous life was plunged once more into darkness. This time for ever.

'On the night Lahawaj Chandra Chatterghee watched his wife being murdered before his very eyes the years of childhood horror turned on him, catapulting him straight back into his own private hell. He had built a whole new life on a pedestal which was now toppling over,

215

and as the flames devoured him, he became convinced that the only culprit in the tragedy was himself and that he deserved to be punished.

'That is why, when Llewelyn ignited the Firebird and the flames engulfed the tunnels and the station, a dark shadow in Chandra's soul swore he would return after his death. He would return as an angel of fire. An angel of destruction, the bringer of vengeance. An angel that would embody the darker side of his soul. It's not a murderer who is after you. Or a man. It's a ghost. A spirit. Or, if you prefer, a demon.

'Your father always loved puzzles, right to the end. You told me about a drawing done by your friend Michael, the picture in which your faces are reflected in a pond. The image that appears on the water is inverted. It's as if the prophecy guided Michael's pencil. If you were to write the name that Chandra's mother gave him when he was born, Lahawaj, on the drawing, the reflection on the pond would give you a different word: Jawahal.

'Ever since that day, Jawahal's tormented spirit has been tied to the infernal machine he created, a machine that, in death, gave him eternal life as a spectre of darkness. He and the Firebird are one and the same. That is his curse: a union between an angry spirit and a machine built for destruction. A fiery soul trapped inside the furnace of that blazing train. Now that soul is searching for a new home.

'That is why Jawahal is looking for you, because the

216

moment you reach adulthood, his spirit needs one of his children so that he can go on living: it needs to inhabit a body and thus extend its power to the world of the living. Only one of you can survive. The other, the one whose soul is not occupied by Jawahal's spirit, must die. Sixteen years ago he swore he would look for you and make you his, and he has always kept his promises – in this life and the next. You must realise that Jawahal has already chosen which child will harbour his accursed soul. But only he knows which.

'Providence granted you a chance sixteen years ago when Lieutenant Peake entered the labyrinth of tunnels at Jheeter's Gate and discovered the lifeless body of Kylian hanging in the void over her own spilt blood. Your cries reached his ears, and the lieutenant, swallowing his grief, searched for you and snatched you from the hands of your father's spirit. But he wasn't able to get very far. His feet led him to my door; he handed you over and then fled.

'When you tell your sister Sheere this story, never, ever forget that the avenging spirit that emerged that night from the flames of Jheeter's Gate and killed Lieutenant Peake when he was trying to save you both is not your father. Your father died in the fire, along with the innocent souls of the children. The figure who arose from the inferno to destroy himself, the fruit of his marriage and his own work is nothing more than a phantom. A spirit consumed by the bitterness, hatred and horror that humans had sown in his heart. That is the truth and nothing and no one can ever change it.

'If there is a god, or hundreds of them, I hope they will forgive me for the harm I may have inflicted on you by telling you exactly what happened.'

WHAT CAN I SAY? WHAT WORDS CAN EXPRESS THE
*sadness I saw in the eyes of my best friend, Ben, that
evening? Delving into the past had unveiled a cruel lesson
– that in the book of life it is perhaps best not to turn back
pages; it was a path on which, whatever direction we took,
we'd never be able to choose our own destiny. I wished
I had already boarded that ship that would take me far
away and was due to leave the following day. Inside me
cowardice mingled with the pain I felt for my friend and
the bitter taste of truth.*

*We had all listened to Aryami's story in silence and none
of us dared ask a question, although hundreds of them
were bubbling over in our minds. We knew that at last
all the strands of fate were converging on one particular
place: an appointment we could not escape at nightfall
amid the shadows of Jheeter's Gate.*

*When we stepped outside, the last rays of the sun
formed a scarlet ribbon in the sky that stretched across
the deep bluish hue of the Bengali clouds. A light drizzle
moistened our faces as we set off down the siding that led
from the back of Lahawaj Chandra Chatterghee's house
to the large station on the other side of the Hooghly River,
passing through the western quarter of the Black Town.*

I remember that shortly before crossing the metal bridge that led straight into the jaws of Jheeter's Gate, Ben made us promise, with tears in his eyes, that never, under any circumstance, would we reveal what we'd heard that evening. He swore that if he ever learned that Sheere had discovered the truth about her father, about the image that had nourished her since childhood, he'd kill whoever told her with his bare hands. We all promised to keep the secret.

There was now only one thing left to complete our story: war ...

© Jackie Freshfield

The Name of Midnight

Calcutta, 27 May 1932

THE SHADOW OF THE STORM HERALDED THE ARRIVAL of midnight as a vast leaden blanket spread over Calcutta, lighting up with every burst of electric fury it unleashed. The power of the north wind swept the mist from the Hooghly River, revealing the ravaged skeleton of the metal bridge.

The silhouette of Jheeter's Gate rose up through the retreating haze. A fork of lightning flashed from the sky, striking the needle of the central dome and fracturing into an ivy of blue light that travelled along the mesh of arches and steel beams before plunging down to the foundations.

The five friends stopped at the threshold of the bridge; only Ben and Roshan took a few steps forward. The rails formed a path edged by two silvery lines that led straight into the mouth of Jheeter's Gate. With the moon hidden behind the clouds, the city was sunk in an eerie gloom.

Ben looked carefully along the bridge in search of gaps or cracks that might send them tumbling down into the turbulent current of the river, but all he could make out was the line of the tracks shining between weeds and rubble. The wind brought a muffled murmur from the opposite bank. Ben looked at Roshan, who was nervously watching the dark maw of the station. He saw his friend approach the tracks and crouch down next to them, his eyes still riveted on Jheeter's Gate. Roshan placed his palm on the surface of one of the rails but quickly removed it as if he'd had an electric shock.

'It's vibrating,' he said, sounding frightened. 'As if a train were approaching.'

Ben went over and touched the metal. Roshan looked at him anxiously.

'It's the vibration caused by the river hitting the bridge,' he reassured him. 'There's no train.'

Seth and Michael came over. Ian knelt down to tie his shoelaces in a double knot, a ritual he reserved for situations when his nerves were as tense as steel cables.

Ian looked up and smiled shyly without displaying a shred of the fear Ben knew was coursing inside him – just as it was in the others, and in himself.

'Tonight I'd give it a triple knot,' said Seth.

Ben smiled and the members of the Chowbar Society exchanged an expectant look then proceeded to imitate Ian and reinforce the knots of their shoes, calling on the lucky ritual that had worked so well for their friend in other predicaments.

A short while later they formed a single line, headed by Ben with Roshan in the rearguard, and began to walk cautiously over the bridge. Following Seth's advice, Ben stayed close to the track, where the structure of the bridge was more solid. In broad daylight it was easy to avoid broken sleepers and see in advance areas that had given way with the passage of time and were now dangling down into the river, but at night, cloaked by the storm, the route was like a forest strewn with traps, and they had to advance a step at a time, feeling their way.

They'd only covered some fifty metres, a quarter of the length of the bridge, when Ben stopped and raised a hand. His friends stared ahead, bewildered. For a moment they stood motionless on the girders that trembled like jelly under the continual pounding of the river.

'What's the matter?' asked Roshan from the back of the line. 'Why are we stopping?'

Ben pointed in the direction of Jheeter's Gate: two arteries of fire were speeding along the rails towards them.

'Get to one side!' shouted Ben.

All five threw themselves to the ground as the two walls of fire sliced through the air next to them. As the fire passed it sucked away bits of the track and left a trail of flames along the bridge.

'Is everyone all right?' asked Ian, standing up. He realised there was smoke and steam coming from his clothing.

The others nodded mutely.

'Let's take advantage of the light from the flames and cross over before they go out,' Ben suggested.

'Ben, I think there's something under the bridge,' whispered Michael.

A strange drumming sound could be heard coming from the other side of the sheet of metal beneath their feet. A vision of steel claws scratching at the surface flashed through Ben's mind.

'Well, we're not staying here to find out,' he said. 'Come on.'

The members of the Chowbar Society pressed ahead, zigzagging along the bridge until they reached the end, not stopping to look behind them. Once they were on firm ground, just metres away from the station's entrance, Ben turned and told his friends to keep away from the metal framework.

'What was that?' asked Ian.

Ben shrugged his shoulders.

'Look!' cried Seth. 'In the middle of the bridge!'

All eyes focused on that point. The tracks were glowing red, the heat radiating in all directions and giving off a light halo of smoke. After a few seconds both rails began to bend. The entire structure of the bridge started to drip huge tears of molten metal into the Hooghly, producing violent explosions as they hit the cold water.

Paralysed with fear, the five boys witnessed the steel structure, over two hundred metres long, melting before their very eyes like a lump of butter in a hot frying pan. The liquid metal sank into the river, its intense amber glow reflected on the faces of the five friends. Finally, the incandescent red faded into a dull metallic tone, and the two ends of the bridge collapsed over the Hooghly like weeping willows caught staring at their own reflection.

The sound of the steel hissing in the water slowly abated. Then, behind them, the five friends heard the voice of the old Jheeter's Gate's siren cutting through the Calcutta night for the first time in sixteen years. Without uttering a single word, they turned round and crossed the frontier into the ghostly setting for the game they were about to play.

ISOBEL OPENED HER EYES as she heard the siren shriek through the tunnels like an air-raid warning. Her feet and hands were firmly pinned to two long rusty metal bars, and the only light she could see filtered through the grille of a ventilation shaft just above her. The echo of the siren slowly died away.

Suddenly she heard something creeping towards the

grille. She looked up at the slivers of light and noticed that the bright rectangle was darkening and the grille was opening. She closed her eyes and held her breath. The metallic hooks that immobilised her feet and hands snapped open and she felt long fingers grab her by the nape of her neck and pull her up through the gap. She screamed in terror as her captor flung her onto the floor of the tunnel.

When Isobel opened her eyes, she saw a tall black silhouette standing in front of her, a figure without a face.

'Someone has come for you,' the invisible face whispered. 'Let's not keep him waiting.'

Immediately two burning pupils lit up, flaring in the dark. Grabbing her arm, the figure dragged her through the tunnel. After what seemed like hours of an agonising walk through total darkness, Isobel at last made out the ghostly shape of a train. She was hauled towards the guard's van and didn't have the strength to resist when she was flung inside and heard the door being locked.

As Isobel fell onto the charred floor of the carriage, a sharp pain seared through her belly. Something had gashed her badly. She groaned. She was seized by panic as a pair of hands took hold of her and tried to turn her over. She shouted out and came face to face with a dirty exhausted boy who seemed even more frightened than she was.

'It's me, Isobel,' whispered Siraj. 'Don't be afraid.'

For the first time in her life Isobel let her tears flow freely as she hugged the bony, frail body of her friend.

BEN AND HIS COMRADES stopped under the clock with the drooping hands on the main platform of Jheeter's Gate. All around them was a vast landscape of shadows and faint slanting light that filtered through the steel and glass dome.

From where they stood, the five youngsters could envisage what Jheeter's Gate must have looked like before the tragedy: a majestic luminous vault held up by invisible arches that seemed to be suspended from heaven, above rows and rows of platforms arranged in curves, like ripples on a pond. Large noticeboards announcing departure and arrival times. Elaborate newspaper kiosks made of carved metal with Victorian reliefs. Palatial staircases rising through steel and glass shafts to the upper levels, with corridors seemingly hanging in mid-air. Crowds strolling about its halls and boarding long express trains that would take them to the furthest reaches of the country … Nothing remained of all that splendour, only a dark broken shell.

Ian noticed the hands of the clock, distorted by the flames, and tried to imagine the magnitude of the fire. Seth had the same thought; they both avoided making any comment.

'We should separate into groups of two. This place is immense,' said Ben.

'I don't think that's a good idea,' replied Seth, who

couldn't get the image of the collapsing bridge out of his head.

'Even if we did split up, there are only five of us,' said Ian. 'Who would go alone?'

'I would,' replied Ben.

The others looked at him with a mixture of relief and anxiety.

'I still don't think it's a good idea,' Seth insisted.

'Ben's right,' said Michael. 'From what we've seen so far, it will make little difference whether we're five or fifty.'

'A man of few words, but always so encouraging,' Roshan remarked.

'Michael, you and Roshan could search the upper levels,' Ben suggested. 'Ian and Seth can check this floor.'

Nobody seemed prepared to dispute the assignment of locations. One area seemed as unattractive as the next.

'What about you?' asked Ian, already guessing the answer. 'Where are you going to search?'

'In the tunnels.'

'On one condition,' said Seth, trying to impose a modicum of common sense.

Ben nodded, listening.

'No heroics or any other such nonsense. The first person to notice something must stop, mark the place and return to look for the others.'

'Sounds reasonable,' Ian agreed.

Michael and Roshan also nodded.

'Ben?' Ian asked.

'All right,' Ben murmured.

'We didn't hear you,' Seth insisted.

'I promise,' said Ben. 'We'll meet back here in half an hour.'

'Let's just pray you're right,' said Seth.

SHE WOKE INTO A nightmare. As she opened her eyes, Sheere vaguely remembered her vain attempts to free herself from the relentless grip of the fiery shape that had pulled her through a maze of narrow passageways. She also remembered Ben's face as he lay writhing on the floor of a familiar-looking house, although she didn't know how long ago that had been. It could have been an hour, a week or a month.

As she regained consciousness and felt the bruises the struggle had left on her body, Sheere realised that what she could see around her was not part of a dream. She was inside a long deep room, flanked on either side by rows of windows which let in enough murky light for her to be able to make out the wreckage of what seemed to be a narrow lounge. The broken skeletons of three glass lamps hung from the ceiling like withered branches. The remains of a cracked mirror shone in the half-light behind a counter that once might have been part of an elegant bar.

She tried to sit up. She worked out that the chains

binding her wrists behind her back were fastened to a narrow pipe, and instinctively understood where she was: inside a train stuck in the underground galleries of Jheeter's Gate.

Straining her eyes, she scanned the mass of fallen tables and burnt debris in search of a tool that might help her free herself from the chains. The interior of the carriage didn't seem to contain anything but the useless remains of scorched objects that had miraculously survived. She struggled, but only managed to make the chains tighter.

Two metres in front of her a black shape that she had taken to be a pile of rubble suddenly turned towards her. A luminous smile on an invisible face lit up in the darkness. Sheere's heart skipped a beat as the figure came within a breath of her face. Jawahal's eyes shone like embers in the wind and Sheere detected the acrid penetrating stench of burnt petrol.

'Welcome to what remains of my home, Sheere,' he murmured coldly. 'That *is* your name, isn't it?'

Sheere nodded, paralysed with terror at the presence before her.

'You don't have anything to fear from me,' said Jawahal.

The girl held back the tears that were fighting to escape; she wasn't going to give up that easily. She closed her eyes tight and breathed deeply.

'Look at me when I'm talking to you,' said Jawahal in a tone that froze her blood.

Slowly Sheere opened her eyes and realised with

horror that Jawahal's hand was getting closer to her face. His long fingers, protected by a black glove, stroked her cheek and delicately pushed away a lock of hair that had fallen over her forehead. Her captor's eyes seemed to turn pale for an instant.

'You look so much like her ...'

Abruptly the hand withdrew like a frightened animal, and Jawahal stood up. Sheere noticed that the chains at her back were loosening and suddenly her hands were free.

'Get up and follow me,' he ordered.

Sheere obeyed meekly and let Jawahal lead the way. But as soon as the dark figure was a few metres away amid the wreckage, she turned and began to run in the opposite direction as fast as her stiff muscles would carry her. She stumbled through the carriage towards the door that led to a small open-air platform connecting to the next coach, then placed her hand on the blackened steel handle and pushed hard. The metal went as soft as potter's clay and Sheere watched in astonishment as it transformed itself into five sharp fingers that grabbed her wrist. Slowly the door panel folded in on itself until it took the form of a shining statue on whose smooth surface Jawahal's features emerged. Sheere's knees buckled and she keeled over in front of him. As Jawahal lifted her in the air she could see the fury in his eyes.

'Don't try to escape from me, Sheere; very soon you and I will be one being. I am not your enemy. I am your future. Come over to my side, otherwise this is what will happen to you.'

Jawahal plucked a broken wineglass from the floor, put his fingers round it and squeezed hard. It melted in his fist, dripping through his fingers in globules of liquid glass that fell onto the carriage floor, creating a blazing mirror among the debris. Jawahal let go of Sheere and she fell only centimetres away from the smoking mirror.

'Now do as I say.'

SETH KNELT DOWN TO examine what appeared to be a shiny puddle in the central section of the station and touched it with his fingertips. The liquid was thick and lukewarm, and had a texture similar to spilt oil.

'Ian, come and see this,' he called.

Ian walked over and knelt down beside his friend. Seth showed him his fingers, which were covered in a glutinous substance. Ian dampened the tip of his forefinger and rubbed it against his thumb, checking the consistency, then sniffed at it.

'It's blood,' the aspiring doctor concluded.

Seth went pale and wiped his fingers on his trouser leg.

'Isobel?' he asked, drawing away from the liquid and trying to stem the nausea rising from the pit of his stomach.

234

'I don't know,' replied Ian. 'It's recent, or at least it appears to be.'

He stood up and looked to each side of the wide dark stain.

'There aren't any marks around it. Or footprints,' he murmured.

Seth stared at him, not grasping the full significance of Ian's remark.

'Whoever lost all this blood couldn't have gone far without leaving a trail,' Ian explained. 'Even if the person was being dragged. It makes no sense.'

Seth considered Ian's theory and walked around the spilt blood, checking that there were no footprints or other tracks within a radius of several metres. The two friends exchanged puzzled looks. All of a sudden Seth noticed a shadow of uncertainty in Ian's eyes and he instantly understood what his friend was thinking. Slowly they both raised their heads and looked up at the vaulted ceiling that rose high above them in the dark.

As they scanned the shadows of the enormous dome their eyes paused on a large glass chandelier hanging from its centre. From one of its branches, tied to a white rope and wrapped in a glittering shawl, was a body, swaying gently over the void.

'Is that a dead body?' Seth asked timidly.

His eyes fixated on the gruesome discovery, Ian shrugged his shoulders.

'Shouldn't we let the others know?'

'As soon as we discover who it is,' replied Ian. 'If the blood is coming from the body, and everything seems to indicate that it is, the person might still be alive. Let's take it down.'

Seth closed his eyes. He'd been expecting something like this ever since they'd crossed the bridge, but knowing that his instinct had been correct only increased the nausea building in his throat. The boy took a deep breath and decided not to wait any longer.

'Fine,' he agreed, his tone resigned. 'How?'

Ian examined the upper reaches of the hall and noticed a metal walkway running around it, about fifteen metres above the ground. From this a narrow gangway connected to the glass chandelier – just a small footbridge, probably intended for the maintenance and cleaning of the structure.

'We'll go up there and take the person down,' Ian explained.

'One of us should wait here, to attend to their wounds,' Seth said. 'I think it should be you.'

Ian studied his friend carefully.

'Are you sure you want to go up there alone?'

'I'm dying to do it ...' replied Seth. 'Wait here. And don't move.'

Ian watched his friend approach the staircase that led to the upper levels of Jheeter's Gate. As soon as the shadows had engulfed him and the sound of his footsteps had grown fainter, he scanned the surrounding darkness.

Gusts of wind from the tunnels whistled in his ears and sent fragments of debris tumbling across the ground. Ian looked up again and tried in vain to recognise the figure hanging in the air. He couldn't bear the thought that it might be Isobel, Siraj or Sheere … Suddenly a fleeting reflection seemed to appear on the surface of the puddle at his feet, but when Ian looked down, there was nothing.

～

JAWAHAL DRAGGED SHEERE THROUGH the corridor of the stationary train until he reached the front car, which preceded the engine. An intense orange light shone through the cracks in the heavy door, and Sheere could hear the furious sound of a boiler raging inside. She felt the temperature rise steeply around her and all her pores opened at the touch of the scorching air.

'What's in there?' she asked in alarm.

Jawahal closed his fingers round her arm and pulled her towards him.

'The fire machine,' he replied, opening the door and pushing the girl inside. 'This is my home and my prison. But very soon all that will change, thanks to you, Sheere. After all these years we have found each other again. Isn't this what you have always wanted?'

Sheere had to protect her face from the blast of heat as she peered at the engine through her fingers. In front of her a gigantic machine made up of large metal boilers joined together by an endless coil of pipes and valves was roaring as if it were about to explode. From the joints of the monstrous device came clouds of steam and gas. On an iron panel bearing a set of pressure valves and gauges Sheere recognised the carved figure of an eagle rising majestically from the flames. Beneath the bird were a few words carved in an alphabet she didn't recognise.

'The Firebird,' said Jawahal, next to her. 'My alter ego.'

'My father built this machine,' murmured Sheere. 'You have no right to use it. You're nothing but a thief and a murderer.'

Jawahal observed her thoughtfully then licked his lips.

'What kind of a world have we built when not even the ignorant can be happy?' he asked. 'Wake up, Sheere.'

The girl turned to look at Jawahal with disdain.

'You killed him,' she said, hatred burning in her eyes. Jawahal distorted his features into a grotesque grimace. Seconds later Sheere realised that he was laughing. Jawahal pushed her gently against the scorching wall of the car and pointed an accusing finger at her.

'Stay there and don't move.'

Sheere watched Jawahal approach the throbbing machinery and place his palms on the burning metal of the boilers. His hands adhered to the metal and there was the stench of charred skin and a ghastly hissing sound as the flesh burnt. Jawahal slowly opened his mouth and seemed to imbibe the clouds of steam floating in the locomotive. Then he turned and smiled at the horrified girl.

'Are you scared of playing with fire? Let's play something else then. We can't disappoint your friends.'

Without waiting for a reply, Jawahal left the machine and moved towards the back of the car, where he picked up a large wicker basket. He drew close to Sheere, a disturbing smile on his lips.

'Do you know which animal is most like man?'

Sheere shook her head.

'I see that the education your grandmother has given you is poorer than I expected. A father simply can't be replaced ...'

He opened the basket and plunged his fist inside, his eyes glittering maliciously. When his hand emerged, it was holding the sinuous shining body of a snake. An asp.

'This is the animal that most resembles humans. It crawls and sheds its skin when it needs to. It will steal the young of other species from their own nests and eat them but is incapable of confronting them in a clean battle. Its speciality, however, is to seize every possible opportunity to deliver its lethal bite. The asp has only enough poison for one bite and it needs hours to recover, but whoever is bitten is condemned to a slow and certain death. As the poison penetrates the veins, the heart of the victim beats slower and slower, until eventually it stop: even in its vicious nature, this small beast has a certain fondness for poetry, just like human beings, although the asp, unlike man, would never attack its own kind. That's a mistake, don't you think? Maybe that's why they've ended up as street entertainment for fakirs and spectators – they aren't quite on a par with the king of creation.'

Jawahal held the snake in front of Sheere and the girl pressed herself against the wall. He smiled with satisfaction as soon as he saw the look of terror in her eyes.

'We always fear what resembles us most. But don't worry,' Jawahal reassured her. 'This one's not for you.'

He picked up a red wooden box and put the snake inside it. Sheere breathed more easily once the reptile was out of sight.

'What are you going to do with it?'

'We're going to play a little game,' Jawahal explained. 'We have guests tonight and we have to provide them with entertainment.'

'Which guests?' asked Sheere, praying that Jawahal wouldn't confirm her fears.

'Your question is superfluous, dear Sheere. Please reserve your queries for matters you really don't understand. For example, will our friends see the light of day? Or how long does it take for a kiss from my little friend to slow down the heart of a healthy sixteen-year-old? Rhetoric teaches us that these are questions with meaning and structure. If you don't know how to express yourself, Sheere, you don't know how to think. And if you don't know how to think, you're lost.'

'Those are my father's words,' Sheere said accusingly. 'He wrote them.'

'Then I see we've both read the same books. What better way of starting an eternal friendship, dear Sheere?'

Sheere listened to Jawahal's little speech, never taking her eyes off the red wooden box that held the asp, imagining its scaly body writhing about inside. Jawahal raised his eyebrows.

'Now, you must excuse me if I leave you for a few moments. I need to add the final touches to the welcome for our guests. Please be patient and wait for me. It will be worth your while.'

Jawahal grabbed Sheere again and led her to a tiny cubicle with a narrow door set into one of the tunnel walls which at one time had been used to house a lever frame for the points. He pushed the girl inside and left the wooden box by her feet. Sheere gave him a desperate look, but Jawahal closed the door in her face, leaving her in the pitch dark.

'Let me out of here, please,' she begged.

'I'll let you out very soon, Sheere,' murmured Jawahal from the other side of the door. 'And then nobody will part us.'

'What are you going to do with me?'

'I'm going to live inside you, Sheere. In your mind, in your soul and in your body. Before day breaks your lips will be mine, I will see through your eyes. Tomorrow you'll be immortal, Sheere. Who could ask for more?'

'Why are you doing all this?' Sheere pleaded.

Jawahal was silent for a few moments.

'Because I love you, Sheere … And you know the saying: we always kill what we love the most.'

～

AFTER WHAT SEEMED LIKE an endless wait, Seth appeared on the walkway that ran around the hall far above the ground. Ian sighed with relief.

'What happened to you?' he demanded.

His voice echoed around the vast space. The chances of them being able to carry out their search without being noticed were rapidly diminishing.

'It wasn't easy to get up here,' Seth called out. 'I can't imagine a worse network of corridors and passageways – except perhaps in the Egyptian pyramids. Just be grateful that I'm not lost.'

Ian nodded and told Seth to go towards the gangway leading to the glass chandelier. Seth went along the walkway but paused after he'd taken the first few steps.

'What's wrong?' asked Ian, watching his friend some fifteen metres above him.

Seth shook his head and continued walking along the narrow gangway until he stopped two metres away from the body suspended by the rope. Very slowly he moved closer to the edge and bent over to examine it. Ian noticed the shock on his friend's face.

'Seth? What's the matter, Seth?'

Visibly agitated, Seth knelt down to untie the rope

holding the body, but when he caught hold of it, the rope wound itself round one of his legs and the suspended body plummeted into the void. The rope then gave a violent jolt and started dragging Seth up into the shadows of the vaulted ceiling like a puppet. He struggled to free his leg and cried for help but his body was now being hauled upwards at a frightening pace and soon he disappeared completely.

In the meantime, the corpse that had been hanging overhead had dropped straight into the pool of blood. All Ian could see beneath the shawl wrapped around it were the remains of a skeleton whose bones cracked as they hit the floor, dissolving into dust. The fabric floated down and slowly became soaked in the dark liquid. When Ian examined it he recognised the shawl he'd seen so many times in the orphanage during his sleepless nights, worn across the shoulders of the luminous woman who visited Ben as he slept.

He looked up again, hoping to see some trace of his friend, but the impenetrable darkness had taken Seth and there was no sign of his presence other than the dying echo of his screams.

'DID YOU HEAR THAT?' asked Roshan, stopping to listen to the shouts that seemed to be coming from the very bowels of the building.

Michael nodded. The screams gradually faded and soon

they were enveloped once again in the sound of the drizzle pattering against the roof of the dome above them. They'd climbed to the top floor of Jheeter's Gate and were looking down at the amazing sight of the immense station from on high. The platforms and tracks seemed very distant and the elaborate structure of arches and multiple levels could be seen much more clearly from that point.

Michael stopped by the edge of a metal balustrade that jutted out over the void, vertically above the large clock under which they had passed when they entered the station. His artist's eye appreciated the mesmerising effect created by the hundreds of curved beams issuing from the geometric centre of the dome. They seemed to vanish in an endless arc, never touching the floor. Viewed from that privileged position, the station seemed to rise towards the sky, spiralling into a vault of steel and glass that merged into the clouds above. Roshan joined Michael and took a brief look at the sight that was bewitching his friend.

'We're going to get dizzy. Come on, let's go.'

Michael raised a hand in protest.

'No, wait. Look down.'

Roshan took a quick peep over the balustrade.

'If I look again, I'll fall over.'

A mysterious smile appeared on Michael's lips. Roshan stared at his friend, wondering what he had discovered.

'Don't you realise, Roshan?'

Roshan shook his head. 'Explain it to me.'

'This structure,' Michael said. 'If you look towards the vanishing point from this position in the dome, you'll understand.'

Roshan tried to follow Michael's instructions, but he didn't have a clue what he was supposed to see.

'What are you trying to tell me?'

'It's very simple. This station, the whole structure of Jheeter's Gate, is an immense sphere. We can only see the part that emerges above ground. The clock tower is situated at the very centre of the dome, like a sort of radius.'

Roshan took in Michael's words.

'OK, it's a stupid ball,' he said. 'So what?'

'Do you realise the technical difficulties involved in building a structure like this?' asked Michael.

Again his friend shook his head.

'I assume they'd be considerable.'

'Radical,' Michael asserted, deploying an adjective he used in only the most extreme cases. 'Why would anyone design a structure like this one?'

'I'm not sure I want to know the answer,' said Roshan. 'Let's go down a level. There's nothing here.'

Michael gave a distracted nod and followed Roshan to the staircase.

Beneath the dome's observation balcony was a kind of mezzanine level barely a metre and a half high flooded by the rainwater that had been falling over Calcutta since the beginning of May. The floor lay under about twenty centimetres of stagnant water, which gave off a nauseating stench, and was covered by a mass of mud and rubble that had been decomposing for more than a decade due to the continual seepage. After crouching down to enter the mezzanine, Michael and Roshan found themselves wading through the mud, which came up to their ankles.

'This place is worse than the catacombs,' said Roshan. 'Why the hell is this ceiling so hellishly low? People haven't been this small for centuries.'

'It was probably a restricted area,' said Michael. 'Perhaps it houses part of the counterweight system that supports the dome. Mind you don't trip over anything. The whole place could collapse.'

'Is that a joke?'

'Yes,' said Michael dryly.

'Then it's the third joke I've heard from you in six years,' said Roshan. 'And it's the worst.'

Michael didn't bother to reply and continued to make his way slowly through the swamp. The stench of stagnant water was beginning to fog his brain, and he started to think that perhaps they should turn back and descend one more level. Besides, he doubted that anything or anybody could be hidden in the impregnable quagmire.

'Michael?' Roshan's voice was a few metres behind him.

The boy turned and saw Roshan's figure bent over a large metal beam.

'Michael,' Roshan said again. He sounded bewildered.

'Is it possible that this beam is moving or is it just my imagination?'

Michael thought his friend had also been inhaling the putrid vapours for too long and was about to abandon the area altogether when he heard a loud crash at the other end of the section. They turned to look at one another. The crash sounded again, only this time the boys felt a movement and then saw something speeding towards them under the mud, raising a wake of rubbish and dirty water. Without wasting a second, Roshan and Michael rushed towards the exit, crouching down as they negotiated their way through the mud and water.

They had only gone a few metres when the submerged object passed them at high speed, then doubled back and headed straight towards them. Roshan and Michael separated, running in opposite directions, trying to distract the attention of whatever was intent on hunting them down. The creature hidden beneath the mud divided into two halves, each half hurling itself after one of the boys.

Gasping for breath, Michael had turned to check if he was still being followed when his foot hit a step concealed under the sludge and he fell headlong into the mud. When he emerged and opened his eyes, which were stinging, a figure of mud was rising in front of him. Michael tried to pull himself up – but his hands skidded, leaving him stretched out in the slush.

The mud figure spread out two long arms, on the end

of which were long fingers curved into large metal hooks. Michael watched in horror as the creature took form, a head emerging from the trunk, then a face with large jaws lined with fangs that were as long and sharp as hunting knives. Suddenly the figure solidified, the dry mud letting off a hiss of steam. When Michael stood up, he could hear the mud crackling as dozens of small fissures spread over it. The cracks on the face slowly expanded revealing Jawahal's fiery eyes. The dry mud fractured into a mosaic of scales that quickly fell away. Jawahal grabbed Michael by the throat and pulled him in close.

'Are you the artist?' he asked, lifting Michael in the air.

Michael nodded.

'Good,' said Jawahal. 'You're in luck, my boy. Today you'll see things that will keep your pencil busy for the rest of your life. Supposing, of course, you live long enough to draw them.'

As this was happening, Roshan ran towards the door, a rush of adrenalin burning through his veins. When he was only a couple of metres from the exit he jumped and landed on the clean, mudless surface of the outer gallery. Standing up, his first impulse was to keep running – the instincts acquired during the years of street thieving before he joined St Patrick's were still there. But something stopped him. He'd lost sight of Michael when they separated inside the mezzanine and now he couldn't even hear his friend shouting as he desperately tried to save himself. Ignoring his instincts, Roshan returned to the entrance of the low-ceilinged floor. There was no sign of Michael or of the creature that had pursued them. Roshan realised that his pursuer had gone after his friend.

'Michael!' he shouted at the top of his lungs.

His call received no reply.

Roshan gave a dejected sigh, wondering what his next step should be: should he go and look for the others, abandoning Michael to that place, or should he go back in and search for him? Neither option seemed to offer much hope of success, but before he could make the decision two long arms of mud emerged from the ground behind the door, aiming for his feet. Claws closed round his ankles. Roshan tried to free himself from their grip, but the arms tugged at him with such force they knocked him over and started to pull him back inside the mezzanine.

OF THE FIVE BOYS who had promised to meet under the clock, only Ian turned up at the appointed time. The station had never seemed so deserted, and he could hardly breathe from the anguish he felt, not knowing what had become of Seth and his friends. Alone in that ghostly cavern, it wasn't hard to imagine that he was the only one who hadn't fallen into the clutches of their sinister host.

He scanned the station nervously, wondering what he should do: wait here and not move, or leave in search of help out there in the night? Small leaks in the roof allowed the drizzle to filter through and drops of water splattered down from a great height. Ian made an effort to keep calm and tried to stop himself thinking that the drops he saw splashing onto the railway tracks were in fact the blood of his friend Seth, dangling somewhere in the darkness above.

He looked up at the vaulted ceiling for the umpteenth time in the vain hope of discovering Seth's whereabouts. The raindrops slid in shining rivulets over the limp smile formed by the hands of the clock. Ian sighed. His nerves were starting to get the better of him and he supposed that, if he didn't get some indication of his friends' presence very soon, he would have to enter the underground network, following the path Ben had taken. He didn't think it was a particularly brilliant idea, but he held fewer alternative aces than ever. It was then that he heard the sound of something approaching from one of the tunnels and he began to breathe more easily, realising he wasn't alone after all.

He walked over to the end of the platform and watched as an indistinct shape emerged from one of the arches. A shiver ran down the back of his neck. A small open wagon was approaching at a snail's pace, and on it he could see a chair and on the chair was a motionless figure with a black hood over its head. Ian gulped. The wagon passed slowly in front of him then came to a dead stop. Ian remained glued to the spot, staring at the cart, and caught himself voicing his worst suspicions.

'Seth?'

The body on the chair didn't move a muscle. Ian went over to the front of the wagon and jumped inside, but there was still no sign of movement from its occupant. With agonising slowness he crept towards the hooded shape until he was only centimetres from the chair.

'Seth?' he murmured again.

A strange sound emerged from under the hood, like someone grinding their teeth. Ian felt his stomach turn. The muffled sound came again. He grabbed hold of the material and mentally counted to three, then he closed his eyes and tugged.

When he opened his eyes again, a manic smiling face with popping eyes was staring up at him. The hood fell from Ian's hands. The doll's face was as white as china and two large black diamonds had been painted over the eyes, the lower tips turning into black tears of tar running down its cheeks.

The doll ground its teeth mechanically. Ian examined the grotesque harlequin and tried to work out what lay behind such an eccentric trick. He carefully put out a hand to touch the figure's face, searching for the mechanism that produced the movement.

Quick as a cat, the robot's right arm grabbed Ian, and before the boy could react, his wrist had been clamped by a handcuff, the other end of which was attached to the doll. The boy pulled hard, but the mannequin was tied to the wagon and all it did was grind its teeth again. Ian struggled desperately but by the time he understood that he wouldn't be able to free himself on his own, the wagon had started to move; this time, however, it was going back into the mouth of the tunnel.

BEN STOPPED AT THE intersection of two tunnels and for a moment considered the possibility that he'd been past the same place twice already. From the moment he'd entered the tunnels of Jheeter's Gate, this had become a recurrent and unsettling feeling. He pulled out one of the matches he was using sparingly and lit it by gently scratching it against the wall. The half-light around him took on the warm glow of the flame and he was able to examine the junction between the railway tunnel and the broad ventilation shaft that cut through it at right angles.

Suddenly a gust of dusty air blew out the flame and Ben was returned to the shadows – a landscape in which, however far he walked in one direction or another, he never seemed to arrive anywhere. He was beginning to suspect that he was lost and that if he persisted in going any further into the complex underworld, it might be hours before he emerged. Common sense told him he should retrace his steps and head back towards the main section of the station. However much he tried to visualise the labyrinth of tunnels in his mind, with its complicated system of ventilation shafts and interconnecting passages, he couldn't rid himself of the strange suspicion that the entire structure was moving around him; if he tried to work out a new route in the dark he would probably only end up back where he started.

Having decided not to be overwhelmed by the confusing web of galleries, he turned round and quickened his pace, wondering whether he was already late for the meeting they'd arranged under the clock. As he wandered through the interminable passageways of Jheeter's Gate, it occurred to him that perhaps there was some secret law of physics by which time moved faster in the absence of light. He was beginning to feel he'd covered whole kilometres in the dark when, at the far end of a gallery, he noticed a brighter area that marked the open space beneath the large cupola of Jheeter's Gate. He heaved a sigh of relief and rushed towards the light, hoping he had come to the end of his interminable pilgrimage through the labyrinth.

But as he reached the mouth of the tunnel and started to walk up the narrow channel between two platforms, he realised his surge of optimism had been short-lived. The station was deserted; there was no sign of any of his friends.

With a jump he pulled himself up onto the platform and covered the fifty metres that separated him from the clock tower with no other company than the echo of his footsteps. He walked round the tower and stood beneath the large face with its deformed hands. He didn't need a clock to guess that the time his friends had agreed on for their meeting had long passed.

Leaning against the blackened wall of the tower Ben had to admit that his idea of splitting up the group to spread their search more widely didn't seem to have produced the expected results. The only difference between the moment he'd first entered Jheeter's Gate and now was that he was alone. He'd lost his friends just as he'd lost Sheere.

Ben decided to start looking. Little did he care if it was going to take him a week, or a month, to find them. He walked along the central platform towards the rear wing of Jheeter's Gate, where the former offices and waiting rooms were situated together with a small citadel of bazaars, cafes and restaurants – all reduced to cinders. It was then that he noticed the glittering shawl lying on the floor in one of the waiting areas. He seemed to remember that the last time he'd been in that place, before he entered the tunnels, the piece of smooth shiny fabric hadn't been there. He hurried forward.

BEN KNELT DOWN AND reached out a hesitant hand. The shawl was soaked in a dark tepid liquid that seemed vaguely familiar but instinctively repelled him. Beneath the material he thought he could see the random pieces of some kind of object. He pulled out his matchbox and was about to strike a match so that he could examine the discovery but realised he had only one left. Resigned to saving it for a better occasion, Ben strained his eyes in pursuit of a clue that might shed light on the whereabouts of his friends. A shadow spread across the dark puddle and he knew he wasn't alone.

'What an experience, to stare at your own spilt blood, don't you agree, Ben?' said Jawahal behind his back. 'Like me, your mother's blood can find no rest.'

Ben's hands started to shake, but slowly he turned round. Jawahal was sitting calmly on the end of a metal bench.

'Aren't you going to ask me where your friends are, Ben?' he offered. 'Perhaps you're afraid of getting a discouraging answer.'

'Would you reply if I asked you?' said Ben, standing motionless by the bloodstained shawl.

'Perhaps.' Jawahal smiled.

Ben tried to avoid his hypnotic eyes, and above all he tried to rid himself of the idea that the grim apparition he was speaking to was his father, or what was left of him.

'Having some doubts, are you, Ben?' Jawahal appeared to be enjoying the conversation.

'You're not my father. He would never hurt Sheere,' Ben blurted out nervously.

'Who said I was going to hurt her?'

Ben raised his eyebrows and watched as Jawahal stretched out a gloved hand and dipped it in the blood lying at his feet. Then he touched his face with his fingers, smearing the blood over his angular features.

'One night many years ago, Ben,' said Jawahal, 'the woman whose blood was shed on this spot was my wife and the mother of my children. It's funny to think how memories can sometimes turn into nightmares. I still miss her. Are you surprised? Who do you think your father is, the man who lives in my memory or this lifeless shadow you see in front of you?'

'My father was a good man. You're nothing but a murderer.'

Jawahal looked down and nodded slowly. Ben turned away from him.

'Our time is coming to an end,' said Jawahal. 'We must now confront our destiny. Each to his own. We're all adults now, aren't we? Do you know what maturity means, Ben? Let your father explain. Maturity is simply the process of discovering that everything you believed in when you were young is false and that all the things you refused to believe in turn out to be true. When are you going to mature, son?'

Ben turned and looked at Jawahal.

'What is it you want?' he demanded.

'I want to keep a promise, the promise that keeps my flame alive.'

'What's that?' asked Ben. 'To commit a crime? Is that your farewell deed?'

Jawahal rolled his eyes patiently.

'The difference between a crime and a deed usually depends on the point of view, Ben. My promise is quite simply to find a new home for my soul. And that home will be provided for me by you two. By my children.'

Ben clenched his teeth and felt the blood throbbing in his temples.

'You are not my father,' he said calmly. 'And if you ever were, I am ashamed of that.'

Jawahal gave a paternal smile.

'There are two things in life you cannot choose, Ben. The first is your enemies; the second your family. Sometimes the difference between them is hard to see, but in the end time will show you that the cards you have been dealt could always have been worse. Life, dear son, is like that first game of chess. By the time you begin to understand how the pieces move, you've already lost.'

Ben hurled himself at Jawahal with all the force of his anger. Jawahal remained seated on the end of the bench as the boy passed straight through him, the image vanishing into the air in a swirl of smoke. Ben crashed to the floor and felt his forehead being ripped open by one of the rusty screws that jutted out from the bench.

'One of the things you'll learn soon enough,' said Jawahal's voice behind him, 'is that before fighting your enemy, you must know how his mind works.'

Ben wiped away the blood trickling down his face and turned to look for the voice in the shadows. Jawahal was clearly outlined, sitting on the opposite end of the same bench.

'Nothing is as it seems,' Jawahal continued. 'You should have realised that in the tunnels. When I designed this place, I kept a few surprises up my sleeve. Do you enjoy maths, Ben? Maths is the faith of those with a brain, that is why it has so few followers. It's a shame that neither you nor your gullible friends are ever going to escape from here. You could have told the whole world about some of the mysteries hidden in this building. With a bit of luck, you'd have been repaid with the same mockery, envy and scorn as the inventor himself received.'

'Hatred has blinded you.'

'The only thing hatred has done to me,' replied Jawahal, 'is open my eyes. And you'd better open yours wide because, even if you do take me for a murderer, you're going to discover that you've been given the chance to save yourself and your friends. An opportunity I never had.'

Jawahal rose and walked over to Ben. The boy swallowed hard and was about to run, but Jawahal stopped about two metres away then clasped his hands together and gave a small bow.

'I've enjoyed our conversation, Ben,' he said politely. 'When you've got your breath back, come and find me. It's going to be fun. I promise.'

Before Ben could utter a word, Jawahal's silhouette transformed into a whirlwind of fire that shot across the station at prodigious speed before diving into the tunnels, leaving a garland of flames in its wake.

Ben gave one last look at the bloodstained shawl, then entered the tunnels once more, knowing that this time, whatever route he took, all the passageways would lead to the same point.

THE SHAPE OF THE train emerged from the shadows. Ben gazed at the endless line of carriages, all of them scarred by fire, and for a moment it was as if he was looking at the skeleton of a giant mechanical snake. As he drew closer he recognised the train he thought he'd seen passing through the walls of the orphanage a few nights before, enveloped in flames and transporting the trapped souls of hundreds of children. The train now sat immobile in the dark, and nothing seemed to indicate that his friends were inside. Yet a hunch led him to believe they were. He went past the engine and slowly walked along the row of carriages, searching for them.

Halfway along, he stopped to look back and saw that the head of the train was already lost in shadow. As he was about to resume his walk, he noticed a face pale as death staring at him from one of the windows of the nearest carriage.

He turned his head abruptly and his heart skipped a beat. A boy of about seven was watching him attentively with penetrating dark eyes. Ben took a step in his direction. The boy opened his lips and flames issued forth, setting fire to the image which then crumbled in front of Ben like a piece of dry paper. Ben felt an icy cold settle on the nape of his neck as he continued walking, ignoring the horrific murmur of voices that seemed to be coming from some hidden place within the train.

When he finally reached the guard's van he walked up to the door and pushed the handle. Inside, hundreds of candles were burning. Ben stepped inside and the faces of Isobel, Ian, Seth, Michael, Roshan and Siraj lit up with hope. Ben gave a sigh of relief.

'Now we're all here, maybe we can start the game,' said a familiar voice next to him.

Ben turned and saw Jawahal's arms locked round his sister. The door of the van slid shut, like an armour-plated hatch, and Jawahal let go of Sheere, who ran over to Ben.

'Are you all right?' he asked, hugging her.

'Of course she's all right,' Jawahal snapped.

'Are all of you all right?' Ben asked the members of the Chowbar Society, who were handcuffed on the floor.

'Perfectly fine,' Ian confirmed.

They exchanged a look that spoke volumes. Ben nodded.

'If any of you has the slightest scratch,' Jawahal said, 'it's only due to your own clumsiness.'

Ben turned to Jawahal, moving Sheere to one side.

'Tell us what you want.'

Jawahal looked surprised.

'Nervous, Ben? In a hurry to get it over with? I've waited sixteen years for this moment; I can wait a little longer. Especially now that Sheere and I are enjoying our new relationship.'

The possibility that Jawahal had revealed his identity to Sheere was gnawing at Ben. Jawahal seemed to read his mind.

'Don't listen to him, Ben,' said Sheere. 'This man killed our father. Whatever he says is as worthless as the dirt covering this dump.'

'Harsh words to say about a friend,' Jawahal remarked.

'I'd rather die than be your friend.'

'Our friendship, Sheere, is only a matter of time,' Jawahal whispered.

His smile suddenly disappeared, and at a signal from his hand, Sheere was sent flying towards the other end of the van, as if she'd been hit by an invisible battering ram.

'Now get some rest. Soon we'll be together for ever …'

Sheere crashed against the metal wall and fell unconscious to the ground. Ben rushed towards her, but the iron pressure of Jawahal's hand restrained him.

'You're not going anywhere,' he said. Then, throwing an icy glance at the others, he added, 'The next person to say anything will have his lips sealed by fire.'

'Let go of me,' groaned Ben. He felt as if the hand

holding him by the scruff of the neck was about to dislocate his vertebrae.

Suddenly Jawahal let go, and Ben collapsed on the floor.

'Get up and listen to me,' Jawahal ordered. 'I hear you have some kind of secret fraternity in which you've sworn to protect one another until death. Is that right?'

'It is,' said Siraj from the floor.

An invisible fist hit the boy hard, knocking him over like a rag doll.

'I didn't ask you, boy. Ben, are you going to reply, or shall we play a little game with your friend's asthma?'

'Leave him alone. It's true,' replied Ben.

'Good. Then allow me to congratulate you on the fabulous job you've done so far by bringing your friends here. First-class protection.'

'You said you'd give us a chance,' Ben reminded him.

'I know what I said. How much do you value the life of your friends, Ben?'

The boy turned pale.

'Do you not understand the question, or do you want me to discover the answer in some other way?'

'I value their lives as I value my own.'

Jawahal gave a fiendish grin.

'I find that hard to believe.'

'I don't care what you believe.'

'Then let's see if your fine words tally with reality,' said Jawahal. 'I promised this was going to be fun, so here's the deal. There are seven of you, not counting Sheere. She's out of the game. For each one of you, there's a closed box containing ... a mystery.'

Jawahal pointed to a row of wooden boxes painted different colours that resembled a set of small letter boxes.

'Each one has a hole in the front that allows you to stick your hand in, but you can't remove it for a few seconds. It's like a trap for inquisitive people. Imagine that each one of these boxes contains the life of one of your friends, Ben. In fact, that's true, for in each one there's a small wooden board bearing a name. You can put your hand in and remove it. Every time you pull out someone's name, I will free them. But, of course, there's a risk. One of the boxes, instead of life, holds death.'

'What do you mean by that?' asked Ben.

'Have you ever seen an asp, Ben? A small beast with a volatile temper. Do you know anything about snakes?'

'I know what an asp is,' replied Ben, feeling weak.

'Then I'll spare you the details. All you need to know is that one of the boxes contains an asp.'

'Don't do it, Ben,' said Ian.

Jawahal gave him an evil stare.

'Ben, I'm waiting. I don't think anyone in the whole of Calcutta could make you a more generous offer. Seven lives and only one possibility for error.'

'How do I know you're not lying?' asked Ben.

Jawahal raised a long forefinger and slowly shook his head.

'Lying is one of the few things I don't do, Ben. You should know that. Make up your mind. If you don't have the courage to play the game and prove that your friends are as valuable to you as you would lead us to believe, say so now and we'll let someone with more guts take their chances.'

Ben held Jawahal's gaze and nodded.

'Ben, no,' Ian said again.

'Tell your friend to shut up, Ben,' Jawahal said. 'Or I will.'

'Don't make it more difficult, Ian,' Ben pleaded.

'Ian is right, Ben,' said Isobel. 'If he wants to kill us, let *him* do it. Don't allow yourself to be tricked.'

Ben raised a hand for silence and turned to face Jawahal.

'Do I have your word?'

Jawahal looked at Ben long and hard and finally nodded in assent.

'Then let's not waste any more time.'

BEN EXAMINED THE SEVEN wooden boxes carefully, trying to imagine in which one of them Jawahal would have hidden the snake. Attempting to decipher the thinking behind the arrangement of colours was like trying to reconstruct a puzzle without being familiar with the image it formed. The asp could be in one of the boxes at the end or in one in the middle, in one of the brightly coloured boxes or the one with shiny black paint. Guesswork was superfluous, and Ben realised his mind had gone blank faced with the decision he had to take.

'The first is the most difficult,' whispered Jawahal. 'Choose without thinking.'

All Ben could see in Jawahal's impenetrable eyes was the reflection of his own pale frightened face. He silently counted to three, closed his eyes and quickly thrust his hand into one of the boxes. The seconds that followed seemed interminable, as he waited to feel the rough touch of a scaly body, followed by the sting of the asp's fangs. None of that happened; after an agonising few moments, his fingers touched a wooden board and Jawahal gave him a smile.

'Well chosen. Black. The colour of the future.'

Ben pulled out the board and read the name written on it. Siraj. He looked enquiringly at Jawahal, who nodded. They all heard the click of the handcuffs restraining the frail boy.

'Siraj,' said Ben. 'Leave this train and get out of here.'

Siraj rubbed his aching wrists and looked sadly at his friends.

'I have no intention of leaving,' he replied.

'Do as Ben says, Siraj,' said Ian, trying to control his tone of voice.

Siraj shook his head. Isobel tried to smile.

'Siraj, go,' she pleaded. 'Do it for me.'

The boy hesitated.

'We don't have all night,' said Jawahal. 'Either you leave or you stay. Only idiots turn down a piece of good luck. And tonight you've used up your life's supply.'

'Siraj!' ordered Ben. 'Just go! Give me some help.'

Siraj looked desperately at Ben, but his friend's expression remained unflinching. At last Siraj bowed his head in assent and walked over to the heavy metal door.

'Don't stop until you reach the river,' instructed Jawahal, 'or you'll be sorry.'

'He won't,' Ben replied for him.

'I'll wait for you,' Siraj called from the steps of the van.

'See you soon, Siraj. Now go.'

The boy's footsteps could be heard receding down the tunnel. Jawahal raised his eyebrows to indicate that the game should continue.

'I've kept my promise, Ben. Now it's your turn. There are fewer boxes. It's easier to choose. Make up your mind and another of your friends could soon be saved.'

Ben's eyes rested on the box next to the one he'd chosen. It was as good as any other. Slowly he stretched out his hand and paused when he was almost touching the flap.

'Are you sure, Ben?' asked Jawahal.

Ben looked at him in exasperation.

'Think twice. Your first choice was perfect; don't go and ruin it now.'

Ben smiled scornfully at him and, without taking his eyes off Jawahal, he thrust his hand into the box. Jawahal's pupils narrowed like those of a cat. Ben pulled out the wooden board and read the name.

'Seth,' he said, 'get out of here.'

Seth's handcuffs opened immediately and the boy stood up.

'I don't like this, Ben.'

'I like it even less than you do,' Ben answered. 'Now leave, and make sure Siraj doesn't get lost.'

Seth nodded gravely, aware that the alternative to following Ben's instructions might put everyone's lives at risk. He gave his friends a farewell wave and headed for the door. When he got there he turned and looked at all the members of the Chowbar Society.

'We'll survive this one, do you hear me?'

His friends nodded with as much hope as the law of probability permitted.

'As for you, sir,' said Seth, pointing at Jawahal, 'you're nothing but a pile of dung.'

Jawahal licked his lips.

'It's easy to play the hero when you're about to abandon your friends to a certain death, isn't it, Seth? You can insult me again if you like; I'm not going to do anything to you. It might even help you sleep better when you remember this night and when some of those present have become food for worms. You can always tell people that you, brave Seth, insulted the villain, can't you? But,

267

deep down, you and I both know the truth, don't we, Seth?'

Seth's face reddened with anger and his eyes flashed with hatred. He began to walk towards Jawahal, but Ben threw himself in the way.

'Please, Seth,' he whispered in his ear. 'Go now. Please.'

Seth gave Ben one last look and nodded, pressing his arm firmly. Ben waited for his friend to leave then confronted Jawahal once again.

'This wasn't part of the deal,' Ben reproached him. 'I'm not going to continue if you keep tormenting my friends.'

'You'll do it whether you want to or not. You have no alternative. Still, as a gesture of goodwill, I'll keep my comments on your friends to myself. Now continue.'

Ben stared at the five remaining boxes. His eyes rested on the one on the far right. Without further ado, he stuck his hand in and groped about inside. Another board. Ben took a deep breath and heard a sigh of relief from his friends.

'There's an angel watching over you, Ben,' said Jawahal. The boy looked at the wooden rectangle.

'Isobel.'

'The lady's in luck,' remarked Jawahal.

'Shut up,' muttered Ben, fed up with the comments Jawahal seemed to enjoy making with each new move in the macabre game. 'Isobel, see you soon.'

Isobel stood up and walked past her friends, her head bowed and her feet dragging as if they were stuck to the floor.

'No last word for Michael, Isobel?' asked Jawahal.

'Leave it,' Ben implored. 'What do you expect to achieve out of all this?'

'Choose another box,' replied Jawahal. 'Then you'll see what I'm hoping to achieve.'

As Isobel stepped down from the van, Ben considered the four remaining boxes.

'Have you decided, Ben?' asked Jawahal.

The boy nodded and stood in front of the box that was painted red.

'Red. The colour of passion,' Jawahal remarked. 'And of fire. Go ahead, Ben. I think tonight's your lucky night.'

AS SHEERE OPENED HER eyes she saw Ben approaching the red box, his arm outstretched. A stab of panic ripped through her body. She sat up abruptly and hurled herself towards Ben as quickly as she could – she couldn't let her brother put his hand in that box. The lives of those boys were meaningless to Jawahal; they were nothing but a convenient way of pushing Ben towards his own destruction. Jawahal needed Ben to hand over his own death willingly in order to clear a path for him. That way the accursed spirit could enter her and escape from those dark tunnels; be reincarnated in a being of flesh and blood.

Sheere had realised there was just one option remaining, one sole action capable of ruining the puzzle

Jawahal had constructed around them. Only she could alter the course of events, doing the one thing in the universe that Jawahal had not foreseen.

The moments that followed became etched in her mind like a series of minutely detailed sketches.

Sheere covered the six metres that separated her from her brother at breakneck speed, avoiding the remaining three members of the Chowbar Society, who lay manacled on the floor. As Ben turned round, his first look was of confusion and surprise, then of horror. Jawahal had risen and each finger of his right hand was ablaze, transforming it into a fiery claw. Sheere heard Ben's scream fade into a distant echo as she crashed against him, pushing him down and pulling his hand away from the hole in the red box. Ben fell to the floor and Sheere saw Jawahal rising above her, stretching out his burning claw towards her face. She fixed her eyes on the eyes of the murderer and read the despairing refusal taking shape on his lips. Time seemed to stand still around her.

Tenths of a second later Sheere was thrusting her hand through the opening in the scarlet box. She felt the flap close over her wrist like the petals of a poisonous flower. Ben yelled out and Jawahal clenched his fiery fist in his face, but Sheere smiled triumphantly and at some point she felt the asp strike her with its mortal kiss. The blast of poison lit up the blood running through her veins like a spark igniting a stream of petrol.

BEN PUT HIS ARMS round his sister and pulled her hand out of the red box, but it was already too late. Two bleeding puncture wounds shone on the pale skin on the back of her wrist. Sheere gave a brief smile as she began to lose consciousness.

'I'm fine,' she mumbled, but before she could utter another syllable her body started shaking, her legs gave way and she collapsed on top of him.

'Sheere!' shouted Ben.

He felt an indescribable nausea take hold of his whole being and the strength seemed to be running out of his body. He held Sheere and settled her on his lap, stroking her face.

Sheere opened her eyes and smiled weakly, her face as white as chalk.

'It doesn't hurt, Ben,' she whispered.

Each of her words felt like a kick to the stomach. Ben looked up in search of Jawahal. The spectre was observing the scene, his expression impenetrable. Their eyes met.

'I never planned it this way, Ben,' he said. 'This is going to complicate matters.'

Ben felt the anger growing inside him like an enormous crack, parting his soul in two.

'You're nothing but a murderer,' he muttered.

Jawahal took one last look at Sheere, who was trembling

in Ben's arms, and shook his head. His thoughts seemed to be far away.

'Now only you and I remain, Ben,' said Jawahal. 'It's heads or tails. Say goodbye to her then come in search of your revenge.'

Jawahal's face was suddenly swathed in a veil of flames and he turned away, passing through the door that connected the guard's van to the rest of the train and leaving behind a breach that dripped with red-hot steel.

Ben heard a crunch as the lock on Ian, Michael and Roshan's handcuffs was released. Ian ran over and, grabbing hold of Sheere's arm, he brought her wound to his mouth. He sucked hard and spat out the poisoned blood, which burnt his tongue. Michael and Roshan knelt down in front of the girl and looked at Ben in despair. He was cursing himself for having allowed precious seconds to go by without realising that he should have done what his friend was doing now.

Ben raised his eyes and noticed the trail of flames Jawahal had left behind him, melting the metal like a cigar burning through paper. The train gave a sudden jolt and began to move through the tunnel as the engine's thunderous roar filled the labyrinth of Jheeter's Gate. Ben looked intently at Ian.

'Take care of her.'

'No, Ben,' Ian pleaded, reading Ben's thoughts. 'Don't go.'

Ben hugged his sister and kissed her on the forehead.

'Will you return to say goodbye to me?' she asked with a trembling voice.

Tears were welling in Ben's eyes.

'I love you, Ben,' she whispered.

'And I love you,' he replied, realising he'd never said those words to anyone before.

The train began to accelerate furiously through the tunnel. Ben ran to the door and jumped through the fresh breach in the metal in pursuit of Jawahal.

As he raced through the next carriage he realised that Michael and Roshan were behind him. Quickly, he stopped on the platform separating the last two carriages, pulled out the bolt that coupled them together and flung it into the void. For a split second Roshan's fingers brushed Ben's hand, but when Ben looked up again, the despairing eyes of his friends had been left behind as the train carried him and Jawahal at full pelt towards the dark heart of Jheeter's Gate. Now only the two of them remained.

WITH EVERY STEP BEN took, the train gathered speed in its descent into the tunnels. The vibrations threw him off balance as he lurched through the carriage, following the glowing trail of Jawahal's footsteps. Ben managed to reach the next connecting platform, holding firmly on to the metal handrail just as the train rounded a crescent-shaped bend and plunged down a slope that seemed to lead to the very bowels of the earth. With another jolt, the train speeded up, careering into the darkness. Ben straightened up and resumed his pursuit of Jawahal as the wheels of the train produced a shower of sparks from the rails.

There was a small explosion beneath his feet and Ben noticed that thick tongues of fire were now flickering along the entire skeleton of the train, tearing away any remnants of charred wood. Flames also fractured the shards of glass that still surrounded the windows, and Ben had to throw himself to the floor to avoid the storm of glass splinters cascading off the walls of the tunnel.

When he was able to stand up, he saw Jawahal advancing through the flames and realised he was very close to the engine. Jawahal turned, and even through a new series of explosions that sent rings of blue fire swirling through the train Ben could make out his criminal smile.

'Come and get me,' he heard in his thoughts.

Sheere's face came alive in Ben's mind, and he began to claw his way towards the last remaining carriage. When he crossed the connecting platform he felt a gust of fresh air; the train must be about to leave the tunnels, he thought. They were heading straight towards the centre of Jheeter's Gate.

IAN DIDN'T STOP TALKING to Sheere during the whole of their return journey. He knew that if she abandoned herself to the sleep that was laying siege to her body, she'd barely live long enough to see the light beyond those tunnels. Michael and Roshan helped him to carry Sheere, but neither of them managed to get a word out of her. Ignoring the anguish that was consuming him and burying it in the depths of his soul, Ian told her amusing anecdotes and made witty remarks, mining every last word in his brain just to keep her awake. Sheere listened to him and moved her head slightly, half-opening her glazed sleepy eyes. Ian held her hand between his, feeling her pulse as it weakened, slowly but inexorably.

'Where's Ben?' she asked.

Michael looked at Ian, who smiled broadly.

'Ben is safe, Sheere. He's gone to fetch a doctor, which, in the circumstances, I find insulting. I'm supposed to be the doctor here! At least I will be one day. What kind of a friend is that? It's not exactly encouraging. At the first sign of trouble he disappears in search of a doctor. Luckily, there aren't many doctors like me. It's something you're born with. That's why I know, instinctively, that you'll get better. On one condition: if you don't fall asleep. You're not asleep, are you? You can't fall asleep now! Your grandmother is waiting for us two hundred metres from here and there's no way I can tell her what happened. If I try, she'll throw me into the Hooghly, and

I have a boat to catch in a few hours' time. So please stay awake and help me with your grandmother. All right? Say something.'

Sheere started to pant heavily. All the colour drained from Ian's face and he shook her. Sheere's eyes opened again.

'Where's Jawahal?' she asked.

'He's dead,' lied Ian.

'How did he die?'

Ian hesitated for a moment.

'He fell under the wheels of the train. There was nothing we could do.'

'You don't know how to lie, Ian,' she whispered, struggling with each word.

Ian felt he might not be able to go on pretending much longer.

'The accomplished liar in the group is Ben,' he said. 'I always tell the truth. Jawahal is dead.'

Sheere closed her eyes. Ian told Michael and Roshan to quicken their pace. Half a minute later they reached the end of the tunnel and could see the station clock silhouetted in the distance. When they got there, Siraj, Isobel and Seth were waiting for them. The first rays of dawn were appearing, a crimson line on the horizon, beyond the large metal arches of Jheeter's Gate.

∾

BEN STOPPED AT THE entrance to the engine and placed his hand on the wheel that locked the door. The ring was burning hot so he had to turn it slowly, the metal biting into his skin. A cloud of steam was exhaled as Ben kicked open the door, but through the humidity Ben could see Jawahal standing by the boilers and gazing silently at him. Ben looked at the machinery and noticed a symbol carved on the metal: a bird rising from the flames. Jawahal's hand was resting on the top of one of the boilers, seemingly absorbing the power that blazed within. Ben peered at the complex framework of pipes, valves and gas tanks.

'In another life I was an inventor,' said Jawahal. 'My hands and my mind could create things; now they only destroy them. This is my soul, Ben. Come closer and you'll see your father's heart beating. I created it myself. Do you know why I called it the Firebird?'

Ben stared at Jawahal without replying.

'Thousands of years ago there was a doomed city almost as wretched as Calcutta,' Jawahal explained. 'It was called Carthage. When the Romans conquered it, such was the hatred aroused in them by the spirited Phoenicians, they were not content with ravaging the town or murdering its women, men and children; the Romans also had to destroy every stone, reducing it to dust. Yet even that wasn't enough to placate their loathing. That is why Cato, the general in charge of the Roman troops, ordered his soldiers to sprinkle salt through every crack in the city, so that not a single sign of life could grow from its accursed soil.'

'Why are you telling me all this?' asked Ben. The sweat was pouring down his body then instantly drying due to the suffocating heat spat out by the boilers.

'That city was home to a divinity called Dido, a princess who had sacrificed her body to the fire in order to appease the gods and cleanse herself of her sins. But she returned and was transformed into a goddess. That is the power of fire. Just like the story of the phoenix, the powerful bird whose flight fanned the flames.'

Jawahal stroked the machinery of his lethal creation and smiled.

'I've also been reborn from the ashes and, like Cato, I intend to destroy every last shred of my destiny, this time with fire.'

'You're a lunatic,' Ben said, interrupting him. 'Especially if you think you're going to be able to get inside me to stay alive.'

'Who are the lunatics?' asked Jawahal. 'The ones who see horror in the heart of their fellow humans and search for peace at any price? Or the ones who pretend they don't see what's going on around them? The world, Ben, belongs either to lunatics or hypocrites. There are no other races on this earth. You must choose which one to belong to.'

Ben stared at Jawahal for a long while, and for the first time the boy thought he could see the shadow of the man who had once been his father.

'Which did you choose, Father? Which did you choose when you returned to sow death among the few people who loved you? Have you forgotten your own words? Have you forgotten the story you wrote about the man whose tears turned to ice when he returned home and saw that everyone had sold themself to the travelling sorcerer? Perhaps you can take my life too, just as you've taken the lives of all those who crossed your path. I don't suppose it would make much difference any more. But, before you do, tell me face to face that you didn't sell your soul to the sorcerer too. Tell me, with your hand on that heart of fire you hide yourself in, and I'll follow you to hell itself.'

Jawahal's eyelids drooped as he slowly nodded his head. A gradual transformation seemed to creep over his face, and his eyes paled in the burning steam. Defeated and dejected. It was the look of a great wounded predator withdrawing to die in the shadows. And that sudden image of vulnerability, which Ben glimpsed for only a few seconds, seemed more horrifying than any of the previous incarnations of the tormented spectre, because in that image, in that face consumed by pain and fire, Ben could no longer see the spirit of a murderer, only the sad reflection of the man who had been his father.

For a moment they stared at one another like old acquaintances lost in the mists of time.

'I no longer know whether I wrote that story or some

other man did, Ben,' Jawahal said at last. 'I no longer know whether those memories are mine or I dreamed them. I don't know whether I committed those crimes, or whether they were the work of other hands. Whatever the answer to these questions may be, I know I'll never be able to write another story like the one you remember, or understand its meaning. I have no future, Ben. I have no life either. What you see is only the shadow of a dead soul. I am nothing. The man I was, your father, died a long time ago, taking with him everything I might have dreamed of. And if you're not going to give me your soul, then at least give me peace. Because only you can give me back my freedom. You came to kill someone who is already dead, Ben. Keep your word, or else join me in the shadows ...'

At that moment the train emerged from the tunnel and passed through the central track of Jheeter's Gate, casting forth its blanket of flames. The locomotive went under the tall arches that formed the entrance to the metal construction and continued along a line seemingly sculpted by the first light of dawn.

Jawahal raised his eyes, and Ben saw in them all the horror and profound loneliness that imprisoned his soul.

As the train crossed the few remaining metres towards the fallen bridge, Ben put his hand in his pocket and pulled out the matchbox containing the single match he had saved. Jawahal thrust his hand into the boiler and a cloud of pure oxygen enveloped him. Slowly he seemed to fuse with the machinery that housed his soul, the gas tinting his outline the colour of ashes. Jawahal gave Ben one last look and Ben thought he could see the gleam of a solitary tear gliding down his face.

'Free me, Ben,' murmured the voice in his mind. 'It's now or never.'

The boy pulled out the match and struck it.

'Goodbye, Father,' he whispered.

Lahawaj Chandra Chatterghee lowered his head as Ben threw the lighted match at his feet.

'Goodbye, Ben.'

At that moment, for a fleeting second, the boy felt the presence of another face – a face wreathed in a veil of light. As the river of flames spread towards his father, those other deep sad eyes looked at him for the last time. Ben thought his mind was playing tricks on him when he recognised the same wounded look as he'd seen in Sheere's eyes. Then the Princess of Light was engulfed for ever by the flames, her hand raised and a faint smile on her lips, without Ben ever suspecting who it was that had just disappeared into the fire.

∾

LIKE AN INVISIBLE TORRENT of water, the blast flung Ben's body to the far end of the engine and out of the blazing train. As he fell, he tumbled through the scrub that had grown up alongside the rails. The train continued its journey following the track on its lethal route towards the chasm. Ben jumped up and ran after it. Seconds later, the cab in which his father was travelling exploded with such force that the metal girders of the collapsed bridge were thrown into the sky. A pyre of flames rose towards the stormy clouds like a fiery bolt of lightning, transforming the heavens into a mirror of light.

The train leaped into the void, a snake of steel and flames crashing into the black waters of the Hooghly. A thunderous blast shook the skies over Calcutta and beneath the city the ground trembled.

The last breath of the Firebird was extinguished, taking with it, for ever, the soul of its creator, Lahawaj Chandra Chatterghee.

Ben fell to his knees between the rails as his friends ran towards him from the entrance to Jheeter's Gate. Hundreds of small white tears seemed to be falling from the sky. Ben looked up and felt the drops on his face. It was snowing.

THE MEMBERS OF THE Chowbar Society met for the last time that dawn in May 1932 by the vanished bridge on the banks of the Hooghly River opposite the ruins of Jheeter's Gate. A curtain of falling snow awoke the city of Calcutta, where nobody had ever seen the white mantle that was beginning to cover the domes of the old palaces, the alleyways and the immensity of the Maidan.

As the city's inhabitants stepped out into the streets to gaze at the miracle, the members of the Chowbar Society walked up to the bridge and left Sheere alone with Ben. They had all survived the events of that night. They had witnessed the descent of the flaming train into the void and seen the explosion of fire rising high into the sky, slicing through the storm like a blade. They knew they might never talk about the events of that night again and that, if they ever did, nobody would believe them. And yet, that dawn, they all understood that they had only been guests, random passengers in a train that had emerged from the past. Shortly afterwards they looked on in silence as Ben embraced his sister beneath the falling snow. Gradually, the day pushed away the darkness of a night without end.

~

SHEERE FELT THE COLD touch of snow on her cheeks and opened her eyes. Her brother Ben was cradling her, gently stroking her face.

'What's this, Ben?'

'It's snow,' he replied. 'It's snowing over Calcutta.'

The girl's face lit up for a moment.

'Have I ever told you what my dream is?'

'To see snow fall over London,' said Ben. 'I remember. Next year we'll go there together. We'll visit Ian. He'll be there studying medicine. It will snow every day. I promise.'

'Do you remember our father's story, Ben? The one I told you the night I went to the Midnight Palace?'

Ben nodded.

'These are the tears of Shiva, Ben. They'll melt when the sun rises and will never fall on Calcutta again.'

Ben gently sat his sister up and smiled at her. Sheere's deep pearly eyes watched him carefully.

'I'm going to die, aren't I?'

'No,' said Ben. 'You're not going to die for years and years. Your lifeline is very long. See?'

'Ben …' Sheere groaned. 'It was the only thing I could do. I did it for us.'

He hugged her tightly.

'I know,' he murmured.

Sheere tried to push herself up and bring her lips closer to Ben's ear.

'Don't let me die alone,' she whispered.

Ben hid his face from his sister and pressed her against him.

'Never.'

They remained like that, hugging each other quietly

under the snow until Sheere's pulse slowly faded like a flame in the breeze. Little by little the clouds receded towards the west and the light of dawn melted away the veil of white tears that had covered the city.

© Jackie Freshfield

THOSE PLACES WHERE SADNESS AND MISERY abound are favoured settings for stories of ghosts and apparitions. Calcutta has countless such stories hidden in its darkness, stories that nobody wants to admit they believe but which nevertheless survive in the memory of generations as the only chronicle of the past. It is as if the people who inhabit the streets, inspired by some mysterious wisdom, realise that the true history of Calcutta has always been written in the invisible tales of its spirits and unspoken curses.

Maybe it was this same wisdom that lit Lahawaj Chandra Chatterghee's path during his final moments, making him realise that he had fallen inexorably into the prison of his own damnation. Perhaps, in the deep solitude of a soul condemned to revisit, time and time again, the wounds of the past, he was able to understand the real value of the lives he had destroyed, and of all the lives he could yet save. It's hard to know what he saw in his son's face seconds before he allowed him to put out the flames of bitterness that blazed in the Firebird's boilers. Perhaps, in the midst of his madness, he was able, for one brief second, to muster the sanity that his tormentors had stolen from him ever since his days in Grant House.

The answers to all these questions, as well as his secrets, discoveries, dreams and expectations, disappeared for ever in the terrible explosion that split the skies over Calcutta at daybreak on 28 May 1932, like the snowflakes that melted even as they kissed the ground.

Whatever the truth may be, I must record that, shortly after the burning train sank into the Hooghly, the pool of fresh blood that had housed the tormented spirit of the twins' mother evaporated. I knew then that the soul of Lahawaj Chandra Chatterghee and that of the woman who had been his companion would rest in eternal peace. Never again would I see in my dreams the sad eyes of the Princess of Light leaning over my friend Ben.

I haven't seen my friends in all the years since I boarded the ship that was to take me to England that very afternoon. I remember their frightened faces when they said goodbye to me on the wharf on the Hooghly River as the boat weighed anchor. I remember the promises we made to stay in touch and never to forget what we had witnessed. I have to admit that, even then, I realised that our words would be lost in the ship's wake as soon as it departed under the flaming Bengali sun.

They were all there, except for Ben. But none was as present in our hearts as he was.

When I look back on those days, I feel that each and every one of my friends lives on in a corner of my soul, a corner that was sealed for ever that afternoon in Calcutta. A place where we all continue to be sixteen years old and where the spirit of the Chowbar Society and the Midnight Palace will remain alive as long as I do.

As for the fate that awaited each of us, time has effaced the footprints of many of my companions. I learned that after some years Seth succeeded the rotund Mr de Rozio as head librarian and archivist of the Indian Museum, and that in doing so he became the youngest man ever to hold that post.

I also had news of Isobel, who married Michael years later. Their marriage lasted five years, and after their separation Isobel went off to travel round the world with a small theatre company. The passing of the years didn't prevent her from keeping her dreams alive. I don't know what has become of her. Michael, who lives in Florence, where he teaches drawing in a secondary school, never saw her again. To this day I still hope to spot her name topping the bill at some show.

Siraj passed away in 1946 after spending the last five years of his life in a Bombay prison, accused of a theft which, until his dying day, he swore he didn't commit. As Jawahal predicted, what little luck he'd had abandoned him that day.

Roshan is now a prosperous and powerful businessman, owner of a good number of the old streets around the Black Town, where he grew up as a beggar without a roof over his head. He's the only one who, year after year, keeps up the ritual of sending me a birthday letter. I know from his letters that he married and that the number of grandchildren who run around his properties isn't far off the figures that make up his fortune.

As for me, life has been generous and has allowed me to journey through this strange passage to nowhere in peace and without hardship. Shortly after I finished my studies, I was offered a post in Dr Walter Hartley's hospital in Whitechapel. It was there that I really learned the job I'd always dreamed of and which still earns me my living today. Twenty years ago, after the death of my wife Iris, I moved to Bournemouth, where my home and my surgery occupy a small comfortable house with a view over the salt marshes of Poole Bay. My only company since Iris departed has been her memory and the secret I once shared with my companions in the Chowbar Society.

Again, I've left Ben to the end. Even today, although I haven't seen him for over fifty years, I still find it hard to talk about the person who was and always will be my best friend. Thanks to Roshan I heard that he went to live in what had once been his father's house – the house of Chandra Chatterghee, the engineer. He moved there with Aryami Bose, who never quite recovered from Sheere's death and was plunged into a long deep melancholy that would eventually close her eyes for ever in October 1941. From that day on Ben lived and worked alone in the house his father had built. It was there that he wrote his books until the year he disappeared without a trace.

One December morning, years after we all, including Roshan, had given him up for dead, I was standing on the little dock opposite my house, gazing out at the marshland, when I received a small parcel. It had been postmarked by the Calcutta Post Office and my name was written in handwriting I could never forget, even if I lived to be a hundred. Inside, wrapped in layers of paper, I found half of the pendant shaped like a sun that Aryami Bose had divided in two when she separated Ben and Sheere that tragic night in 1916.

This morning, as I sit writing the last words of this memoir in the early light of dawn, the first snow of the year has spread its white mantle before my window and the memory of Ben has come back to me, after all these years, like the echo of a whisper. I imagine him walking in the crowds, through the fevered streets of Calcutta, among a thousand untold stories such as his own, and for the first time I realise that my friend, like me, is now an old man and that his journey is about to complete its circle. It is so strange to think how life has slipped through our fingers ...

I don't know whether I'll ever hear of my friend Ben again. But I do know that in some part of the mysterious Black Town the boy I said goodbye to that morning when it snowed in Calcutta lives on, keeping the flame of

Sheere's memory alive, dreaming of the moment when at last he'll be reunited with her in a world where nothing and no one can ever separate them.

I hope you will find her, my friend.

The Midnight Palace
Reading Group Notes

© Jackie Freshfield

In Brief

May 1916

Lieutenant Peake rested a moment on his oars – but just for a moment. He knew he had only a short time left to live, perhaps minutes, and he had to get his charges to safety. Behind him in the mist loomed the outline of Jheeter's Gate Station, where he had been forced to leave the woman he had sworn to protect. But he would not leave her children – they were hidden in the bilge and were crying with cold and hunger – and he rowed on towards Calcutta.

The storm broke as he reached the bank, and rain lashed down on him and the babies clutched to his chest. The violent electrical storm broke the stifling heat of the Indian summer, and the temperature tumbled thirty degrees. Through the rain Peake saw the boat holding his relentless pursuers closing on the shore behind him – and he ran.

Peake hurried towards the streets known as White Town – his one remaining hope was to get the children to the house of Aryami Bose – but it was a long way to the heart of North Calcutta and his enemies were close behind him.

Somehow Peake kept ahead of them and reached the home of the last woman in the Bose family line. Peake had to pound on the gates for what seemed an age before he was heard through the storm, and he saw Aryami's face appear, illuminated by the candle she was holding. 'She was already dead when I got there,' was all he could say. After momentarily closing her eyes, she moved aside to let him in. He stayed long enough for the babies to be settled by the warming fire, before he once more slipped into the night. As he had no more reason to live, he moved towards his fate in the pounding storm.

Aryami took a pendant from a box belonging to her daughter. Aryami had had it made for her daughter years before, but somehow she had never had a chance to wear it. Aryami pressed the centre, and the pendant separated into two parts, which she placed around the necks of the two babies. She had only one chance of keeping them alive – they must be separated. Their beginnings must be erased and they could never be together. No matter how painful, it must be done. Taking only one, she headed out into the storm.

May 1932

Ben looked intently at the girl who was waiting at the main entrance to St Patrick's. The woman she had arrived with had clearly gone in to see the head, Mr Carter. Mr Carter's arid social life as head of the orphanage made a visit by anyone so close to midnight unheard of, let alone a woman with a pretty girl in tow.

Ben was shaken from his thoughts by the other members of the Chowbar Society. It would soon be the end of their mutual support club, as they were all reaching the age of sixteen when they would be set loose on an unsuspecting world. This momentous meeting should not have been interrupted by a woman and a mysterious girl – but Ben was drawn inexorably to the girl. She told him her name was Sheere, and he found himself inviting her along to their meeting. Reluctantly drawn from the spot where her grandmother had left her, Sheere followed the others to the

Midnight Palace, where all their meetings were held.

As Sheere told her story and became a member of the group, they were all drawn into the terrible storm that was approaching as the events of sixteen years before caught up with them. The ruin of Jheeter's Gate station would prove to be the epicentre of the storm, and whilst the horrific events of 1916 were still all too fresh, new terrors would be unleashed on the Chowbar Society members, not all of whom would emerge to tell the tale . . .

About the Author

Carlos Ruiz Zafón is the author of six novels, including the international phenomenon *The Shadow of the Wind* and *The Angel's Game*. His work has been published in more than forty different languages and honoured with numerous international awards. He divides his time between Barcelona, Spain, and Los Angeles, California.

For Discussion

- 'You could spend a hundred years in this city and not understand half of what goes on here.' How has the author created such a strong sense of place in the novel?

- 'Most likely a bank. Isn't that what they always build when they knock something down in any city?' What does this tell us about society, and Ben's view of it?

- 'Michael always looks at what others don't see.' What does this tell us about Michael – what sort of boy is he?

- 'We had yet to learn that the Devil created youth so that we could make our mistakes, and that God established maturity and old age so that we could pay for them . . .' Is this your experience?

- Is hatred more powerful than love?

- 'The fact is that nothing is more difficult to believe than the truth.' Is this a recurring theme in *The Midnight Palace*?

- 'Nothing seduces like the power of lies.' True, do you think?

- 'Whoever said that childhood is the happiest time of your life is a liar, or a fool.' Do you agree? Was childhood the happiest time of your life?

- 'The main difference between a man and a woman is that the man always puts his stomach before his heart and a woman does the opposite.' Is that the main difference?

- Is it acceptable to lie to protect someone?

- 'In the book of life it is perhaps best not to turn back pages.' Can we help ourselves?

- 'We always fear what resembles us most.' True, do you think? How does this apply to the novel as a whole?

- 'Maturity is simply the process of discovering that everything you believed in when you were young is false and all the things you refused to believe in turn out to be true.' Is this your experience? To what extent is this the theme of the novel?

Suggested Further Reading

American Gods by Neil Gaiman

■

Harry Potter and the Deathly Hallows
by J. K. Rowling

■

The Ruby in the Smoke by Philip Pullman

■

A Study in Scarlet by Sir Arthur Conan Doyle

■

David Copperfield by Charles Dickens

■

Jack Cloudie by Stephen Hunt

© Jackie Freshfield

The PRISONER OF HEAVEN

CARLOS RUIZ ZAFÓN

Translated by Lucia Graves

Available now in paperback, ebook and audio from
Weidenfeld & Nicolson

I have always known that one day I would return to these streets to tell the story of the man who lost his soul among the shadows of that Barcelona of long ago whose name lay buried amid the ashes and silence of a city of troubled dreams. This is a story born in the city of the damned, its words etched in fire on the memory of a man who returned from the dead with a promise nailed to his heart and the price of a curse upon his head. The curtain rises, the audience falls silent and before the shadow hovering over their destiny descends upon the set, a chorus of white spirits has taken the stage to give voice to a comedy. With the blessed innocence of those who believe that the third act is always the last, the chorus embarks on a Christmas story, unaware that even as they turn the last page, the inky stain of its words is creeping into their hearts, dragging them slowly, but inexorably, towards the darkness.

Julián Carax
The Prisoner of Heaven
(Éditions de la Lumière, Paris, 1992)

Part One

A CHRISTMAS STORY

1

Barcelona, December 1957

That Christmas, each day dawned frosty beneath leaden skies. A bluish hue hung over the city and people walked by, wrapped in coats and scarves, their breath leaving a trail of vapour in the cold air. Very few stopped to gaze at the shop window of Sempere & Sons; fewer still ventured inside to ask for that lost book that had been waiting for them all their lives and whose sale, poetic flights of fancy aside, would have helped shore up the bookshop's ailing finances.

'I think today will be the day. Today our luck will change,' I proclaimed, buoyed up by the first coffee of the morning.

My father, who had been battling with the ledger since eight o'clock, twiddling his pencil and rubber, looked up from the counter and eyed the procession of elusive clients disappearing down the street.

'May heaven hear you, Daniel, because at this rate, if we don't win our Christmas campaign, we won't even be able to pay the electricity bill in January. We must do something.'

'Fermín had an idea yesterday,' I remarked. 'He thinks it's a brilliant plan that will save the bookshop from bankruptcy.'

'Lord help us.'

I quoted Fermín, word for word: *'Perhaps if I stood in the shop window wearing my underpants, some female with a passion for literature would be drawn in and want to spend money in the shop. According to expert opinion, the future of literature depends on women, and as God is my witness no woman can resist the animal attraction of this rugged physique.'*

I heard my father's pencil fall to the floor.

'Thus quoth Fermín,' I added.

I thought my father was going to laugh at Fermín's insane idea, but he remained silent. Not only did Sempere Senior not appear to find the suggestion the least bit funny, but he had adopted a pensive expression, as if he were seriously considering it.

'Funnily enough, perhaps Fermín has hit the nail on the head,' he murmured.

I looked at him in disbelief. Maybe the drought of customers that had struck in the last few weeks was affecting my father's sanity.

'Don't tell me you're going to let him wander around the bookshop in his Y-fronts?'

'No, of course not. It's about the shop window. What you said has given me an idea . . . We may still be in time to save our Christmas.'

He disappeared into the back room then emerged sporting his winter uniform: the same coat, scarf and hat he'd worn since I was a child. Bea suspected that my father hadn't bought any new clothes since 1942, and by all indications my wife seemed to be right. As he slipped on his gloves, my father gave an absent smile, his eyes twinkling with an almost child-like excitement. It was a look we only witnessed when he was about to embark on some momentous task.

'I'll leave you on your own for a while,' he announced. 'I'm going out to do an errand.'

'May I ask where you're going?'

My father winked at me.

'It's a surprise. You'll see.'

I followed him to the door and watched him as he set off at a brisk pace towards Puerta del Ángel, one more figure in the grey tide of pedestrians advancing beneath the ashen skies of another long winter.

2

Making the most of my solitude, I decided to turn on the radio and enjoy a bit of music while I reorganised the collections on the shelves. My father thought that it was bad manners to have the radio on when there were customers in the shop, and if I tuned in when Fermín was around, he'd warble along to the melody like a flamenco singer or, even worse, start doing what he called his 'sexy Caribbean moves', which grated on every nerve in my body. Taking such considerations into account, I'd come to the conclusion that I should limit my enjoyment of the radio to those rare moments when there was nobody else in the shop but me and a few thousand books.

That morning, Radio Barcelona was broadcasting a rare recording of a magnificent Louis Armstrong concert, made when the trumpeter and his band had played at the Windsor Palace hotel on Avenida Diagonal, three Christmases earlier. During the advert breaks, the presenter insisted on calling the music 'yazz', warning that some of its indecent syncopations might not be suitable for Spanish listeners brought up on theatrical *tonadillas* and boleros, or the popular *ye ye* movement that currently ruled the air waves.

Fermín used to say that if the composer Don Isaac Albéniz had been born black, jazz would have been invented in Camprodón, along with its other claim to fame – tinned biscuits. The sound, he said, was one of the few real achievements of the twentieth century, together with the pointed brassieres worn by his adored Kim Novak in the matinees we saw at the Fémina Cinema. I certainly wasn't going to argue with that.

I spent the remainder of the morning lulled by the magic of the music and the perfume of the books, savouring the calm satisfaction that comes from a simple job well done.

Fermín had taken the morning off to finalise the preparations for his wedding to Bernarda, which was due to take place at the beginning of February – or so he said. The first time he'd brought up the subject, just two weeks earlier, we'd all told him not to rush into it. More haste, less speed, we'd recommended. My father had tried to persuade him to postpone the wedding for at least two or three months, arguing that it was better to get married in the summer when the weather was good. But Fermín had insisted on sticking to his date, saying that, having been weathered in the harsh, dry climate of the Extremadura hills, he perspired profusely in the Mediterranean summers, and he didn't think it would be appropriate to celebrate his nuptials with sweat stains the size of saucers beneath his armpits.

I was beginning to think that something odd must

be happening if here, in a Spain so dominated by religious fervour and state-controlled propaganda, Fermín Romero de Torres – standard-bearer for civil disobedience against the Holy Mother Church, banks and good manners – was displaying such urgency to get himself hitched in a church. In his pre-matrimonial zeal he'd even befriended Don Jacobo, the new parish priest at the church of Santa Ana. Don Jacobo, who hailed from Burgos, professed a relaxed ideology and had the manners of a prize fighter. Fermín had infected him with his boundless passion for dominoes and together they played epic matches at the Admiral bar on Sundays after mass. Don Jacobo would split his sides laughing when my friend asked him, as they sipped glasses of Aromas de Montserrat liqueur, if he could confirm that nuns did indeed have thighs, and if they did, were they as soft and delectable as he'd suspected ever since he was a boy?

'You'll get yourself excommunicated,' my father scolded him. 'Nuns are not to be looked at, or touched.'

'But that priest is almost more of a tart than I am,' Fermín protested. 'If it weren't for his uniform . . .'

I was recalling this conversation and humming along to the sound of maestro Armstrong's trumpet when I heard the soft tinkle of the doorbell. I looked up, expecting to see my father returning from his secret mission, or Fermín ready to start the afternoon shift.

'Good morning,' a hoarse voice intoned from the doorway.

Set against the light from the street, the dark figure resembled the solid trunk of a tree lashed by the wind. Sporting a dark, old-fashioned suit, the visitor was leaning on a stick, and when he took one step forward, he had a visible limp. As he came into the glow cast by the small lamp that hung above the counter, I could see a face lined by many years. The man stared at me for a few moments, sizing me up, rather like a bird of prey, patient and calculating.

'Are you Señor Sempere?'

'I'm Daniel. Señor Sempere is my father, but he's not here right now. Can I help you?'

The visitor ignored my question and began to wander around the bookshop examining everything with almost covetous interest. His limp was so pronounced that I thought the wounds hidden beneath his clothing must be severe indeed.

'Souvenirs from the war,' said the stranger, as if he'd read my thoughts.

I kept my eyes on him, following his reconnaissance of the bookshop and wondering where he was going to drop anchor. Just as I'd imagined, the stranger stopped in front of the ebony and glass cabinet, a relic dating back to the founding of the enterprise in 1888, when great-grandfather Sempere, then a young man recently arrived from his adventures in the Caribbean, had borrowed some money in order to buy an old glove shop and turn it into a bookshop. That cabinet now occupied a place of honour in the store, and it was where we traditionally kept our most valuable items.

The visitor drew so close to the cabinet that his breath misted on the glass. He pulled out a pair of spectacles, put them on and proceeded to study the contents. His expression brought to mind a weasel examining freshly laid eggs in a chicken coop.

'A beautiful piece,' he murmured. 'Must be worth something.'

'It's a family heirloom. Its value is mostly sentimental,' I replied, feeling uncomfortable at the stranger's piercing gaze, which seemed to be weighing up even the air we breathed.

After a while he put his spectacles away and spoke in a measured tone.

'I hear that a certain gentleman, well known for his wit, works for you.'

When I didn't reply immediately, he turned round and gave me a withering look.

'As you can see, I'm the only one here. Perhaps, sir, if you tell me which book you're after, I could try to find you a copy.'

The stranger gave me a smile that was anything but friendly then nodded.

'I see you have a copy of *The Count of Montecristo* in that cabinet.'

He wasn't the first customer to notice the book. I gave him the official sales patter we reserved for such occasions.

'The gentleman has a good eye. It's a magnificent edition, numbered and with illustrations by Arthur Rackham. It belonged to the private library of an important collector in Madrid. A unique piece, and it's catalogued.'

The visitor listened without interest, focusing his attention on the ebony shelves and making it clear that my words bored him.

'All books look the same to me, but I like the blue of that cover,' he replied disdainfully. 'I'll take it.'

Under other circumstances I would have jumped for joy at the thought of being able to sell what was probably the most expensive book in the entire shop, but there was something about the idea that it should end up in the hands of this character that made my stomach turn. I suspected that if the book left the shop in his possession, nobody would even read the first paragraph.

'That is a very expensive edition. If you like, sir, I can show you other editions of the same work that are in perfect condition and more reasonably priced.'

People with a miserly soul always try to make others feel small too, and the stranger, who could probably have concealed his on the head of a pin, gave me his most disparaging look.

'Some of them have blue covers too,' I added.

He ignored the impertinence of my irony.

'No, thank you. This is the one I want. I don't care about the price.'

Reluctantly I agreed and walked over to the glass cabinet. As I pulled out the key and opened the glass door, I could feel the stranger's eyes boring into my back.

'Good things are always kept under lock and key,' he muttered.

I removed the book with a sigh.

'Is the gentleman a collector?'

'I suppose you could call me that. But not of books.'

I turned round with the book in my hand.

'So what do you collect, sir?'

Once again, the stranger ignored my question and reached out for the book. I had to resist the urge to put the volume straight back in the cabinet, but my father would never have forgiven me if I had lost such a sale when business was so bad.

'The price is thirty-five pesetas,' I said before handing the book to him, hoping the figure would make him change his mind.

He nodded without batting an eyelid and pulled out a one hundred peseta note from the pocket of a suit that could not have been worth more than fivepence. I wondered whether the note was forged.

'I'm afraid I don't have change for such a large note, sir.'

I would have asked him to wait a moment while I ran down to the nearest bank for change – perhaps also taking the opportunity to make sure the note wasn't a fake – but I didn't want to leave this man alone in the shop.

'Don't worry. It's genuine. Do you know how you can tell?'

The stranger held the note up against the light.

'Look at the watermarks. And these lines. The texture . . .'

'Is sir an expert in forgeries?'

'In this world, everything is a forgery, young man. Everything except money.'

He placed the note in my hand and closed my fist over it, patting my knuckles.

'I'll collect the change on my next visit,' he said.

'It's a lot of money, sir. Sixty-five pesetas . . .'

'Loose change.'

'I'll give you a receipt then.'

'I trust you.'

The stranger examined the book.

'It's a gift. I want you to deliver it in person.'

For a moment, I hesitated.

'We don't normally do deliveries . . . but in this case I'm more than happy to take care of the package myself, free of charge. May I ask whether the address is in Barcelona itself or . . . ?'

'It's here,' he said.

His icy look seemed to be filled with years of anger and resentment.

'Would you like to include a dedication or add a personal note before I wrap up the book, sir?'

With some difficulty, the visitor opened the book at the title page. I noticed then that his left hand was artificial, made of porcelain. He pulled out a fountain pen and wrote a few words, then gave the book back to me. I watched him as he limped towards the door.

'Would you be so kind as to give me the exact name and address where you would like the book to be delivered?' I asked.

'It's all there,' he said, without turning his head.

I opened the book and looked at the page that bore the inscription:

> *For Fermín Romero de Torres, who came*
> *back from the dead and who holds the key*
> *to the future.*
>
> 13

I heard the tinkle of the doorbell, and when I looked up, the stranger had already left.

I dashed over to the door and peered out into the street. The visitor was limping away, disappearing into the crowd of figures that surged through the mist veiling the Calle Santa Anna. I was about to call out to him, but

I held back. The easiest thing would have been to let him go, but my instinct and my usual lack of common sense got the better of me.

IMPRINT OF THE YEAR 2015

For literary discussion, author insight,
book news, exclusive content,
recipes and giveaways, visit the
Weidenfeld & Nicolson blog and
sign up for the newsletter at:

www.wnblog.co.uk

For breaking news, reviews and exclusive competitions
Follow us 🐦 @wnbooks